"YOU KNOW YOU AREN'T WELCOME HERE," Said the Stranger.

"Yes. I've heard that no upriver fishermen are," replied Keven.

"That's a fact. Lord and his former mate bucked us with high hand last season," rejoined the stranger. "We don't intend to let you get away with it this year. You won't have any sale for your fish. And that's why I'm giving you a hint."

"Thanks," replied Keven dryly. "But I think it's a bluff."

"You'll soon find out it's no bluff. You'll be out in the cold."

"But look here! Isn't this a free country? Can't a man get his wages for honest work?" shot back Keven, growing nettled.

"Take it or leave it," snapped the other crisply. From his face a mask of persuasion dropped to expose craft and, less clearly, menace. "If you signify your willingness to quit Garry Lord and join the ring, then—"

"Say," interrupted Keven. "You look like a crook and you talk like a crook. Go to hell!"

ZANE GREY

ROGUE RIVER FEUD

PUBLISHED BY POCKET BOOKS NEW YORK

This story was published serially under
the title of *Rustlers of Silver River.*

**POCKET BOOKS, a Simon & Schuster division of
GULF & WESTERN CORPORATION**
1230 Avenue of the Americas, New York, N.Y. 10020

ISBN: 0-671-83427-4

First Pocket Books printing July, 1975

10 9 8 7 6 5 4 3

POCKET and colophon are trademarks of Simon & Schuster.

Printed in the U.S.A.

ROGUE RIVER
FEUD

chapter one

Deep and dark green, swift and clear, icy cold and as pure as the snows from which it sprang, the river had its source in the mountain under Crater Lake. It was a river at its birth; and it glided away through the Oregon forest, with hurrying momentum, as if eager to begin the long leap down through the Siskiyous. The giant firs shaded it; the deer drank from it; the little black-backed trout rose greedily to floating flies. And in sunlit glades, where the woods lightened, the wild lilac bloomed in its marvelous profusion of color, white and purple and pink, scenting the warm drowsy air with sweet fragrance.

Then suddenly, with a gurgling roar, the river performed a strange antic. It sank underground to reappear far below, bursting from a great dark hole at the head of a gorge and sliding down in glancing green inclines that ended in silvery cascades. Below Prospect the river tumbled off the mountain in mellow thundering music, to meet its main branch, and proud with added strength and beauty, it raced away between its timbered banks down the miles to the sheltered valley, through Burnham's Ranch, and by Gold Hill, slowing in a long still reach that ended in Savage Rapids. Then on to Pierce Riffle, and skirting Grant's Pass, the river twisted and chafed and fought its way through Hell Gate, and rushing over the Alameda rocks, and the ledges of the Argo Mine, it entered the canyoned wilderness of the Coast Range.

Long before the towering crags above Horseshoe Bend looked down upon the hurrying green and white stream it had grown to superb maturity, and flowed on, here with brooding peace and there with eddying poise, yet ever and oftener breaking into fierce rapids, down into the thundering cauldron of Reamy Falls and through the

1

Plowshare, a white furrow in the mighty boulders, and over the constricted Graves Creek Rapid.

Tyee Bar and Russian Bar and China Bar, where the miners had washed away the sand for gold, and shed their blood and left their strange graves, made wide curves for the river. It raced and eddied by turns; it tarried under the high golden meadows that shone like jewels on the black mountain slopes; it glided on in glancing ripples around Winkle Bar, gentle and reluctant and sweetly vagrant, as if to lull and deceive, only to bellow sudden rage at the confines of Blossom Bar, and to prepare itself for a sullen surrender to treacherous Mule Creek Canyon. When it emerged from that narrow black-walled crack it was a subdued and chastened river, yet glad to be free once more, and to receive graciously the amber brook that tumbled off the mossy cliffs, on to the winding beauty of Solitude, where the black firs encroached to the water's edge, and the sun shone only at midday down upon the ledged and barred river, and the wild ducks played among the reeds, and the weird and lonely water ouzels built their mud nests under the overhanging rocks, and the eagles screamed aloft, and the deer and bear made trails along the shores. But at last the leaps of Clay Hill and Two Mile Rapids released the river from the hundred-mile grip of the mountains.

Here it opened out and slowed down and spread wide over shallow gravelly bars, and ran on merrily, its fury spent, its mood changed, its age realized, on through the pastoral country of the coast, past the picturesque farms of the Indians and the rude shacks of the fishermen, broadening and meandering, smiling from its shiny pebbled bed at the retreating banks and the low colorful hills, and so on down to Gold Beach, assuming a deep, calm majesty when it found its home in the infinite sea.

Outside the mouth of the Rogue lurked a motley swarm of salmon, steelhead, forked-tails and silversides, and the hungry wolf-jawed jacks.

They began to gather early in the spring and every day thereafter the specked ranks grew. A marvelous instinct of nature brought them from out the ocean depths to the river which had given them birth. That same strange instinct actuated them with this restless waiting urge.

Sharks and seals moved them to and fro, but never drove them from this inevitable wait at the river's mouth. In great shadowy shoals they drifted close to the gateway through the breakers and listened for that mysterious call. When it came it was as if an irresistible command had united them. It was the first rise in the river, the freshet from mountain rains, and the water carried a sweet cold scent of the springs and the gravel beds. The run was on. First over the bar were the great brown leather-backed, white-bellied salmon, and the others followed, in a long endless stream, like deer migrating from north to south.

Their next obstacle was a man-made one, the wall of nets stretched across the wide river to intercept and capture and kill. Thousands strangled by the gills in the close meshes, but hundreds got through or around or over. The run was on and only death could end that instinct to survive and to reproduce. All day fish came over the bar into the river, but it was at night when they ran in heavy numbers. The fishermen knew this and cunningly spread their nets across the deep channels.

Those fish that escaped went up the river, steadily while the high water was on, sooner or later, when it fell again, to be halted by shallow bars over which they could not swim, or by rapids which they could not mount. Here in deep pools and where cool springs bubbled out of the ferny banks they waited again for another rise in the river, and ever their number grew. Days, sometimes weeks, passed before they could resume their journey. But most years nature provided the means by which the fish could move on upstream. At last they climbed above the region of obstructing shallows, and from then on the progress depended on strength and endurance. They shot the rapids and leaped the falls.

Gradually their number thinned out. The long two-hundred-mile climb was beset by perils and obstacles. The forked-tails and steelhead had no such battle for life that faced the salmon. They were smaller and nature had endowed them with endurance to get back to the sea. But the great scar-sided salmon sacrificed life in this struggle. Many weakened on the way, only to drop back; others, leaping high to get over the falls, sometimes hit rocks and crippled themselves; all rested longer and longer in the

3

still pools above the rapids; none ever reached the spawning beds without the wounds of battle.

Upon the shallow gravel bars of the upper reaches of the river the surviving salmon made their spawning beds. When the sun shone brightly they could be seen almost motionless, huge brown-and-silver shapes, heroically absorbed in their task of procreation. And below them, wavering in deeper water, like wolves on the edge of a flock, hung predatory jacks. They were salmon, too, but the cannibals of the species. Often one of these would glide forward, suddenly to shoot head on into the plump side of a spawning salmon, to burst from her eggs that floated down. And the wolf would drop back to fight his fellows for these floating eggs.

Nevertheless the spawning proceeded, perhaps inscrutably benefited by this cruel preying of nature. Salmon eggs were laid and fertilized and hatched—a procedure which ended in death for the progenitors. Out of millions of tiny little salmon, almost too small to be seen, some survived. And this survival was a monstrous and marvelous thing, in that the little fish lived off the rotting carcasses of their parents. As if by magic they grew.

When the time came the same mysterious call that had brought their parents up the river drew them instinctively down toward the sea. In shiny schools they glittered on the surface, sometimes leaping like a swarm of silver minnows. And they went on down the river to be swallowed up by the fertile salty sea, into which they vanished until maturity roused the same urge that had given them existence, when, strong with life and immutable to extend it forever, they sought the rolling Rogue to fulfill their part in the cycle.

chapter two

KEVEN BELL, returning home to Grant's Pass after two terrible years in an army training-camp hospital, seemed to see all things strange and unfamiliar except the beloved river of his boyhood—the errant and boisterous Rogue.

He had not gone home at once, but wandered about the town, finally lingering at the river bridge. It troubled him that he could not remember well. But he knew his mother had died during his four-year absence from home, and his father's last letter had acquainted him with more misfortune. Watching the green gliding, rolling river brought a break in his thought and feeling. A poignant spasm gripped his breast. His jaw quivered, and his eyes smarted and dimmed with tears. How long had it been since he had cared for anything?

Surely still for Rosamond Brandeth, whom he had loved before he left home to train for war! Long since her letters had ceased—so long that he could not recall when. He knew what to expect and had no bitterness then. Indeed he meant to release her from a claim that honor, at least, held binding. The river brought back memories of Rosamond.

At length he turned away. He had to ask a man, who peered strangely at him, how to find his father's house. It looked old and dilapidated. He sat down on the porch, slowly realizing. Yes, he knew the rose vine, just budding green, and the flagstones in the walk.

The day was a Sunday in May. He had arrived from Seattle on the morning train. The streets appeared deserted. New houses across the common hid the banks of the river. Finally, hearing steps within, he knocked on the door. It opened.

There stood his father, greatly changed, now slight of

5

build and stoop-shouldered, his hair gray, with amazed and slow recognition dawning in his mild blue eyes.

"Dad, don't you know me? It's Kev."

"My son!" replied the older man, and reached for him. "I—I didn't know you. . . . Come in."

When Keven saw the sitting room, with its open grate, where a fire burned, he suffered another pang. That empty armchair by the table told him of the vacancy in this home. His father clasped his hands hard and gazed up, puzzled and anxious.

"Son, you're not the same," he said. "Taller. . . . Thin. You used to be big. . . . And your face—"

"I couldn't write," replied Keven, a hand going to his father's shoulder. "But you heard of my accident?"

"I think I did. Long ago, wasn't it? But I forget what. Once we thought you'd died. Then it was in the paper about your being in the army hospital. That was before your mother went. . . . What happened to you, Kev?"

"A lot. Cannon blew up. I stopped the breechblock with my face," replied Keven. "I was pretty badly mussed up. But I didn't know anything about it for months. They thought I'd die. I was in hospitals for two years. Then I pulled through. But my mind is bad. I notice it most in not being able to remember. Can't see well out of one eye. . . . And look here—at my iron jaw."

He drew down his lower lip, to expose the hideous thing that served for his lower maxillary.

"What's that?" queried his father, nonplussed.

"I lost most of my lower jaw. The dentist patched it up with iron. I can chew with it. But I hate the taste. They said I could get a gold-and-platinum jaw someday, with teeth in it. Ha! Ha! When I strike gold along the Rogue!"

"Well! Well! . . . Sit down, son. So you never got to France?"

"No, worse luck. Four years! My health shattered—my eyesight impaired—my brain injured somehow. I'd been better if I'd gotten to the front. Four years for nothing."

"My God!" replied his father huskily. "It seems hard. . . . And now you're only twenty-six. Ruined! . . . What a miserable farce! All that patriotic hokum! That wonderful training camp. What did they do for my son?"

6

"Worse than killed me, Dad," replied Keven sadly. "I suffer pain all my waking hours. And I don't sleep well. In the Army I learned a lot of rotten things. But you get so you don't care. They wanted you not to care—to revert to savagery. Yet they fed us on saltpeter bread. . . . Whisky gives me relief, though. . . . I'm sorry to tell you this, Dad. Better from me, though, than from anyone else. I had to come home. I'm a wreck. No money. Nothing but this uniform on my back. That's all."

"God has failed us," replied the older Bell bitterly.

"I don't remember where I stood in regard to God once. But sure He didn't linger around that camp."

"Son, if we lose faith we're lost," said his father, poignantly regretting his momentary confession. "It could have been worse. You might have been killed—or have been sent to an asylum. While there's life there's hope. Kev, I implore you to have hope."

"For what, Dad?"

"That you've something left to live for," was the earnest reply. "Find it—make it! *They* have failed you. Your country—your sweetheart! And you'll find no friends now. But I say—by God, as long as you can wag, rise above it all! The damned sordid, rotten part of the world that seems in power. The destructive forces! . . . Don't let them kill your soul."

"I understand, Dad. . . . Thanks. I know there'll always be a bond between us. It's something—it's enough. I'll try. . . . Tell me about Mother."

"Kev, she just gradually went downhill," returned Bell. "You should remember she was a sick woman before you left. She had a long, lingering illness. She was glad to go. Before she died she told me to get you back home here by the Rogue—that the river would cure you. She loved that river. . . . Well, I had to take more and more time away from the store, until gradually my business failed. I lost it. . . . Since then I've been carpentering. You know I was always handy with tools. They were my hobby. And now that hobby stands by me. You can never tell."

"If only I had learned a trade!" sighed Keven. "I'm not so weak. I could work—I could stick at something that didn't require thinking. But I never learned anything, except how to fish. I spent more time fishing than in school."

"Kev, you can go back to the river," said Bell thoughtfully.

"What? You don't mean fishing?"

"Yes, I do. For a living. The market fishermen do well now. Some of them own their homes. Brandeth has gotten control of the canning factory at Gold Beach. He pays big wages. It's an established business now. He got rich during the war."

"Brandeth. You mean Rosamond's father?"

"Yes, no one else than John Brandeth. Of course he never was poor. But now he's rich. Built a magnificent new house. Has a big fruit ranch down on the river. He's in everything. And, by the way, he got my store."

"Straight or crooked, Dad?" queried Keven.

"All business is straight, since the war," replied his father evasively. "But John Brandeth could have saved me from failing."

"Business must be like war. . . . Dad, how about Rosamond?" returned Keven, averting his eyes.

"Grown into a beautiful young woman. Fine feathers make fine birds. She sure flies high. Drives her own car. Drinks and dances. Engaged to this high-stepper from Frisco and then some fellow round here—so the gossip runs. She never speaks to me, though it's not so long since she begged candy from me at my store. . . . But, Kev, you haven't any hopes, have you—about Rosamond?"

"No, indeed, Dad. . . . But she never broke our engagement. At least I never had word of it. . . . Was—that reported about town?"

"Lord, no, son. You've been long forgotten."

"Ah, I see."

"Forget all that, too, my son. . . . Let's talk of other things. We'll fix up your old room. And come out to the shed. I've built a new river boat. The same old model, Kev. I sell one now and then to a market fisherman. This one is spruce, twenty-one feet long, deep gunwales, sharp fore and aft, with watertight compartments. It's a dandy."

Sight of that Rogue River boat seemed to open a door in Keven's heart to let memory in. For he had known every

8

stone in the river from Savage Rapids to Blossom Bar, and beyond. To run the rapids, to drift with the still current, to listen to the singing waters, to fish the pools—these had been his joy from boyhood up. And sight of this long deep boat, sharp fore and aft, with its beautiful lines and its strong frame, brought that old forgotten joy surging back.

"Dad, it's sure a dandy. Better than you used to build," Keven said heartily.

"Necessity is the mother of improvement, son," replied his father.

"What do you charge for these boats, Dad? I've forgotten."

"Forty dollars to the market fishermen. They furnish oars, locks, lines."

"This one sold?"

"No. But Garry Lord has his eye on it. Wanted to pay me ten on deposit. Garry can never keep money long enough to save up that much."

"Garry Lord! . . . Somehow that name seems familiar," returned Keven ponderingly.

"Humph, it ought to be. You used to play hooky from school to fish with Garry Lord. How that distressed your mother! Garry never was any good, and now he's worse. He's grown up now. Just a lazy drunken low-down riverman!"

"Does he still live out on the edge of town, in a tumble-down shack under the pines by the river?"

"No. Brandeth bought that pine grove and the river front. He ousted Garry and the other loafers out there. Garry moved farther down the river."

"I'll hunt him up. . . . Dad, here's your forty dollars for the boat. It about cleans me out."

"Son, I can't take your money."

"Yes, you can. If you don't some bootlegger will get it," replied Keven, and forced the money into his father's unwilling hands. "Is my old room available?"

"It has never been used. Mother locked it after you went to be a soldier. And she lost or hid the key. That room has never been opened. . . . But we can force the lock."

Presently Keven Bell stood on the threshold of the

room where he had lived his childhood and boyhood days. And on the threshold of the dim past, where vague scenes arose, like ghosts, like the musty cobwebbed things under his piercing gaze!

In the afternoon he walked out the broad avenue to the Brandeth mansion that lifted its shiny tiled red roof among the pines on a bench high above the river. He wanted to get something over—a duty he imagined he owed himself—something for which no letter would suffice. The fine-graveled road, the smooth path, the green lawn with its plants and statued fountain, the stately house that seemed to frown at his insolence—these made but momentary impressions. The maid who answered his ring informed him that Miss Brandeth was out motoring.

Keven returned to the main street and strolled its long length, passing many persons, not one of whom he recognized. Automobiles full of gay young people whizzed by him. Keven was used to being stared at. The attention he created, however, was not due to recognition. He went to the park, which was dotted with strollers and loungers, and from there back to the railroad station. An hour's walk on Sunday afternoon assured Keven he was not known in his home town. But four years was an age and he had greatly changed. He ended upon the river road, from which he crossed a meadow to the pine-fringed bank.

He sat down in a shady fragrant brown-carpeted spot. It was lonely there. The road, the bridge, the town with its noisy cars and young people were out of sight. Suddenly the dull thoughts that had been stirred in him ceased to operate. And he felt the pleasantness, the welcome of the place.

The river ran clear, swift, and green over the rocky ledges. From the bend below floated a low musical roar of a rapid. It mingled with the sound of the wind in the pines. A crow cawed from the hills. In the shallow water red crayfish backed over the mossy stones.

Keven closed his eyes and lay back upon the pine mat, and all these sensations seemed magically intensified. At last, thought and remembrance encroached upon the first peace he had felt for years. How strange that it should

10

come to him here on the bank of the Rogue! Even his physical pain had been in abeyance. It was something he must inquire into. Rising, he strode on down the river, past the white rapid that stopped his heart with a recollection. Here as a boy he had experienced his first upset and had drifted, clinging to his skiff, through the ugly rocks and rushing channels to the safety of shallow water below. How much better it would have been for him to perish then! But a doubt mocked his sadness.

At the end of the fringe of pines he espied a fisherman's shack. He knew the type, though this one appeared more hastily and flimsily thrown up. It had been constructed of boards and stones and flattened gasoline cans, with a stovepipe sticking out of the roof. Yet it appealed to Keven. No location could have surpassed that upon which it stood. A giant pine spread wide branches down over the roof, to brush against it. Keven was calculating doubtfully about its being above high-water mark when he saw a man bending over a net which evidently he was repairing. Keven had to gaze keenly to make sure this was Garry Lord. Finally convinced, he slipped aside so that the shack hid him and went cautiously down the bank, with a warm, inexplicable desire to surprise Garry. And he peeped out from behind the shack, in time to see Garry throw aside the old net in disgust.

"Rotten!" he ejaculated. "Rotten as the damned nettin' game itself! . . . It ain't no use. No net—no boat. An' jail yawnin' at me again!"

Keven stepped out. "Hello, Garry."

The fisherman started quickly to rise and turn. He had a leathery, weather-beaten face, homely and hard, unshaven and dirty, yet despite these features and the unmistakable imprint of the bottle, somehow far from revolting. Perhaps that was due to the large, wide-open, questioning blue eyes. His ragged apparel further attested to his low estate.

"Fer the love of Mike!" he yelled suddenly. "It ain't Kev Bell?"

"Yes, it is, Garry. All that's left of him."

"But, my Gord! Last I heerd you was dead!"

"No, worse luck, I'm alive." There was no mistaking the glad-eyed, warm-fisted welcome of this fisherman, to

11

which Keven felt strange reaction. He returned that hard grip.

"Gord, I'm glad to see you, Kev. An' you hunted me up? Or was you jest walkin' down the old river?"

"Dad told me where to find you," replied Keven. "I got home today. The old place is changed, Garry. I didn't see anyone I knew. Mother's gone—Dad's old and broken. . . . It's tough to come home to—to all that. . . . Well, I'm lucky to get home at all. Garry, I was at the butt end of a gun that blew up. Breechblock hit me in the face. I've a bum eye, an iron jaw, and a sunspot on my brain. Ha! Ha! But that's all, Garry, about me."

"Set down, Kev. You are changed a lot. I'd knowed you, though, out of a thousand. You can still ketch the eyes of the girls."

"Honest, Garry, I'm a cripple. Look here." And Keven gave proofs of several of his physical defects.

"I heerd you'd been bunged up somethin' fierce an' was slated to cross the big river. Fact is, Kev, I heerd about you before an' after you was hurt."

It was Garry's manner of speech, more than its content, that roused Keven's curiosity. The fisherman regarded him gravely, as if remembering that before the war there was a certain definite barrier between them, and as if wondering now if that had been leveled.

"You remember Gus Atwell?" he queried guardedly.

"Yes, I guess so. Though I can't recall his face."

"He got a major's commission."

"Oh, yes. He lorded it over us at camp. God, that seems long ago. Atwell went to France long before I was injured."

"Like hell he did," retorted Garry with contempt. "He came home. Invalided they called it. We all called it nogutseted! . . . Kev, he was as healthy as me."

"Is that so? News to me. I guess there'll be a lot of news."

"You said it. An' I'm wonderin', Kev. . . .Wal, I'll tell you straight. Atwell spread such talk about you thet it got to the ears of us fishermen."

"Gossip? What about? My accident? How near death I came—and all that time in the hospital?"

"Not on your life," snapped the riverman, with those keen bright eyes studying his visitor. "He spread a lot of rotten stuff. I can only remember one of the things. Thet was so queer no one'd ever forget it. About five girls in one family. Name Carstone. They lived near the trainin' camp. Five girls from fifteen years old up to twenty-two, an' every damn one of them had a baby. Five sisters! . . . Thet's the worst I ever heerd."

"Carstone? Five sisters? That runs in my mind somehow—not exactly strange."

"Well, Atwell said you was mixed up in thet. An' there sure was a nine-days' gabfest here at the Pass."

"Garry, it's a lie," replied Keven hotly.

"I'm right glad to hear that, Kev," returned Garry fervently. "An' if I was you I'd face Atwell with it. Make him crawl or beat hell out of him. Us upriver fishermen sure have it in for Atwell. You see he's superintendent of the biggest cannery on the coast. Belongs to Brandeth, who's gettin' hold of everythin'. He about runs Gold Beach. Well, Atwell's gang of downriver fishermen are against us, an' we've had hell these last two years. Fights every Saturday night durin' the nettin' season. There's been two killin's. There's a tough crowd down the river. They're tryin' to freeze us out."

"Don't stand for it, Garry," said Keven stoutly.

"What can we do, Kev? Why, there's only a few upriver fishermen who go down to the coast. An' they shoot the Rogue, which you ought to remember is some job. No, we're up against it. Atwell dominates the market here an' on up the river. An' at Gold Beach we have to sell to opposition canneries, none of which can afford to pay what Brandeth pays. . . . It sure riles me to see Atwell drivin' around here in his fast cars. Spends as much time here as at Gold Beach. He's chasin' Brandeth's girl now. Hell of a lot of good thet'll do him. Fer there's too swift a little lady fer him. She's playin' him fer a sucker."

"You mean Rosamond Brandeth?" asked Keven quietly.

"Sure. She's the only daughter. She's as swift as she's pretty. . . . By gosh, Kev, I forgot!" exclaimed the fisherman, slapping his knee. "You used to be sweet on her. I

13

remember you used to borrow my boats to take her ridin' on the river. When you was kids, an' later, too."

"Yes I remember, Garry. It seems long ago. . . . But let's talk fish. When does the season open?"

"Open now. But there's no run yet. If I had a boat an' a net I'd take another try at Gold Beach, if only to spite Atwell. Kev, I'm very suspicious about thet guy. But my boat won't hold together no longer. If I tried to shoot Tyee or Mule Creek I'd be feed for little salmon. An' I haven't got no net, either. Last season I hand-lined salmon. Hard job an' poor pay!"

"Is it enough to live on?"

"Well, yes, if you can make a little durin' winter to help out."

"What's a net cost?"

"Around two hundred dollars. I could make one for less, but it takes time, an' I'm lazy."

"Garry, I've a little money. And Dad will lend me the balance. He's just built a dandy new boat. Come in with me, Garry. We'll be partners. I furnish equipment to start. We'll share profits."

"Kev, what are you talkin' about?" asked the fisherman incredulously.

"I mean it, Garry."

"You be a market fisherman!"

"Yes, I'd like it. I see no disgrace in it. I've got to work at something. And I never could do anything but handle a boat and fish."

"You could do them, by gosh! But, Kev, you're dotty. I've got a bad name. I'm only a lazy no-good, rum-guzzlin' riverman. It'd ruin you to be braced with me."

"Ruin? Ha! I'd like to know what I am now. The Army sounds great. But it's a hideous lie! . . . Garry, I don't believe you're as bad as you make out. Or perhaps as bad as the majority of Grant's Pass believes. You know the Rogue. It's about all there's left for me. I always liked you. I'd swear by you. So come on. Let's be partners. Let's give Atwell a whirl."

"By Gord, Kev, I'll take you up!" shouted Garry, extending a horny hand. There was a birth light of love and loyalty in his eyes. "I taught you to run a boat an' mebbe you can make a man of me. Shake!"

14

chapter three

THE RIVER CALLED KEVEN. At night he lay awake listening to its low roar. In the darkness his memory seemed clearer. He longed to drift into the wilderness, into the mountain fastness which the Rogue penetrated. And that was the first longing he had felt for years—except to die. Pictures wavered before his wide eyes in the dark—Chair Riffle, with its glancing slide along the ledges under which the steelhead lurked; Whisky Creek, where the otter and the wild boars fought; Solitude, so sweet and wonderful in all that had given it name.

But obstacles arose. The sheriff arrested Garry Lord on a belated warrant. Fishing out of season was the charge, and it required no effort to trace it to the factor now dominant in river affairs. Keven had to raise money to get him out, as well as for the necessary equipment of market fishermen. His father at length found the means. So it came about that Keven had to remain at home, during which time occurred inevitable meetings with old acquaintances. And every one probed deeper into what had seemed a closed wound.

Girls he had been friends with, now grown into modern young women, eyed him in curiosity as if they had never known him. That, however, was a relief. It was the honest gladness and warmth of Minton, the tackle dealer, whom Keven had once fished with many a summer day, that hurt him. For here was faith and loyalty he had not expected. "To hell with all that rot!" Minton had exclaimed, when Keven had haltingly hinted of the calumny which had been heaped upon him. "Nobody believes it. Sure I don't. Chuck that uniform, Kev, and forget the war. It was a dose of hell for all of us. Drop in at the store. I'll show you some of the new tackle we've de-

15

veloped. Steelhead fishing has become a great booster for the old town. But there's only a few of us to fight the canning hogs at Gold Beach. If we don't unite and restrict them the grand fishing on the Rogue will soon be gone."

He met Clarke and Dugan, likewise former fishing comrades, and old Jim Turner, and the Negro Sam Johnson—all of whom were cordial in their welcome. No reference to his army training—no hint of any change in him! They were glad. How significant that each associated him with the past and the river they loved!

Then he turned a corner to be confronted by a tall, blond, sweet-faced girl who appeared strangely familiar. He swerved.

"Kev Bell! You can't dodge me," she called in a high treble. "Don't you know me?"

"I—I do and I don't," replied Keven confusedly, hastening to take her proffered hand.

"Guess," she said archly. "I was one of your schoolgirl sweethearts."

"Indeed. It's good of you to remember that," he responded, stirred by unfamiliar emotion. "Your face I know. But I—I can't place you. . . . I sustained an injury to my head. It affected my memory."

"You fickle soldier! I am Emmeline Trapier," she said reproachfully.

In a flash Keven linked the name with that pretty face and bygone associations. "Well, I know you now," he replied heartily, and wrung her hand. "Lord, I'm glad you spoke to me, Em. I've been snubbed until I'm leary."

"Have you seen Billy yet? Oh, of course you haven't, or you would have known me. We heard you had come home. Billy is crazy to see you."

"Billy who?" inquired Keven.

"Why, Billy Horn, your old chum."

"Oh! . . . No, I haven't run into Billy yet," replied Keven hesitatingly.

"You will soon, for he'll hunt you up. Come, Kev, walk out home with me."

"I'd like to. But it wouldn't do for you to be seen talking to me."

"I'll risk it, Kev. We're not all snobs. And you've friends still in Grant's Pass. Mother will be glad to see

16

you. . . . Did you know my brother Hal was killed in France?"

"Hal! No, I didn't. I've heard so little. . . . My God, that's terrible, Emmeline, I'm sorry. . . . I never got over there."

They walked down the street toward the residence quarter.

"You were badly hurt, though, I heard," she said solicitously.

"Yes. It'd been better if I'd gone west, too."

"No. Don't say that. Kev, you mustn't be bitter. How silly of me! Yet I mean it. For your own sake."

"Emmeline, it's good of you. I thank you. It makes me feel there are a few people who understand a little. But there's no place in the old life for me. I can't delude myself."

"Then you've seen Rosamond?" she asked gravely.

"Not to speak to. I called Sunday. She wasn't home. And again last night. The maid took my name. But Rosamund was not at home—to me. . . . I saw her through the window. Seemed as though she suited that gaudy place."

"Don't take it to heart, Kev."

"Well, it hurt so little I was surprised. Perhaps I can't feel deeply any more. I only wanted to see her a moment. . . . Em, I wish you'd tell her I felt honor bound to release her—no, never mind. That's ridiculous. I've fallen behind in these quick modern days. But I'm no jackass."

"I don't see Rosamond often," rejoined the girl. "She belongs to the new set. While I—well, Kev—I'm engaged to Billy."

"Fine!" ejaculated Keven, thrilled at the blush that flushed her cheek. "I congratulate you both. I wish you everything life can give, Em. There are two kinds of people: the destroyers and the builders. You belong to the latter."

"Thanks, Kev," she said, stopping at a gate. "Won't you come in and speak to Mother? She'll weep over you. But don't mind. It'll do her good to see you back alive."

"Yes, I'll come. It might do *me* good to have someone shed a tear over me. . . . But wait just a moment, Em. I want to ask you something. Was it Atwell who started this

17

vile gossip here? I mean that scandal about a family named Carstone, who lived near our training camp. Five sisters who—But did you hear it?"

"Yes, Kev, I did, and I—we never believed it," she returned warmly, her face scarlet. "It was Atwell who started that talk. Billy told me so. He heard him."

"Emmeline, I swear it's a lie," returned Keven appealingly. "God knows I got tough enough in the Army. They wanted us—made us tough. . . . I wasn't concerned in that Carstone affair. I thought I didn't care what anyone believed. But, Em, meeting you again and remembering—well, I'm afraid I *do* care."

"Kev, you needn't have denied that," she replied, with tears in her eyes. "Come in now."

That visit with Emmeline and her mother was an ordeal Keven did not want to undergo twice. It apprised him of his unsuspected weakness. It left him raw. A dull and thick lethargy passed from his consciousness.

Turning once more into the main street, he strolled down, revolving in mind the need to get away from town, from home that was no longer home, from an awakening, brooding self he did not trust. And it was while thinking thus that he espied Rosamond Brandeth. She was driving a flashy car. Bareheaded, bare-armed she sat at the wheel. Keven stopped stock-still. It was a recognition that staggered him, wrenched his sore heart; yet her bobbed hair and her painted face had something to do with the pang. She saw him. She knew him. That he realized in the flash of her eyes. The sleek, handsome head went up. She drove on with no other sign and her gay laugh trilled back. Keven turned to see her companion was a man, young, and bareheaded, too.

"Well, that's over and I'm glad," muttered Keven, resuming his walk. But the meeting left no warmth in him. Love was dead. He could be tolerant towards anyone whom the war had changed, for better or worse. Did it change anyone for the better? Souls did not require war to be tried in fire. Yet he wished Rosamond had been big enough to regret his misfortune, if not to repudiate the ignominy cast upon him.

Keven went into Minton's store and straightway forgot

the episode. Here Keven had spend many an hour in the years gone by selecting and rejecting the varieties of fishing gear. He had stepped out of a void into the pleasant and sunny past, over which the river reigned.

"I'd bet you couldn't keep long out of here," laughed Minton, sure of his man. "Kev, you'll have to get some to catch up. These four years have changed fishing tackle, same as the other and less important things. Lighter rods, smaller flies, fewer spoons. Oh, boy, the steelhead I hung last summer!"

"It's nice to see you once more among your treasures," replied Keven. "'How I used to slave, beg, and borrow, almost steal money to spend here! . . . I'd forgotten. . . . Joe, I—I guess I'll never cast a fly again."

"Ha! Ha! Listen to him! Once a fisherman always a fisherman, Kev. The old river will get you back. You were born on it. So was I. Do you imagine you can resist? Never, and don't think you're too weak or sick or bitter ever to fish again. That's what you need. The Rogue will cure you, Kev. Give you back all you've lost!"

"Mint, you were always a great salesman," said Keven admiringly.

"Sure! But, you darned fool, I'm just glad to see you home. I don't want your money."

"I haven't any," replied Keven. "Just got Garry Lord out of jail. Dad's going to raise enough to buy us a net. I've decided to try the market-fishing game with Garry."

"Deuce you have! That's not a bad idea, Kev. You two ought to clean up. Garry is the best salmon fisherman on the river. If you can keep him sober!"

"Mint, I may need some keeping myself," laughed Keven.

"Oh, say, Kev, you didn't learn to hit the booze?"

"Afraid I did, Mint."

"Then you gotta quit. I hate a drinking fisherman. That old gag about fishermen going out in the morning to return smelling of rum, with the truth not in them—that always gets my goat. It's not true."

"Mint, I got in the habit of drinking because it relieved my pain," replied Keven sadly. "I don't know which is worse now."

19

"You take to fishing again, Kev Bell," said Minton with earnest bluntness. "It's your best bet. There's a living in it. And more—for you. Jobs are hard to get in this valley, and there's none for crippled soldiers. Market-fish for a few years—save your money—and put it in an apple farm. Oregon apples! Fortune in them, Kev. I'm raising an orchard now."

"Apple farm? Well, not so bad, Mint. I'd like it, and if I can save some money! . . . You make me feel sort of hopeful."

"That's the fisherman of it, Kev. Always anticipating, always hopeful. Every bend of the river beckons—every pool may bring better luck. Life should be like that. Then the joy of fishing! The fun, the peace, the sport! Who would ever tire of the music and the beauty of a running river? Especially the Rogue! It's the best in the world, Kev."

"You make me wish I had the dough to buy a lot of tackle," replied Keven dejectedly.

"Say, you don't need any dough," retorted Minton. "Buy what you like and pay me when you can. I don't care if you never pay, far as I'm concerned. I owe you something."

Keven was powerless to resist this offer, and straight-way plunged into the old delight of choosing a rod and suitable outfit to go with it.

"No more," he vowed, finally, waving back the generous and enthusiastic dealer.

"Well, when you bust that come in for more," declared Minton. "Say, the steelhead ran big last year. Late in the season, though. Funny about it. We used to get some twelve-pounders in the first run."

"Twelve pounds! And you've sold me a six-ounce rod?" ejaculated Keven, awakening to the old argument over heavy versus light tackle.

"You bet. Wait till you hang a big one on that rig," replied Minton. "And now listen to your Uncle Dudley. This talk is looking to the future and it's serious. Keep it under your hat. Find a likely flat or bench down the river. And locate it. File a mining claim. Do your assessment work faithfully. Someday it'll be valuable property, even if you don't strike gold."

"Gold! What are you driving at, Mint?"

"Have you forgotten the Rogue has given up its millions to miners?" went on Minton earnestly. "There's gold down the river. Gold in sand bars, gold in quartz ledges. Fall in with one of those old prospectors and learn from him. Whitehall is one of them. He has a claim at Whisky Creek. If you're going to run the Rogue cultivate him. Make friends with the half-breeds. Most of them are good fellows. Get acquainted with the trail packers, too."

"Thanks for the tip, Minton," said Keven gratefully. "You make me feel like a regular fellow."

"Now one last word, Kev," went on the dealer, with lowered voice. "There's a nigger in the woodpile down at the mouth of the river. Every year fewer salmon and fewer steelhead come up! Find out why. This partner of yours, Garry Lord, is keen as a bloodhound. Tough runt, yes, but if I don't miss my guess he has a heart big as a hill. Anyway he's a riverman. There's none better. Get him on the job. We fishermen up here fear Brandeth will ruin the river. He'll hog the fish and kill the runs—if he isn't stopped. Don't get the idea only us few anglers are interested. The people all along the river, from Galice to Prospect, are complaining. Fish used to be easy to catch. They are no more. There're a hundred thousand people, more or less, who are vitally concerned. The netting at the mouth ought to be stopped. Or if not that, restricted. One man particularly and a few more getting rich at the expense of the people of Oregon. It's an outrage."

"Minton, I certainly agree with you, if that's the condition," rejoined Keven earnestly. "Comes as a surprise to me. But it's in line with everything—since the war. . . . How does this Gus Atwell stack up to you?"

"Not very high, Kev," replied Minton. "He was a slacker. He rolls in money now. Rolls a Rolls-Royce around. Yet it's like squeezing juice out of a rock to get him to pay his bills—so the town gossip goes about him. He's against the upriver market fishermen. And for that matter all kinds of fishermen. During the canning season he drives a car between Gold Beach and here. But he sticks there pretty close."

"Garry told me as much," replied Keven meditatively. "Somebody ought to put a crimp in Atwell."

"I'll tell the world," agreed Minton. "Kev, he lined you from soda to hock when he came home, 'invalided' from training service."

"You don't say?" inquired Keven, with affected mild surprise.

"He stood right there, in this store, and told some of the boys you had been mainly responsible for the ruin of five sisters. Ghastly story! Of course we got hardened to the doings of soldiers. But that was the limit!"

"It is pretty bad, even for soldiers," admitted Keven. "Did everybody believe that particular yarn?"

"No, not everybody. I remember Bill Hall, who was one of the fellows in here when Atwell gabbed so loud—he called him sarcastic enough. And I cursed him. Never speaks to me now. But, Kev, that yarn hurt you with the women."

"I suppose Atwell swaggered around in a uniform and dazzled the ladies."

"He did. And made us fellows sick."

"Well, I might tell a yarn about him if I'd happen to get sore."

The thing rankled in Keven and gradually clouded the better mood inspired by Emmeline and Minton. The resentment thus engendered rather augmented than otherwise. Even work with Garry over fishing nets and boat equipment did not suffice to soften it. They planned to pack camp duffle and provisions on Saturday, preparatory to their departure early on Sunday.

If Keven had not had anything to drink on Saturday night he would have gotten away from town without giving the gossips more to wag their tongues over. But out of deference to his father he had left the bottle severely alone, and not until he had left home to stay at Garry's camp to facilitate an early start next day had he transgressed.

Still he was sober that Saturday night when he encountered Atwell in the crowded lobby of the principal hotel. Liquor seldom made Keven drunk. But it found a hidden devil in his depths.

"Hello, Major, I've been looking for you," he said, confronting the well-groomed and well-fed Atwell.

"Sorry I can't return the compliment," replied Atwell,

in cold contempt, his dark, rather handsome face flushing with annoyance. He turned his back.

A tiger leaped up inside Keven Bell. His swift outflung hand spun Atwell around.

"You lied about me, you—skunk!" exclaimed Keven, in ringing voice. "I'm going to call you to your face. It was *you* who was mixed up in that Carstone outrage. Not I. . . . Why, didn't you tell Grant's Pass that the soldiers burned you in effigy? Why didn't you tell them your company could have gone to France if you hadn't been a coward? . . . For that's the truth and I can prove it."

Atwell's face grew livid. "You filthy soldier bum! Everyone knows that crack you got made you weak in the head. But take care——"

Keven struck him, causing him to stagger along the rail of the stairway to the wall. The blow brought blood. It was not violent, but it unleashed a devil in Keven.

"What I said goes," he shouted, in scathing passion. "Invalided home! Yes, you white-livered cur. But the soldiers know. Let your friends ask any soldier in your company. . . . And as for the dirty lie you spread—if you accuse me again of that Carstone muck, I'll kill you!"

Fiercely Keven grasped a vase from a table and swung it on Atwell's head. With a sharp crack it flew into bits. But it knocked Atwell flat to the floor, where he lay stunned or unconscious.

No one made any move to interfere, and Keven walked out into the night.

chapter four

KEVEN, REMEMBERING HIS FATHER, regretted his violence, and hurried home to tell of it, and that arrest would surely follow unless he got out of town. To his surprise the old man took the news with satisfaction. "Good! Glad you

23

soaked Atwell. I'd done it myself," he said spiritedly. "So his soldiers burned him in effigy because he reneged on reporting his company fit for France. Well, that's the other side of the story."

"It is, Dad, and straight goods. I'll beat it now. Will keep you posted about what's doing at Gold Beach. Good-by." Keven took his pack and tackle and went out. He crossed the meadows to the dark pines, and holding outside the edges of these he groped his way down to Garry's shack. No answer to his whistle! The fisherman was not at home. A fire smoldered in the stone circle. Keven replenished it, feeling a strange, pleasant vibration of his pulses. The blaze crackled up cheerily; the dull embers underneath took on a live red glow. The smell of burning wood was sweet.

His next action was to remove his uniform and don in its stead the flannel shirt and overalls he had bought. He had also a heavy waterproof coat lined with wool. With something of violence and finality he flung the army uniform into the fire. "That'll be about all," he muttered, as he watched it burn. "No more of that patriotic bunk for me." He believed he voiced the opinion of several million young Americans. "Fight? Hell, yes! If your country was invaded!" Sitting down, he watched the suit burn down to gray ashes. "That ends that." And he meant all concerning the last few miserable years.

A rattling of gravel startled him. Someone was stumbling down the low bank under the pine. "That you, Garry?"

"Wash masher?" came in Garry's voice, now thick in utterance. And Gary staggered into the firelight, red of face, panting for breath, drunk as a lord.

"Nothing the matter with me, Garry," replied Keven, with a relieved laugh. "You're three sheets in the wind, though. How'd you escape the police?"

"All lookin' fer you, b'gosh."

"Me? What for?"

"Heerd you mashed Majjer Atwell on the coco."

"Well, for once, rumor is right. I sure did."

"We gotta beat it."

"Downriver at night?" queried Keven, alarmed.

"Sure Mike. Little ways. An' we'll camp on the other side."

"Skiff all packed, Garry?"

"Yep. But I'll hev anozzer look."

Keven took his bag and tackle and carried them down to the river. He flashed his light. The skiff had been neatly packed. Keven made a thorough survey of it, satisfied himself about the four oars in place in the rowlocks, two extra oars on the floor of the boat, and particularly the long rope coiled in the bow. Then he deposited his belongings below the stern seat and went back up the bank. Garry came out of the shack with a roll of blankets and a canvas.

"Here, man, let's roll them up in the tarp," said Keven. "That river will be wet and cold. . . . There. Now I'll put out the fire."

He spread the blazing sticks and kicked sand over them. Suddenly all was pitch dark. Feeling his way down, he finally made out Garry's shape and the pale outline of the boat. He was about to flash the electric light again when a police whistle deterred him.

"Garry, they're after me," he whispered.

"Sojer boy, they're after *us,*" returned the fisherman, chuckling.

"What'd you do, Garry?"

"I shure beaned thet ossifer. He ast me where you was. An' when I swore didn't know he pinched me."

"Get in the skiff. Easy now. I hear footsteps. . . . What's the dope?"

"Watz me, Kev, old boy," rejoined Garry, who had taken the seat facing the stern.

Keven stepped softly into the skiff and, sitting down upon the other seat, he carefully pushed off with an oar.

"Garry, you won't shoot this rapid below in the dark? We'd better line the boat down."

"Line nuthin'."

"But man, you're drunk!"

"Whassthell's difference?"

Out from the gloom of the pines the skiff moved and the current caught it. The river gleamed under the stars. Garry faced downstream, his oars dipping noiselessly. Evidently, drunk or sober he knew his business on that river. Another shrill whistle rang out from the dark shore, followed by a hoarse call: "Hyar's the shack, Bill. Come on."

Keven roused to keen and vibrant feeling. Long had authority weighed like a yoke upon him. He poised his oars and watched the guarded movement of Garry's. Then a dull heavy roar of tumbling waters smote his ears. His hair seemed to freeze at the roots and stood up stiff. From boyhood he had been taught to respect the Rogue. Companions of his youth had defied the river to find watery and unknown graves. The skiff was now in the middle of the stream; the current was quickening; the roar grew clearer. Garry turned to whisper. "All we gotta do is hit the middle where she dips."

Keven stood up, the better to see. Somewhere beyond them the livid gleaming river appeared to end. Bold black banks stood up on each side, and sharp treetops pierced the sky. Keven resumed his seat, only to rise again, bending somewhat to hold the oars. With this movement of the boat, the swelling of the roar, an old daring, pulsating spirit of adventure seemed to be having a rebirth. Or was he just remembering? Then, not so far ahead, he made out white tips of wild waves upflung. Next he saw a long silvery incline, V-shaped, rolling and bobbing, from which thunder rose. His skin tightened cold on his face as he felt the wind of the rapid. Many a time had he run this stretch of river. He knew it. His eyes pierced the gloom. He bent over his companion, to speak in his ear.

"Garry, we're square in the middle."

What the hoarse answer was Keven could not distinguish, but it rang full of the daredevil assurance of the riverman. Keven sat down to grip the oar handles. Swifter current caught them; the banks blurred; the stern of the skiff rocked and dipped; then they shot down, to smash into the curling backlash. They bounced high between spread sheets of water and went over straight as a die into the long buffeting incline. Then Keven saw only Garry's oars, the action of which he duplicated so swiftly as to be almost in perfect time with them. His arms felt like those of a giant. He could have yelled above the roar of the rapid—a liberation of long pent-up agony. But he bit his tongue. He was aware of cold, stinging water on his face; of the solid lessening thumps on the gunwales; of the dim canopying sky, studded with stars. Garry began to pull hard, edging to the right. Below, the rapid split bellowing round a black rock. Keven had hit it once. He bent powerfully on his oars. The skiff slowed, slanted diagonally across the channel, moving inshore while on the breast of the current, and missed the ugly obstacle by a yard. Garry racked his oars, to turn and grin at Keven in the pale gloom. Keven followed suit. They drifted on below the rapid into smooth deep water where the river glided darkly.

"Loike swipin' candy from the baby," whispered Garry hoarsely. Then he turned the skiff and rowed downstream. Keven rested on his oars. His face felt damp. His breast labored. The turmoil of his veins slowly subsided. He felt a sudden wave of admiration and appreciation of Garry Lord. While he rested and pried into these unfamiliar sensations, the skiff covered water to the long sweeping strokes of the riverman. They turned a bend. Black rose a high wooded hill. The river broadened. Garry kept to the side opposite to that on which the road ran. The cool night breeze brought a faint low roar. Another rapid! This river was indeed a rogue! Keven felt that itch at the roots of his hair. Would Garry run another rapid that night? Still this next one was far away yet.

Keven gazed back up the river, over the fringed shores to the bold mountains which encompassed the town. What was he leaving there? Home—a bad name—an old father to whom he refused to be a burden—to——But he suddenly raised a wall before his consciousness of that which flayed.

The roar of the next rapid grew louder. It began to disturb Keven. Yet if Garry meant to run it Keven would say never a word. The riverman, however, rowed ashore and beached the boat on a sandy bar, under the shade of trees. After Keven stepped out he pulled it well up and made the bowline fast to a root.

"Kev, lez sleep some," said Garry, tugging at the bedroll. "Wake me early, fer I'll be dead to the world."

They spread tarpaulin and blankets on a level grassy plot, and removing coats and shoes they went to bed.

27

Garry was asleep as soon as he stretched out, but Keven felt wakeful. He found he was extremely tired. His body throbbed and burned. Such exertion, not to say excitement, was new and very exhausting to him. It amazed him that he had not collapsed. Perhaps he was not so weak as he had imagined. Nevertheless his sensations were distinctly pleasant. He began to get warm and to rest. His heart ceased its abnormal pounding. Then he attended to outward stimulations. Cold bright, thoughtful stars peered at him through the dark foliage; the branches of the trees rustled; and the river sent up its melancholy sounds—the lap of tiny waves on the sand, the gurgle of gliding current, the mellow roar of the next rapid.

Lying there in the still darkness, Keven felt a drawing power in this strange mountain river. As a boy he had loved it; as a man he realized an affinity in it somehow, if only the freedom and loneliness it embodied. How singular that he was to earn his livelihood now from its swift waters! He marveled at that. There was something inscrutable in the causes which had led to this. A great burden welled up and out of his heart. He had come back to the Rogue. It could never be denied him. What would poverty and privation mean to him? Nothing. He would glory in them.

At last, with the dreamy hum of the falls in his ears, Keven fell asleep. He awakened at the first streaks of dawn, and it took a moment for him to realize where he was. The dark spreading branches above bewildered him. But the gray misty curtain and the murmur of the river stirred him to glad facts. He had to shake Garry hard to awaken him.

"My God, I thought—thet jailer was—proddin' me," yawned Garry, sitting up. "Mornin', soldier boy."

"Cut that, Garry. Call me anything but that," replied Keven. "I'm your fishing mate now."

"Ex-coose me, Kev. . . . Gosh, I gotta have a drink," said the riverman, throwing off the blankets. "I fetched a bottle fer this very gol-durned thing. Hev a drink on me. We don't want to risk buildin' fire an' cookin' breakfast along here."

"What's your plan, Garry?"

"We'll run down an' stop short of Hell Gate," replied

28

Lord speculatively. "Them cops will drive along the river lookin' fer us. They can't see the river except in certain places, where you bet we won't be. We'll camp an' eat, an' tomorrow mornin' early get by the bridge an' Galice. But sure as hops them cops will be waitin' at the end of the road. We'll fool 'em though, fer the Alameda bridge went out this winter. An' all they can do is watch us run through."

It was daylight when they rowed out from the shore. A cloud of mist overhung the river like a lowering pall. Under its cover the fugitives could safely pass on to where the river wound out of sight from the road.

When they reached the rapid, which was in no wise terrifying by day, Garry turned to his partner, while poising his oars: "Take her through, Kev. Let's see if you've forgot."

"I'm on, Garry," said Keven, and stood up some distance above the incline, to get his bearings. A cool tickling ran along his spine. But he awakened to Garry's confidence. It was a slow rapid, necessitating a varied course to avoid rocks. Keven sat down to pull a little to the right, and when he dipped over the incline he had the skiff in hand, half diagonally across the channel, and once below the fall, a few strong tugs with the aid of the current worked her out of line with the first submerged rock. Then he turned straight, stern forward, to take the main volume of water, his eye keen on the next rock. Some rods above it he pulled slantingly to the left and let the current take him by. The rest of the rapid was trivial.

"You ain't forgot nuthin'," declared Garry, taking up his oars. "That was apple pie."

Keven stifled a yell which swelled in his throat. That he could feel so good again—alive—strong—active—bold! He warmed to Garry. They would get along together. They had much in common. The river was a bond.

On they rowed, down the still stretches, where the wild ducks scuttled in great flurry out of the coves, and drifted down the long ripples, and shot the rapids which repeated themselves every mile or so, while the mist lifted, and deep blue patches of sky showed through, and the green wooded slopes. Soon the sun burst through to flood the

valley with light. By afternoon the fugitives had reached
the constriction of the valley, where the river cut through
under cliffs of bronze. Hell Gate was close. They could
hear the low thunder of this dammed-up and furious
rapid. Garry pointed to a shady bench.

"There we are, Kev," he said, grinning. "We'll make
camp an' take it easy. They can't see us or our smoke. An'
by golly, if they did they'd never get to us, 'cept by
runnin' the river. Ketch them lousy cops tryin' out the
Rogue!"

Ashore Keven found a wonderful covert, yet which
opened out to the glancing river, and the mounting wall of
ferned and mossy granite. Leisurely he helped at making
camp, at the chores around the campfire. Every hour
more came back to him—a regurgitation of past and
forgotten joys. Could the future possibly hold more for
him than pain and drink and degradation? He pondered.
And in the late hours of afternoon he lay idly, dreamily,
fighting a drowsiness that threatened to drag him into
oblivion. A short pink-flushing of the sky heralded the
sunset, and then twilight soon settled down. With dusk
came the cool of the river. Garry kindled the fire, and
Keven had a long unthinking hour lounging before it,
listening and feeling. But soon sleep claimed him, and
scarcely had he closed his eyes, it seemed, when Garry
routed him out.

"Hey, are you dead?" called Garry. "Hop up an' feed
your face. We gotta dig."

The morning appeared scarcely to have broken, or the
banner of mountain mist hung thicker. It was like gray
twilight. Before they shoved off Garry said: "Kev, I'll
take her through Hell Gate. You jest watch. The river's at
thet stage when the current is bad. I can't let it do the
work. An' a stroke of oar from you, thet wasn't jest right,
could sure spill us. I want you to get broke in again before
takin' risks."

"All right, Garry. But I'll gamble it'd come to me,"
replied Keven.

"Mebbe. But the Rogue is cold as hell this early in the
mornin'."

Garry rowed into the center of the narrowing river.
Keven could not see the tips of the cliffs, which were

30

obscured. He turned a corner, whence came a sullen wrestling roar. Garry wheeled the boat to face that threatening sound. Keven had been through here many a time, but in summer, at low water. The river was two feet above that now, and running like a millrace. The channel narrowed to a box, and dimly ahead Keven made out the gate. Passage looked impossible and shook his heart. Then he bent his faculties upon the boatman and the current. They entered the box, rode a swelling ridge of water, and shot like a plummet into the gray roaring hell of that sinister gateway. Garry pulled with swift powerful short strokes. They were lifted toward the corner of the wall, where the water climbed in whirling fury. But they fell back with the wave and sped by through the gate. The angry waters spread hissingly. Garry rested on his oars, and when they drifted beyond the roar, he said: "Run it easy. But I ain't stuck on Hell Gate."

"Garry, would a saw log or an empty boat hit that corner?" asked Keven.

"Nine times out of ten, I bet," Garry returned, and took to his oars. "Fall in, Kev. Let's get by the bridge an' Galice."

Soon the even powerful strokes propelled them to the bridge, dim in the gray fog, and under it, and beyond to where the river turned out of the gorge into a valley again. Galice appeared a sleeping village, without one column of smoke from its cottage chimneys. Below Galice another thunder of rapids greeted the boatmen.

"S rapids ahead," said Garry. "She's a right-angle triangle. A humdinger to shoot sometimes. But apple pie at this stage. We can't hit nuthin'."

They navigated a series of ripples between shallow islands and bars, to run into a circling pool, which curved to the right and leaped with a bellow into gray darkness under a high black overhanging slope. It would have been frightful but for Garry's assurance. They backed the skiff until an invisible hand seemed to snatch at it and fling it over a runway into a choppy crested channel, down which it bobbed like a cork, rising over the white mounds, to pound at last once more into open, spreading river.

Here they passed the Lewis Ranch and sped on over the rock ledges and gravel bars and ripples which had once been Keven's favorite fishing waters. Floods might come and go, but Keven knew the river there, and he sat as one in a trance. Garry was whistling. The mist was breaking away to reveal the timbered slopes, ever rising higher. A mile-long stretch of river followed on a sharp bend. Chair Riffle! Here ran the famous steelhead pool, beloved alike by native spooner and the effete fly-fisher. How many times had Keven sat in that rocky chair from which the riffle derived its name! Then on they went round the bend, over the rapids that had cost Keven many a game trout; on under a sunny blue sky.

The quiet stretches of river grew few and far between, but the current took its fall gradually, as if preparing for a big drop round the bend, above which the green slopes sheered mountain high. Alameda! The end of the road and the entrance of the Rogue into the wilderness! Soon Keven sighted the gaunt and rusted ore mill, abandoned and falling to ruin, that despoiled the beautiful slope. Another turn fetched them within sight of the wide pool above Alameda Falls. Here a great gap yawned in the bridge that spanned the head of the fall. Keven's quick eye espied a motorcar, and men standing on the left bank.

"Told you so," shouted Garry, turning to Keven. "Them lousy cops!"

"What'll we do?" queried Keven quickly.

"Nuthin'. They'll reckon they'll halt us above the fall. But we'll go right on over—an' then to hell with 'em!"

They rode the long swift stretch that ended in the huge eddy. The current here slowed for a hundred yards, then converged towards the gap in the bridge, where the river disappeared. From below soared up a hollow boom.

The policemen on the bank began to make authoritative gestures, which grew violent as the boatmen made no effort to row out of the current. Then the pull of the fall caught the boat and it was too late. The officers saw that. They yelled:

"Row ashore or we'll shoot!"

Garry stood up to reply in stentorian voice: "We gotta go over!"

Alameda Falls, without any officers of the law, or any broken bridge, was ticklish enough to run. The drift swung to the left and circled over black knife-edge rocks on the lip of the fall. Garry pulled well to the right of the middle and had to keep pulling to hold that position. Keven for the moment forgot the two policemen, crowding to the edge, now brandishing their automatic pistols. When Garry shipped his oars Keven knew all was well for that descent. As the skiff careened on the curved green crest of the incline he let out a wild yell, which he scarcely heard in the din. Down they slipped—crash! And then fast indeed did they speed down the diminishing waves away from the falls. It was when Garry turned his smug red face that Keven remembered the policemen. He turned. They were bouncing up and down, waving weapons and evidently yelling like Indians. A few seconds had carried the skiff two hundred feet and more beyond.

Again Garry stood up, and this time he put his thumb to his nose and spread his fingers.

"Com mon!" he yelled from leather-bellowsed lungs. "Come an' get us—you lousy loafers!"

No doubt the policemen heard; at least they could not have misunderstood Garry's defiance. And they began to shoot.

"Wow! Low bridge, Kev. Duck your nut!" he shouted, and fell into the bottom of the boat.

Kev crouched low behind a gunwale, while the bullets whanged and splashed all about the boat, until it drifted out of range.

chapter five

BELOW ALAMEDA the river wound around a bend in the green mountain-sloped canyon. Keven had a last glimpse at the broken bridge, the watching policemen, and the abandoned mill. Then swiftly they disappeared, and he realized he had left civilization and law behind. For more than a hundred miles the Rogue bisected a wilderness that was a law unto itself. The great slopes slanted to towering crags where eagles soared. Then another heavy roar filled Keven's ears.

"Snap out of it, Kev," called Garry. "Thet's the Argo, an' she ain't no slouch to run. We gotta pull like hell to keep close on the right. There's a ledge we can slip over."

Another turn brought into view a rocky black gap, where huge ledges, striped with white quartz, obscured the river. It jumped into a pit, but a goodly part of the current kept to a long bench. Keven always used to line down this bad fall, as did all but the most reckless rivermen. But now it pulled a yelp of delight to his lips. Garry began to sing: "Pull for the shore, sailor, pull for the shore."

Keven lent himself with all his power to aid Garry in making the desired place. Soon they were in the heavy current, from which there was no backing. A hundred feet below the main body of water thumped into a hole from which rose clouds of mist. They could not now see the slanting ledge that was to help them over. But they knew where it lay. They rowed with deep strong strokes. When within six feet of the butting black bluff, and twice as far from the dip, Garry slipped his oars. He was still singing, but Keven could not hear him. Like a swan the skiff took the leap into the narrowing millrace that sped high above and alongside the cauldron below. With plummet speed they went over, and such was the celerity of the new boat that, despite Garry's sudden and tremendous exertions, she bumped hard into the cliff. Keven was thrown off his seat, and one of his oar handles hit Garry a sudden blow in the back. The backlash drew them away from the wall, and when Keven had righted himself and gotten his oars fixed, they were drifting safely into the pool below. Only then did Garry turn, grievous pain and amaze showing on his face.

"What t'hell you doin', soakin' me thet way?"

"Accident, Garry. When you tried to knock down the cliff I went flying off my seat."

"By gosh, Kev. Our boat's a hummer. She's too good.

34

Too fast. We gotta load her, or Lord only knows where we'll jump when we hit Kelsey Canyon."

"We'll line the rapids, you broncho-busting riverman."

"Line nuthin'. There ain't no bad runs till we get to Kelsey an' thet ain't bad."

So they drifted and rowed, glided and eddied, and drove on into the deepening wilderness of the range. Except at the head of long stretches they could not see the tips of the high mountains, but when they were able to gaze far down the valley, crags and domes and peaks greeted their eyes, piercing the blue sky. And ever the river murmured and sang and roared on into solitude. Cloud ships sailed across the gold-green slopes; troops of deer stood on the sand bars, heads erect, long ears up, to bound away only at near approach of the skiff. Wild ducks winged rapid flight down the canyon. Eagles streaked across the blue gap above. And at the end of every still stretch boomed a rapid.

They ran Graves Creek Fall, and once more Keven's skin prickled. To look back and up at that fall, where a green flood poured between narrow gray confining cliffs, and turned white and spread fan-shape into the great pool below, stirred both daring and dread in his tormented breast. Garry beached the skiff at the head of Lower Graves.

"Gotta start linin' sometime," he said. "An' this bird is a good one to break in on."

They took the long line out of the bow and, shoving the skiff adrift, waded down along the shore, holding back and letting loose as the exigency of the case demanded. But when the boat shot over they had to run, hanging on as best they could, while the line whizzed through their hands. Keven slipped on a rock that was like ice, and down he plunged at Garry's heels, to have the line wrenched out of his hands, and to plunge down, striking on his shoulder and face. He saw a million stars and lay stunned, half in and half out of the water, until he recovered and awoke to excruciating pain.

Garry waited below the fall. "Kev, you can't move these river boulders with your face," he said.

"Don't kid me, old man," gasped Keven, his hand to his jaw. "That was awful."

"It wasn't nuttin' to what we'll hit at Blossom or Mule Creek. Com mon. Don't you hear Reamy Falls bellerin' fer us?"

They went on, but it was long before Keven regained the spirit of the voyage. Reamy Falls was a big drop, where the river roared into a foaming hole. It could not be run. They had to portage their cargo around the fall, over tremendous stones between which deep ruts yawned. And lastly the skiff had to be dragged, and hauled, and skidded over the bare ledges to the channel below. After that ordeal Keven was exhausted. But the river, as if to make up for that violent break, glided smoothly and evenly for a distance, then rippled on to Whisky Creek, which was the voyagers' objective for that day.

It was high time, Keven thought, as he labored and floundered up the sandy bank with his pack. The valley widened here, in confluence with the intersecting valley, down which the clear creek babbled. Huge pine trees stood upon the bench, and back of them a rudely fenced garden and a log cabin. Here dwelt Whitehall, a prospector, and a lover of the wilds.

The barking of his dogs brought him down to welcome his visitors, a stalwart man, still in the prime of life, rugged and weather-beaten, with the still clear eyes of the backwoodsman.

"Hullo, Whitey," Garry greeted him. "Guess who's with me this run."

"Kev Bell, or I'm a lonely sinner!" replied the prospector.

The meeting was not without its gladness and pathos for Keven. He had stopped often with this hospitable dweller of the mountains. Yet how far back in the irrevocable past! Keven could not get rid of a horrible, immeasurable span of years.

"Boys, don't make camp," he went on. "Come up to the cabin. I haven't seen a white man since last fall."

"How's the gold pannin' out?" asked Garry.

"I'm on the track of a strike."

"Whitey, you've been on thet for ten years I know of."

"Yes. But there's gold in these hills. I'll show you. I've struck it at last."

He led them into his one-room cabin, most comfortable wilderness quarters, with its rude furniture and trophies of the chase, its wide yellow stone fireplace and neat cupboard and shelves. A ham of jerked venison hung on the wall. Sight of that made Keven's mouth water, and he frankly announced the fact.

"Take it along. An' if you want a deer get up early. You'll find some in my garden patch. . . . But look ahere, Garry."

Whitehall showed them gold—in dust, in nuggets, in quartz. He handled it lovingly; not as one who thought of what gold could buy, but for the hazard and the glory of its discovery.

"Jumpin' silversides!" ejaculated Garry, his eyes alight, as he scratched his sandy hair. "You didn't have this on my last run."

"No. I've struck it, Garry. An' I won't be here on your next," replied the prospector significantly.

"By gosh, I'm glad fer your sake—sorry fer us fellers who have to come down the Rogue. . . . Whitey, you musta made thet strike over around Tyee Bar somewhere?"

"No, I wasted years on Tyee, just because the Chinks took millions off that bar in years gone by. Garry, the gold on the bars came down the river, in floods. I found mine in the hills, back of here. . . . But that's enough about myself. Tell me the news from upriver. What're you doin' down here, Kev? It's too early for steelhead, if they ever come again."

While the prospector got supper for them he talked incessantly, as one thirsty for communication with the outside world. When Keven's story came out, as it soon flowed from Garry's voluble lips, he did not voice the sadness his face expressed, and his only comment was: "Kev, you're wise to take to the river. But pass up the salmon. Garry hasn't sense enough to see the day of the salmon is almost done. But you're young. Hunt for gold!"

His words sunk deeply home to Keven. The idea of hunting for the yellow metal had never before seriously crossed his consciousness. How fascinating it was now! It far outweighed the fruit farm in satisfying romance, in other appeal that he could not analyze on the moment. Was it not food for thought? Best of all it meant living away from people!

In the morning Whitehall accompanied them down to the river and bade them a cheery farewell. "Good-by, boys. Good luck. Have a care at Mule Creek." And as they shoved off into the current he called: "Send me word by the trail packers about the fish-hog business down there."

"We'll send you one of Brandeth's ears. Haw! Haw!" shouted Garry.

Then the current of the Rogue caught them. Whitehall waved from the high bank, until the swift curving channel raced them round a timbered corner into the long chute that ended in Tyee Bar.

"Garry, oughtn't we go ashore and look the rapids over?" called Keven, as the sullen thunder floated up the river.

"Sure, but I can run Tyee with one hand tied," was the gay reply.

"But a river changes with every winter flood."

It mattered not to Garry. His shoulders squared, his neck bulged, as he faced the unknown around the rocky bend, whence lifted swelling menace. Then it seemed to Keven that the famous Tyee leaped at their faces until he was blind and deaf. When they flashed out of the big waves, on to the long glistening, glassy runway, something of Garry's wild spirit had taken permanent hold of Keven. He screamed his freedom to the soaring eagles above the crags. He laughed at the black rock-studded Russian Bar. And the frothy China Bar lent only added power to the oars and lustier voice. So they ran the Corkscrew, Devil's Ribs, Black Bar, and on down sunlit lanes past the meadows, and the gentle lingering, rippling Winkle Bar, on and on through still gorge to the boulder-jumbled constriction of the river at Blossom, where not even a saw log could have passed unscathed. A shattered mountain had obstructed the river in this cool dark melodious left angle, where the firs stood up, and the amber brooks poured off the mossy cliffs, and the current hissed its way. They packed the outfit round this rapid and slid the boat over rocks and between rocks to the open channel below.

Then on into an endless murmuring solitude the voyagers drifted, rested, rowed and glided, silent under the cool gleaming walls and the fern-covered cliffs, until at last the solemn roar of Mule Creek Canyon assailed their ears and shocked the flint into their veins.

In the open sunlight, at the head of a wall of bronze rock which barred the valley, they rowed ashore on the left side, to beach the skiff on a gravel bar.

"We'll climb up an' take a look," said Garry, as if reluctantly forced. A hundred yards beyond, the sliding sullen Rogue abruptly turned into a bronze break, from whence it sent forth a terrific bawl, enough to quake the stoutest heart.

They climbed up and out across the rock to the split, where far below the river waved like a white ribbon in the wind. Garry walked half a mile farther, ever and anon taking a peep over the brink, and halted above the Narrows.

"It ain't no joy ride," he remarked soberly, "but since we gotta run it, let's hurry back an' pile into her."

Whereupon they swiftly retraced their steps. Before Garry shoved off he said: "You never run Mule Creek?"

"No," replied Keven seriously. "We brought wheels and dragged our boat down the trail."

"Damn good idee. . . . Well, there ain't nothin' till we hit the Narrows an' then there ain't nuthin'. If we don't fill when she jumps off here we'll be okay till we come to the Narrows. There it's jest luck. If thet whirlpool's open you gotta pull your very guts out until it closes. Com mon."

No beauty or music in the river here! Even under the sun it had a steely glare. Beyond the bronze corner of wall an appalling spectacle riveted Keven to his seat. The boat poised on a green curve, then plunged, suddenly to be lifted by colossal power, to smash over the backlashing wave, into a seething maelstrom, out of which she was propelled as if by a catapult. Then she rode a swelling

39

ridge of green, between sinister overhanging walls, against which the water curled and boiled with millions of bubbles. Garry held his oars poised. They drifted like a feather. The sky appeared as a blue flowing stream above. The green slopes were hidden. Soon the thunder of the rapid at the entrance lulled and ceased. The river sped on, almost quiet. Little sucking gurgling sounds rose from the chafing margin, where the bubbled circles eddied. How sinister these boils! Then the crest of current in the center spread, and great eddies caught the boat, turning her round.

"Let her turn!" boomed Garry, as the amazed Keven dipped an oar. And so they whirled, sometimes several times in one giant eddy, before they were released and sent on. The poised oars scraped the walls.

Soon a strange sound struck Keven. It came from water. But water doing what? Hollow, deep, mocking, subterranean, it ended in a stupendous suck.

Round a jut of wall they swept. Keven saw a jagged ledge crossing diagonally to within ten feet of the opposite cliff. This was the Narrows. He had only seen it from above. Down in the canyon how monstrously different!

Garry began to row in desperation. Keven caught his stroke and bent with every ounce of weight and strength. They checked the speed, they held her back, so that inch by inch she drifted toward the hellish hole now visible. It was the whirlpool, open and engulfing. The current did not look so terribly swift. But it was the swell of the river, passing that obtruding corner, that caused the whirlpool.

Keven's terror broke when he saw the hole closing and filling. But the resistless and unbeatable current carried the boat past the corner, through the narrow gateway, right upon that whirlpool. It gave a horrible gurgle, as if a demon below emitted sullen anger. Keven's right oar was wrenched out of his hand. It stood upright. It whirled as if upon a rapid lathe. It sank straight down before his eyes; and the boat, caught in the toils, whirled and whirled. Suddenly then the river bulged where the suckhole had been.

Garry pulled the bow from threatened collision with the wall, and on the skiff drifted, slower and slower, round more corners, at last out again into the sunlight of the open valley.

"Jest an incident in a riverman's life," remarked Garry facetiously. "Thet's all thet's bad today. We'll camp below Solitude.'"

Keven fished out one of the extra oars from under the packs and put it in place. But not soon did he row.

Indeed there appeared little need of rowing. The river ran in every mood, except that of fury; and each succeeding vista gathered beauty, until the gleam of water and the glory of the slopes seemed supernatural. The sun was westering; the ripple took on a golden sheen, and the rocks over which they glided were gold; black and dense rose the forested mountains to the white clouds, and ever the river seemed flowing on into endless solitude.

On they traveled through a narrow gorge above white water, where at the brink natives had gathered to watch the voyagers pass their lonely homes, and down a long swift beautiful racecourse of shimmering water, and on still into wide peaceful reaches, to turn the curve which led into the river lane ending in magnificent Solitude.

Keven knew the long lovely lane. It pierced his heart with strange unsatisfied emotion. This was the wildest stretch, the sweetest and shadiest, that ran down to the bend of Solitude—a mining camp of early days—and to the finest pools and ripples, for steelhead, of all the Rogue. Yet it was not only the fishing that had chained Keven. The beauty of the great bend, perhaps, the loneliness, and that for which it had been so perfectly named, and yet for some vague and poignant thing, illusive and haunting—this caught at Keven's heart.

The boat went on, and no longer lingeringly, much to Keven's regret. He was all eyes, all senses. Still he did not see.

"There's Aard," said Garry. "Let's stop an' have a word with him. Best feller on the river."

Keven espied a man at a sand-bar edge. High above the green-gold bank a column of blue smoke curled against the background of forest fir.

Garry rowed ashore, to step out and shake hands with a tall lithe man, dark as an Indian, whose piercing eyes stirred that chary chord of remembrance in Keven's brain.

"Hello, Aard. Glad to see you. I'm late on the run this season. Shake hands with my new pard."

"Keven Bell. Reckon I know him," replied the other, extending a hand that slapped Keven heartily on the shoulder. "He stayed with us once. . . . How are you, boy? You growed some—an' changed. We heerd you'd been killed in France. An' then read you was hurt at some army camp."

"How do, Aard?" replied Keven ponderingly, trying to remember. "Wasn't it you who first put me on to Solitude steelhead? . . . Years ago, it was."

"Not so long, at thet, Keven," replied Aard, with a smile that brightened his dark face. "But I wasn't your first guide here at Solitude."

"No? . . . Doggone, but I hate that crack I got in the Army. It's ruined my memory. . . . But, Aard, I do remember you—and the river—and the steelhead."

"Thet's fine, boy. But come up to the cabin, an' mebbe you'll remember more."

Keven looked at his comrade. Garry spoke for both: "Thanks, Aard. But not tonight. We want to make camp at the spring below Solitude. Mebbe in the marnin'."

"Aard, how has the steelhead fishing been these last years?" queried Keven eagerly.

"Poorer all the time. Never a big steelhead gets up here till after October first."

"Hell you say!" ejaculated Garry meaningly, with a gleam in his eye, as he hitched up his belt.

"That's funny," added Keven, puzzled. "Till after October first!"

"Nuthin' funny about it," replied Aard. "You'll see if you're goin' through to Gold Beach. Are you?"

"Yes. I'm Garry's fishing partner now. See the net?"

"Reckon I seen thet right off an' thought Garry had made a raise. Well, I don't want to discourage you, but thet nettin' down at the mouth is bad medicine for upriver fishermen."

"What'll they do to us, Aard?" asked Garry.

"Reckon they'll kill you," replied Aard grimly. "I was

42

down to Gold Beach with my winter's catch of fur. An' I heerd some things."

"Ahuh. Well, don't discourage my young pard here," replied Garry, as he resumed his seat in the boat. "How was the trappin' this last winter?"

"Fair too middlin'. Mink an' coon plenty. Otter scarce, same as other fur."

"Aard, I jest wonder about you," rejoined Garry sagely, as he wagged his head. "By gosh, I'll spend a winter with you sometime. . . . Shove her off, Kev."

"Sorry you won't come up," said Aard, his fine eyes on Keven. "Someone will be disappointed."

· Keven laughed that off, as he bent to the oars, but somehow Aard's words, his look, struck him strangely. Kind and hospitable man, trapper Aard. Probably he meant his folk, whom Keven did not recall.

And straightway Keven, looking to the river below, was again gripped by the enchantment of Solitude, and after waving a hand to the watching Aard forgot all about him. Scarcely did he hear Garry, who was remarking: "Thet Jim Aard is a queer duck. I mean mysterious. Always has money. His cabins are the best on the river. He sends his family out often. An' he never packs enough fur to Gold Beach to make thet much money."

When they shot the last incline, over the rocky shelves that gleamed under the water, and turned the blue bend where the old mill stood moldering under its moss, and the great fir trees, Garry said they had time yet to make Missouri Bar, and as that was important, Keven reluctantly bit his tongue to keep from objecting. So they ran on, through the beautiful canyon, down to Missouri, where at sunset they hauled ashore and made camp.

Next morning at dawn they went whistling on their way, by the hamlets Illahe and Agness, to get through Two Mile Rapids and Clay Hill, both of which they ran. As they cleared the last wild plunge, Garry threw up his cap and let it go. From there on the mountains melted back, the valley widened, the river slowed and spread. Its fury was spent. It had cut and plowed through the Cascades. It ran now over wide shingles, between sandy bars and around gravelly islands. Shacks and huts, and high up on a grassy ridge a farmhouse, heralded the return of the habitations of men. The wilderness had been passed. The river flowed wearily, on into a wide bay, from whence it cut its way through low dunes of sand to the sea. On the fresh salt breeze floated the boom-boom of the surf.

chapter six

HIGH ON THE pine-fringed south shore of the bay stood the town, picturesque and inviting, its white houses shining in the sunlight. Low on the north shore, in a deep bight, the long flat piers and canning factories showed gray against the green. A mile stretch of sand curved out from the wooded hill and was cut by the river, where it had its narrow deep outlet to the sea. Across on the other shore sand dunes piled their monotonous gray. Inland, through the haze, rose the blue domes of the Cascades.

"Looks peaceful as it's pretty now," said Garry. "But wait till the salmon begin to run! Reckon we're early an' thet's good. I don't see many fishin' boats."

"Where's the netting done?" asked Keven.

"Out in thet bay, everywhere an' anywhere, except across the mouth of the river. Law against thet. But it's done on the sly, an' not by upriver fishermen, by gosh."

Garry made a deal with an Indian he knew to camp on his land and have a mooring. "If we strike fish I can hire a big flatboat from Stemm," said Garry. "Let's unload an' put up our tent under thet tree. Me an' Bill Malone camped there last year. Better fer us not to board uptown. Lord knows we'll blow our dough fast enough. Kev, are you strong on poker?"

"Nope. I'm too unlucky to gamble."

"Humph. Luck ain't nuthin' to do with nuthin' but fishin'. What'd you learn in the Army, anyhow?"

"To drink and cuss, for two things."

"Well, they ain't so bad, to start market fishin' on. Fightin' comes jest natural then."

44

"Say, Garry, don't they have any law and order here?"

"Sure. Finest little town on the coast. But in the salmon season there's crowds of fishermen an' oodles of money. Gamblin' an' bootleggin' on the sly. An' there's a couple of joints as tough as any frontier dive ever was. They're a hard crowd, these fishermen. Seafarin' men from Portland an' Seattle. Canucks from Puget Sound. Half-breeds from the Cascades. Coast fishermen from Crescent. From May till October first Gold Beach is sure prosperous."

"October first? Then that ends the netting season, and the fishermen leave?"

"You said it, bucko."

"Aard told us no big steelhead ever got up the river until after October first. Remember that, Garry?"

"Sure do. Your mind's operatin'. You may have a rotten memory, Kev, old top, but you can sure figger."

"There's a connection between the close of the netting season here and the run of large fish up the Rogue."

"You bet. An' thet connection is somethin' damn important to a hundred thousand people who live between the mouth of this river and Prospect."

"Ahuh. It's up to us to find out what that connection is."

"I should snicker to sneeze," rejoined Garry, with fire in his eye. "I've got my idees about it. Never cared so much, till last season, when I got sore. My pard, Jeff Dunn, was bumped on the head by some of these fishermen who hate us upriver fellers. Jeff never has been no good since."

So they talked while pitching camp and cooking a meal. After that they spread out the long new net, handling it with care and affection. Garry assured Keven that few nets on the river could beat it, and none owned by independent fishermen. Toward sundown Garry went off towards the town, while Keven strolled along the river, around the south shore of the bay, and out upon the strip of sand. It was the second time in his life that he had come in sight of the sea; and the first occasion had been at Crescent, where the coast lacked the ruggedness and loneliness of this one. The sun was setting out behind the white-ridged horizon, rose and gold, under purple clouds.

But the swell and break and boom of the surf claimed Keven's attention. He would walk on a few steps, then linger to listen and watch. At length he reached the spit of sand, the farthest point he could attain between the sea and river. Gulls and cormorants were screaming along the edge of the sand, where the tide was coming in. It had a resistless flow. Here Keven sat down.

Sound and movement were on a large scale here. They dwarfed Keven's familiar impressions of the river. Yet how wild and wonderful the sea! He did not think, however, that he could love it. But it was the mother of the steelhead and salmon, about which he had been concerned since childhood. As a boy he had learned the significant expression: "Fresh run from the sea." And that meant a fighting fish in the best of condition, like speckled silver, or as pink as a rainbow. Salt water gave the salmon and steelhead the qualities beloved of anglers. The steelhead, after their long climb up the rapids, returned to their mysterious regions in the sea. But the salmon died. What a pity that was! Hundreds of times Keven had lain on a rock or a bank to watch salmon spawn on their beds. He had seen them, spent, scarred, spotted with ulcers, wag wearily and die. And he had watched the cannibalistic offspring feed and thrive off their rotting remains. It was all so interesting, yet obscured in mystery.

Keven believed that he would profit through these coming months of sojourn by the seashore. But more than ever the black forests of fir that stood almost on end, the amber-mossed and fern-laced banks dotted with white flowers, the pure cold crystal brooks tumbling off the cliffs, called to him to return. The Rogue was destined to dominate the rest of his life, whatever that might be. Solitude haunted him. Here by the chafing tide and with the squall of fierce sea fowl in his ears, the grand peaks of the Cascades and the canyons with their singing river lured him with strong, sweet power. The sea would have no Lorelei for Keven Bell. It was too big, too restless, too cold and aloof ever to rival the Rogue in his affections.

The sun sank, the afterglow spread its pale gold over the sky, to flush and fade and die, and the pale gleaming light, herald of dusk, stole down across the bay to the narrow outlet. Suddenly Keven's meditations were disrupted by a heavy souse in the water. He knew that sound. "Salmon!" he cried, in delight, even before he saw the circling break, and a dark tail lazily slip out of sight. Keven had an eye for fish. Rising salmon had been to him what spinning tops and flying kites were to most boys. Wherefore he watched. And before dusk settled down he saw the breaks of many salmon. They were coming in from the sea on that rising tide. Keven remembered then that just before Garry had set out for town he had said: "Little raise on. She's come up a couple of inches. There's been some rain somewhere upriver. Reckon not enough, though, to start a run of fish."

The Rogue was as sensitive and temperamental, as changeable as a woman. It would rise and lower without warning, between sunset and sunrise. It had a habit of running clear as green glass one hour and pale amber the next. A thundershower in the Cascades would precipitate a flood. But such occasions were rare, at least in the season of salmon running.

Keven imagined the fact of salmon showing on the surface at the mouth of the river would be interesting news for Garry Lord. Certainly where one salmon broke water there must be a hundred underneath. It might mean the opening of the season. Certainly they could troll in the bay next day and catch fish.

He wended his way back along the resounding beach, and rowed the curve of the bay, in the melancholy cool dusk. In camp he found Garry squatting before a fire.

"Where in hell have you been?" queried that worthy, with manifest relief.

"Down by the shore."

"You gotta stay in camp," growled Garry. "Somebody might bump you off in the dark. An' steal everythin' we own."

"Any news from town?"

"Lord, yes. Heaps. Good an' bad. New cannery opened, in opposition to Brandeth's. It'll be about the only one at thet, an' on a small scale, I reckon. Town's full of hulligan fishermen from everywhere on this dinged coast. All waitin' for the leather-backs to run."

"Well, they're running," said Keven nonchalantly.

47

"Wh-at?"

"The first run is on."

Garry shook his tousled head dubiously and eyed Keven askance. "See here, boy, if you spring thet on me I'll reckon you've got wuss than a bum memory. You'll be goofy."

"Garry, I've got as good an eye for salmon as you or anyone else, and when it comes to steelhead I can beat you all hollow."

"Listen to my new pardner!"

Whereupon Keven calmly stated the facts about the salmon he had seen on the incoming tide.

"Jerusalem!" shouted Garry, and scrambling up he ran down to the river. Presently he came thumping back, puffing hard. "By gosh, Kev, the river's up half a foot. Sure as guns a bunch of salmon out there have got a snootful of mountain water, an' they're on the move. . . . You're sure a pard after my heart. There I was uptown drinkin' with them muckers, an' you go off to find fish! Com mon."

He dragged Keven down to the boat. "Grab a big long stone while I roll up the net. . . . We gotta have anchor, rope, buoy. . . . But no lantern. We're moles, an' we can see in the dark. A light would give us away to some of them rivermen. Gosh, this's great. Me an' my pard stole a march on them last season. Surer'n hell we're agonna do it this year."

In short order they were in the skiff and rowing out down the river towards the bay. The shore lines were indistinct. Lamps flickered in the shacks. Up on the bluff the electric lights shone brightly. Soon they were in the bay, feeling the slow press of the tide. A cool, damp, salty breeze came over the sand dunes.

"Pretty nifty, huh?" queried Garry, in low voice of exultation. This drink-sodden fisherman had the soul of adventure in him. He felt the thrill of the night, of the wide gleaming bay, of the booming sea so near at hand, of the pursuit of their quarry. He reveled in the prospect of surprising and outdoing their rivals. And somehow, to Keven, it seemed more than a game. There was an intimation of hazard in it.

"I heard a fish break," he whispered.

"Got a ear like your eye, huh? By gosh, Kev, I'm cottonin' to you somethin' fierce," rejoined Garry.

"Took you long, Garry," replied Keven with a laugh. "I did that to you, just after we shot Alameda Falls."

Souse! A heavy fish rolled on the surface close to the boat.

"Kazoozle! Did ye hear thet loafer? Too big and fat to cut the water. He'd go about fifty pounds."

"Garry, will we get paid by weight or just so much for every salmon?"

"So much a pound, first off, if we make a haul. An', Kev, by gosh, I feel it in my bones. We're gonna do it. Tide's just well in. Mebbe they'll hit in before flood. mebbe after. . . . Listen to thet hunker. Wow!"

Garry rowed noiselessly across the bay, where on the pale, gleaming surface, in the reflected starlight, the boat might have been espied by keen eyes. When, however, it reached the shadow of the dunes it would be invisible. Garry enlarged upon a stretch of water close to where the bay converged again into the river, preparatory to its confluence with the sea. Here in days past, on the early runs, he and his partners had made great hauls. There was a shelving bottom, over which the current flowed quickly. and here the salmon, keen to taste the fresh cold water from the river, swam in bunches.

"Kev, the idee is to locate your fish, then anchor one end of your net, tie on a buoy, stretch her across the run, an' hang at thet end with the boat," expounded Garry, as he paddled to and fro in the shadow, evidently jockeying for position. "No picnic fer one fisherman. I swore I'd never have another pard. But you're different. . . . Kazoozle! Thet was a buster."

"Garry, they're all around us now," returned Keven, whose eyes were keen as those of a cat in the dark. "Heads upstream, lazy, just rolling along. But they're moving. I'd say it was a run."

"Say! My Gord, man! You can whoop it to the skies. Mebbe only the vanguard. Mebbe the big run will be days later. But here's salmon, an' we're gonna ketch a ton."

"Not a boat on the bay!" exclaimed Keven, gleefully as a boy.

"What's worryin' me is we can't load any big haul in this skiff,'" went on Garry.

"Well, when we get the net out there'll be lots of room for fish."

"By gosh, I'll tell you what," returned Garry, as if inspired. "If there's a good run I'll swim ashore, mozy back to Stemm's an' fetch out the big flatboat."

"Excuse me from swimming in this Rogue water. With a freshet on? Nix."

Eventually Garry found a location to his liking. It was perhaps a quarter of mile from the mouth, just where the river broadened into the bay, and close to the north shore. The current ran fairly swiftly.

"Why not make a set across the mouth?"

"It'd be great, but thet's forbidden," said Garry. "An' we upriver fishermen observe the law."

"Oh, I see. I suppose there are all kinds of regulations."

"You take the oars now, Kev." He carefully slid the big stone overboard. When it touched bottom he tied a buoy on the rope, where it joined the net, and let that over. "Now row toward shore, Kev. . . . Not so fast."

"Do you anchor both ends?" asked Keven.

"*I* don't. You bet I stick with my net. These cannery favorites ain't above stealin' your fish. Not to say nuthin' about nets! I anchor my skiff an' tie the net onto it. Then when the salmon come I pull up anchor an' go over the net. It's slow, but beggars can't be choosers."

Presently Keven found himself idle in the skiff, watching Garry, who kept a hand on that taut net rope. By this time Keven had gotten used to the darkness and could see very well. There was charm, not to say excitement, in the place. Outside, the surf fell with resonant hollow boom; close at hand the current drifted by with silky swish. Faint splashes and here and there a souse told of rising fish. Then came a break near the boat.

"B'gosh, I felt one hit," said Garry with a chuckle. "Kev, old top, we'll have salmon steak for breakfast an' tenderloin steak for supper. . . . Wow! Another! Another! . . . Gosh, this is gettin' good! So early in the evenin'! Com mon, you leather-backs!"

Far out toward the buoy a salmon leaped the net with

50

cutting splash. The breaks on the surface occurred oftener, here, there, all around. Souse! A big fellow hit the net high up, but did not get over. He stuck fast and threshed with whizzing sound.

"Kev, would you believe it? Our swell net has already begun to sag," said Garry. "We've gilled some hunkers. . . . Aw, wake me up, I'm dreamin'."

"Strikes me they're running pretty thick," returned Keven eagerly.

"Nope, not yet, an' mebbe they won't a-tall. But gosh, consider. Here we are, ahead of thet whole tribe of hoags. We're broke, too, an' in debt. An' a few salmon's like strikin' gold."

The moments passed, fraught with ever keener stir and thrill for Keven. There were lulls in the breaks on the surface and again continuous though scattered splashings. Salmon leaped the net in considerable numbers.

"Pull up anchor, Kev," said Garry finally. "I jest can't wait no longer. I know we've got this damn skiff full, but I can't believe in no such luck."

Keven did as directed, and the skiff slowly drifted with the current up the bay. Garry began to haul in the net. The first ten feet fetched in two salmon, big fellows over forty pounds. They had to be big to catch by the gills in an eight-inch mesh. Garry swore softly to himself as he, with difficulty, extricated the fish. Then he slid them into the skiff. Both net and skiff now had drifted straight upstream, in line with the buoy, which Keven could just barely make out, a black dot on the surface. The next ten feet of net came in heavy with a number of kicking salmon. As Garry tugged and tore he talked to himself. He was happy. He was rich. He might have been meeting old friends among these salmon. He called this one Old Sock-eye and that one Leather-back and another Big-jaw and still another Fatty. The bottom of the skiff was soon covered with flapping, tail-flipping salmon. It did not take many to crowd Keven out of his seat. And still they came, all huge, black-humped fellows, plump-sided, with silvery bellies that shone in the starlight.

"It's a swell run, Kev," said Garry. "Lord, if they come thick an' fast later, as I reckon, we'll be swamped."

51

"We're going to be swamped right now," declared Keven.

"Turn the skiff, you amateur. This ain't nuthin' yet, an' it won't be nuthin'. . . . Kev, I've stopped countin' 'em; an' when I do thet it's good night."

It required an hour for Garry to clear the net, and then the skiff was so full that its gunwales were only a few inches above water.

"Row carefully now," instructed Garry. "Back where we were, inshore from the buoy." As Keven rowed, Garry again let out the net, until he came to the end. "Drop anchor, Kev. . . . Hurry."

The skiff swung heavily, almost careened, then dragged to a stop.

"Okay. Couldn't be better. Here, take the rope," said Garry. "Jest you set there an' feel yourself gettin' rich. I'll go after the big flatboat. Don't you get nervous now, pard."

"Careful, you'll swamp us," rejoined Keven, as Garry slipped over the side into the water.

"Aggh! . . . My Gord!" ejaculated the fisherman huskily. "If this water ain't from Crater Lake I'll drink it all."

He let go of the skiff and struck out for the shore, his head and shoulders darkly parting the pale gleaming shadow. Finally he disappeared, but Keven could hear him swimming. He felt relieved when he heard the fisherman wading out. Then Keven attended to the vibrating rope in his hands, and the many other sensations that assailed him. Tug! A salmon had hit the net hard. For a space around, the water appeared quiet, though he heard distant splashes. The stars seemed to watch. How the rising tide outside roared and crashed in mounting waves on the strand! The night breeze was cold. Tug! Tug! And that was the beginning of an onslaught on the net. Salmon began to pound against the cork line, to swish in the air, to split the water like plummets. If there were so many on the surface, how many more would be deep down? Wet salmon piled against his legs. He could find no room to sit comfortably, and he began to get cold. But this was fun, this was fishing and more—it was business. Tug! Tug! Soon the net sagged so heavily that he could no longer

52

feel when another salmon hit. He had to loop the rope around the oarlock. Then followed a spell of quiet, when he attended to his more distant surroundings. The bold Cascade Range stood up against the fretwork of stars; the tide glided faster, with more of hiss and gurgle; a plover passed overhead with weird cry; dogs barked across the bay, and the lights of the town glimmered through openings in the pines.

Suddenly there came a surge on the net that rocked the overloaded skiff. Keven thought it was a stronger thrust of the tide. But, as there followed a quick flurry of water along the rope, then sharp splashes, culminating in a roar, he realized that he had been struck by a wall of fish. He could have yelled in his excitement. Then the skiff anchor began to drag. The burdened net was swinging upstream. At first Keven was alarmed. But a moment's calculation convinced him that if he were careful he was in no danger, and could not lose the fish, so long as the tide was flooding in. Whereupon he cautiously drew the anchor off the bottom. After that the boat, dragging the net, drifted upstream, until in line with the buoy. Would the heavy rock at that far end suffice to hold both net and skiff? Keven let down his anchor. Also he released the net rope, and let it slowly out, until the drag was perceptibly lessened. The floundering of salmon along the net ceased as soon as it sank. But soon again the tremendous weight reasserted itself, until Keven was hard put to it to keep the skiff afloat. He was now in a pretty predicament, and he racked his brain to meet the situation. It would not help matters much to lighten the load in the skiff, though he feared he would have to do it. What would happen if he let go of the net rope altogether?

He gazed around helplessly, and in desperation, up the bay in the direction from which Garry must return. The gloom could not be penetrated for any considerable distance. It was opaque and weird. The incoming tide flowed by the skiff, drawing it perceptibly. When would Garry come? In any event he must have a hard row against that current.

Keven located his position by a tuft of brush on top of one of the sand dunes, and when he gradually edged out of line with this he knew the net anchor was dragging. At last, when he was about to abandon the net to row ashore and save at least the skiffload of salmon, he heard something that was not splashing fish. He listened, his ear turned upstream. The slight breeze came in from the sea, and it brought the almost incessant moan and beat the surf. But presently he heard squeaky oarlocks. And he felt a rush of glad excitement. That would be Garry coming. So he held onto the net rope, while he tried to peer through the gray obscurity. It seemed a long time before he made out a dark object on the water. The sound of oars grew louder. Indeed Keven feared they could have been heard ashore by some watchful, keen-eared fisherman. Garry was a long time heaving up. The flatboat was wide and heavy. But at last Garry reached him.

"Gord—what—a pull!" he panted.

"Got an anchor?" queried Keven, sharp and low.

"Sure Mike."

"Drop it quick. Don't grab hold of me. I'm drifting with the net. It's chock-full of salmon. That rock is dragging. You didn't get back any too soon."

Garry wasted no time. He thumped over a heavy anchor, after which he reached an oar to Keven and pulled the skiff alongside the big flatboat. Indeed it looked like a barge.

"Gimme hold of—thet net rope," demanded Garry hoarsely, and as Keven complied he added: "Well, I'm a son of a gun! . . . Kev, slide your fish over into this boat. . . . Careful now. If you rock her it's good night."

"I've been aware of that for a couple of long hours, Garry Lord," replied Keven, as he began to transfer the heavy salmon.

"Gosh, you must have had a nice time out here, waitin' an' fightin' this tide. How'n hell did you hold on? This net is bustin' with fish. Never but once in my life did I feel the like. Kev, we've got a haul. An' if we can make a few more sets tonight we're rich."

"We'll make 'em, Garry. Didn't you even know what a lucky fisherman I was?"

"Sure. I remember how steelhead used to crawl out on the bank an' die at your feet. . . . You was lucky with the girls, too, Kev."

"I never noticed that," declared Keven decidedly.

When at length he had lightened the skiff Garry stepped over out of the flatboat and began the laborious job of hauling the net, while Keven stood by the oars. The net sagged with salmon. Garry raved while he worked. He was jubilant. He bragged about how he and his new partner were the slickest fishermen on the river.

Before he had hauled twenty feet of the net the skiff was once more dangerously laden. "My Gord! Packed solid! . . . Row back to the flatboat, Kev. Slow now, fer I'm hangin' onto the rope, you bet."

They emptied that load, and this time Garry risked fastening the net rope to the flat boat. That faciliated the work. The heavy anchor held. And Garry told Keven he would give him an exhibition of how to pick a net. "Like a starvin' tramp pickin' blackberries. . . . Ha! Ha! . . . My Gord, look here, Kev. Whopper of a steelhead. First one. He'll go sixteen pounds."

"Heavens!" gasped Keven, as he eyed the beautiful gleaming silvery fish. He knew the graceful lines, the small game head. "Let me have him. . . . He's alive yet, Garry. I don't see how I can do it—but I'll let him go."

Reluctantly he consigned the wonderful steelhead to the dark murky water, glad to see it swirl and disappear. "If I ever hooked one like that I'd fall in and drown."

Garry filled the skiff four times. "Now, Kev, we gotta get back to thet place. How far have we dragged, do you reckon?"

Keven took his bearings from the sand dunes. "Hundred yards or so."

Garry pulled up the rock anchor, and then left Keven to manage the skiff while he returned to the flatboat. He had another tremendous pull to follow Keven back to their original spot close under the shadow of the sand dunes. Here he anchored the larger boat.

It was long past midnight and cold. The sea wind pierced Keven through. Numb and wet, he stuck to his oars, while Garry handled the net. Salmon continued to come in, and in four sets they filled the flatboat to the top of the gunwales. In the cold dim grayness of dawn, at slack tide, they rowed across the bay and up the river to beach the boats on the sand.

"Go to bed, pard. You sure done noble," advised Garry.

"I'm a dead one myself, but I'll set on this haul of salmon till it's sold."

Keven could scarcely drag himself up to the tent. He was wringing wet, slimy as an eel, so frozen and exhausted that only by dint of the last expenditure of strength could he get out of his clothes and into bed. But his heart was warm and glad. What a night for a fisherman! And there was something singing within him when his weary eyelids glued shut.

chapter seven

WHEN KEVEN AWAKENED the day appeared far spent. He rolled his aching body out of the blankets and found he was stiff and bent, like an old man. His sore and blistered hands fumbled over his bag, to get out a flannel shirt and pair of blue jeans. Of socks he had plenty, and one extra pair of shoes. It was labor to dress, during which time he wondered what had become of Garry and the carload of salmon they had caught. But had that been a dream?

He went outside. The clothes he had worn, sight of which attested to the truth of that night haul, lay spread in the sun. Garry was nowhere to be seen. The big flatboat, with its heaped-up shining freight of salmon, was likewise missing. No doubt Garry was absent on the pleasant and profitable task of selling their catch. Whereupon Keven set about getting a meal, which would do for both breakfast and supper.

After starting a fire he went down to the river to fetch a bucket of water. The Rogue ran clear again, at just about the same level. That little freshet, merely a wave from some upriver rain, had come and gone in the night. But it had started a run of salmon, to his considerable profit. The changeable, deceitful, roughish river! Keven conceived an idea the river would bring him good fortune, maybe his old strength, possibly happiness. But that seemed a mad dream. Nevertheless, as he sighed he said: "Good old river! I sure love you."

He had slept three quarters of the day, as he could tell by the sun, already gilding the wooded hills in the west. And he felt as if he had been pounded with a club. Yet as he moved about, his muscles gradually loosened, his joints lost their stiffness, and much of the cramp and soreness left them. When he had the meal almost prepared Garry appeared, treading as if on air. He wore a smile as wide as his ruddy face, and his blue eyes honestly beamed upon Keven.

"Two an' a half tons!" he announced grandiloquently. "An' I sold to Brandeth's manager—by weight! He had to buy. He couldn't let the first haul of the season go. . . . Looka here, pard. Look at this roll of dough. Thet's yours. Fifty-fifty. You could choke a cow with thet."

With much extravagant speech he forced upon Keven a sizable roll of greenbacks. Then he produced a smaller one. "Pard, I'm askin' you to keep this much of my share. Hold it out on me. If I fall for celebratin'—an' thet's a cinch—hide it from me."

"You bet I will," replied Keven warmly, as he pocketed the money. "Garry, I'll pay Dad as soon as I can get to the post office."

"Right an' proper. I forgot. I'm in on thet," rejoined Garry, sitting down. "I can't eat till I get this off my chest. . . . Kev, we've shot the works! News of our ketch spread like wildfire. Stemm saw thet mess of salmon first off this mornin', and he scooted off like the Indian he is. Before I'd cooked breakfast fishermen began to flock down here. None of 'em would believe. They had to see for themselves. Then Jarvis, the new cannery man, came down an' made me a swell offer. I said I'd see. 'Cause I was layin' fer Brandeth's man. Sure he come, an' when I chirped double what he paid last year he snapped me up without battin' an eye. Reckon I was a sucker. He'd have paid three times. . . . Well, I rowed the boat over to the cannery an' cashed in."

"Will that price hold for the season?"

"Yep, prob'bly will. Mebbe not. Last night was jest a flash in the pan, Kev."

"I had that notion myself."

"Sure it's early fer the real thing. But mebbe not. Stemm's an Indian. He says they used to run thet way, years ago. An' he predicts an early season an' a big one. We started somethin'. Fishermen ranted around. Them thet are ready to start stand round in little crowds talkin', as if there was a prize fight on."

"Sit down and eat, Garry," said Keven gaily. "I'm no swell cook. But I'll learn. . . . So we started up the machinery, eh? Well, I had no idea of this salmon-fishing business down here. I always hated it. Stretching nets across the mouth of the Rogue when the fish begin to run! It's a rotten, cruel, greedy business."

"Sure, Kev, it is. But people gotta eat. Consumption of fish growin' every year. Cost of livin' hell! An' we fishermen gotta earn our keep. The way I look at it is we oughter thank God there are fish to catch an' sell an' eat."

"I suppose mine is the sportsman's point of view. It oughtn't have much weight with the legislature, though I think the steelhead should be preserved."

"You're right both ways. I reckon the ideal would be to live an' let live. But Brandeth will hog the river an' kill the salmon runs, if he's not stopped. Every year fewer salmon get up to spawn. The day will come when there will not be any salmon. Steelhead, now, they are different. They are a smaller, faster, stronger fish. An' after they spawn they run back to the sea. If they don't get stopped altogether they've a chance to survive. An' the upriver folks ought to fight fer them."

"They will, Garry," returned Keven enthusiastically.

"Well, I've my doubts about the survival of anythin' there's money in. What do men care fer the future? Not a damn! Take the case of the California redwood trees. Them grand trees—they're bein' *cut*. Or the Oregon cedars. Thet's a still grander tree, but not so big. An' where are they? Only one stand in the whole world, Kev. Thet's north of here a ways, on the coast. The Japs bought thet stand before the war. An' they cut an' they're still cuttin'. I worked there one winter. White cedars, Kev. You should see them trees once before they're gone. If you love trees."

"I sure do. Pines and firs. What's more beautiful than an Oregon fir? Why, they make shipmasts of them, everywhere ships are built."

"An Oregon fir is a pretty nifty tree, I'll not gainsay, Kev. An' as we jest passed through millions of them thet won't never be cut—if Uncle Sam stays put—we ain't worryin' none over them. But the redwoods an' the cedars are in much the same boat as the salmon an' steelhead."

Later when Keven asked his partner if they would make any sets that night, Garry scratched his stubbled chin:

"Reckon we'll lay off. The river's back again. I ain't seen a fish break water all day, an' you bet I've kept my eye peeled. Thet run was jest a school of lunkers. They've gone up. But gosh, my fish sense says you can never tell what'll come off. The only way to ketch fish is to keep on fishin'."

"It's just as well we lay off tonight," replied Keven. "I'll be laid out if we have two such nights in succession. I haven't been long out of the hospital, Garry. I'm not very strong."

"Thet was worryin' me, Kev. But you sure did noble last night. I see I gotta break you in easy. We'll let them yannigans lambast the river tonight all fer nuthin'."

After supper Garry went to town and Keven made his way by slow stages to the sand dunes, where he spent the hour of twilight and dusk beside the sea. It seemed new and strange; it helped to keep his mind off the unjustness of his fate; it roused in him a conception of the vastness of the world and the inscrutability of life. More, too, it increased his yearning for the tranquil solitudes of the mountains, where instead of all this boisterousness of the sea, the boom of billows, and the ceaseless, marvelous crawling of the white foam up the strand, there were the sweet, low-singing river and the deep solitude of the green canyons.

Garry did not return to camp that night, which omission in no wise surprised Keven. In the morning he got up late, rested and refreshed, and after cooking breakfast started for town. Down by the river he encountered

Stemm, to learn from him that no salmon had been netted by the fishermen. Keven passed a group of them, and appreciated that they appeared a hard-looking disgruntled crew. Soldiers were tough—and here again he wiped an encroaching thought from his consciousness. What he ought to remember he had forgotten; what he should forget was always recurring.

Gold Beach appeared to be quite a place, clean, widestreeted, with a fine stretch of business houses, and colorful residences in the background. It was certainly not a sleepy town at this time. Keven leisurely sauntered down the main thoroughfare, and upon locating the post office he went in and dispatched two money orders to his father. They almost canceled his debt, which fact afforded him great satisfaction. He added a note to acquaint his father with his safe arrival at Gold Beach and the wonderful good luck of his first market-fishing venture.

The clerk in the post office was a pretty girl. She made eyes at Keven, and he reflected that he might have returned the compliment if she had not had bobbed hair. Somehow he hated that. Then he went out to look for Garry.

It looked a vain task even before he started, and it certainly proved to be one. There were in fact not many places where Garry Lord might have been found. At last far down the main street he came to a sign "Sock-eye." That was the name of a certain species of coast salmon, as were "humpback," "tyee," "quinnat," "silversides." Keven went in the Sock-eye.

A cigar and newsstand occupied the front. From this a door led to a smoky, noisy poolroom, full of boys and men. Keven did not need to be told that he had happened upon a rendezvous of the market fishermen, such as Garry had described to him. Tired from the walk, which had been a long one, Keven sat down to rest and watch. Nobody paid any attention to him, and he gathered that strangers in Gold Beach were plentiful enough not to excite notice.

Snatches of conversation he overheard betrayed a twofold occupation of these loungers' minds—fishing and gambling. Keven doubted not that there was a secluded hall somewhere near, and most probably upstairs. For the building was two-storied. He lingered there until he felt rested. On his way out a sharp-eyed man behind the cigar stand accosted him:

"What you want, stranger?"

"I stepped in to look for my partner," replied Keven easily.

"An' who's he?"

"Garry Lord."

"Lord, huh? Are you another upriver fisherman?"

"Yes. And I gather from the way you speak that the upriver fishermen are not so welcome in Gold Beach."

"You gathered correct, young man. But that doesn't apply here at the Sock-eye. All fishermen are welcome."

"Glad to hear that. Are you the proprietor?"

"Hardly," replied the man, with a wry smile.

"Who is?"

"Don't you know?"

"I certainly don't. Never was in Gold Beach before."

"Well, it won't be long till you find out who runs the big interests here—the Sock-eye included."

"Ahuh. I'm not a nosy fellow, though. And it doesn't matter to me. Do you have any idea where I might find Lord?"

"Jail mebbe. He was drunk last night. I heard he slugged some fisherman."

"Quite likely. Garry's quarrelsome when he's drunk. Where's the jail?"

Upon being directed, Keven walked toward the jail with perturbing thoughts. Garry was the best of fellows, but that besetting sin of his might well spoil his usefulness as a business partner. Presently Keven encountered a middle-aged man, who stood in the doorway of the building designated, and who wore a star on his vest.

"I'm looking for Garry Lord," said Keven, without any beating about the bush.

"What'd you come here for?" queried the man, looking Keven over with shrewd eyes. He had a stern, yet not unprepossessing face.

"I was told I'd find Garry in jail."

"Who said so?"

"A man at the Sock-eye."

61

"An' who're you, young feller?"

"My name's Keven Bell. I'm Garry's partner, and I want to get him out of jail."

"What'd you tell me your name for?"

"Because that's my real name," replied Keven, puzzled. This was surely the sheriff, and he appeared a dry, curt, yet not unkindly man.

"No reason for you to hide it?"

"Not on your life!" retorted Keven

"Come inside," said the other.

Keven followed him across the threshold into a small, barely furnished office. From a desk he picked up a sheet of yellow paper and handed it to Keven, manifestly for his perusal. It was a telegraph blank. Keven's heart sank. He read rapidly. The message came from Grant's Pass, ordered the arrest of one Keven Bell, for assault and resisting officers, and was from the chief of police.

"So that's—that," replied Keven, returning the telegram. "I—I should have expected it. Guess I've spared you the trouble of hunting me up."

"Bell, I read in a Seattle paper about you—if you're the soldier who spent two years in a training-camp hospital."

"Yes, I'm the—the fellow."

"Had a queer accident, didn't you? Gun busted in practice. Backfired on you."

"I should smile it did. Look here," replied Keven, beginning to realize that this sheriff was not unsympathetic, and he pulled down his lower lip to expose the iron jaw.

"Hell! Knocked your teeth an' jaw out?"

"That was nothing, sheriff. It near killed me—and left me with a clouded brain."

"You don't say! Wal, you look a bright an' handsome young feller. No one would guess it. . . . I had a boy who got to France. He—he never came back."

"That's damn tough for you. I'm sorry." Keven hastened to say. "Some boys were taken and some left behind. For my part I wish to God I could have gone in place of your son."

"Why? That's no sane attitude. Your mind must be clouded."

Briefly then Keven recounted the misfortune and shame he had fallen upon when he returned home.

"By God! I heard about that Carstone family. An' you was innocent?"

"Yes, I was—of complicity in that."

"An' you slugged this Atwell for ruinin' your character at home?"

"Guess that was an excuse—to be perfectly honest, sheriff," returned Keven ruefully. "But I was jealous. I left a sweetheart behind. . . . When I came back Atwell was rushing her hand. It galled me."

With slow and deliberate action the sheriff tore up the telegram. "I don't know any Keven Bell. . . . An' I do happen to know Mister Atwell. *He's* no stranger hereabouts."

"Then—then you're not going to pinch me?" asked Keven, trembling.

"Not on the strength of that. . . . But you keep it under your hat."

"Oh—thanks—sheriff. I—you——" Keven suddenly sustained an unaccountable emotional upset. He who could have laughed sheriffs and jail to scorn felt weak as water before unexpected kindness.

"I met Garry last night," went on the sheriff, ignoring Keven's agitation. "Early in the evenin'. Garry an' me are not bad friends. He told me he had a new pard. 'Prince of a feller,' Garry said. An' he was tellin' me about you when he was interrupted. Later I had to go on Garry's trail. He'd got drunk an' beat up one of Brandeth's pet fishermen. An' Austrian. I dragged Garry out. But instead of pinchin' him I led him out of town an' told him to go sleep it off."

"He didn't come back to camp," returned Keven anxiously.

"Wal, he might have got slugged by one of these roustabouts. Bad blood here, Bell, as you'll find out. But Garry is cute, drunk or sober. He's safe in the woods, somewhere. Don't worry about him."

"What's your name, sheriff?" asked Keven.

"Blackwood. I'm from up the river myself. Ashland. Born on the Rogue. But you needn't blow that around," rejoined the officer, grinning at the last. "We're bound to

63

get acquainted. So drop in to see me. Not on Saturday, though. That's my busy day."

Keven went out, confronted by two unfamiliar conditions of mind—gratitude, and a reversion of bitter, set opinion. All the world was not against the returned, broken soldier. He would have to reconstruct his opinions. This kindly, sad-eyed sheriff added another to the slowly growing number of persons who reached to the frozen depths of Keven Bell. He was going to have another kind of fight to contend with presently. It made him uneasy. He would rather have remained callous, hopeless, defiant, aloof, and therefore lost.

In front of the busy-appearing hotel, where cars were parked, and people passed in and out, a slim, fox-faced man accosted Keven.

"Are you the young man who helped Garry Lord make that salmon haul?" he queried.

"Yes, sir. I'm he."

"What might your name be?"

"It might be Jeff Davis or Jesse James—only it isn't," returned Keven tartly. He had recalled Blackwood's remark about his name.

"No call to be funny. But your name doesn't matter," said the man conciliatingly. "Any relation of Lord's?"

"Just a fishing partner."

"Do you know he isn't liked here?"

"Yes. I've heard that no upriver fishermen are."

"That's a fact. They are independent fishermen. They buck the game."

"Ahuh. Is there a labor union of fishermen here at Gold Beach?" inquired Keven curiously.

"No. But there's an inside ring which you want to join. You agree to sell your fish to one buyer."

"But Garry and I prefer to be free to sell to anyone," replied Keven sturdily. "Whoever offers the most will get our fish. I understand there are two canneries now, besides the large one which Brandeth operates. That'll surely make better prices for all fishermen."

"It looks that way to a newcomer. And probably will fetch more money at the start. But you'll find yourself out of it altogether, when the big run's on."

"Bunk. That doesn't sound American to me," declared Keven, with more force than elegance.

"Lord and his former mate bucked us with high hand last season," rejoined the man. 'We don't intend to let him get away with it this year. He won't have any sale for his fish. And that's why I'm giving you a hint."

"Thanks," replied Keven dryly. "But I think it's a bluff."

"You'll soon find out it's no bluff. You'll be out in the cold."

"But look here! Isn't this a free country? Can't a man get his wages for honest work?" shot back Keven, growing nettled. "I'll bet two bits you want me to join a clique to freeze out upriver fishermen. And probably this new rival cannery."

"Take it or leave it," snapped the other crisply. From his face a mask of persuasion dropped to expose craft and, less clearly, menace.

"Whom do you represent?" inquired Keven.

"That's none of your business. If you signify your willingness to quit Garry Lord and join the ring, then——"

"Say," interrupted Keven. "You look like a crook and you talk like a crook. Go to hell!"

chapter eight

BY JUNE THE season was at full blast at Gold Beach. Likwise life at the Sock-eye.

The element foreign to the town, except during the salmon runs, constituted its clientele. Keven Bell dropped in there often, first in a futile attempt to hang onto Garry, and then through a habit that formed. Money was Garry's downfall. He would slave for days and nights when a run of fish was on, only to squander his earnings on the bottle and the cards. A master fisherman at his trade, he was a poor and unlucky gambler, and he could not stand liquor. Yet he was withal such a splendid fellow that Keven grew deeply attached to him and sought to influence him.

The Sock-eye roared that Saturday night. On flood tide the night before, and at flood the morning after, a magnificent run of salmon had swamped the fishermen. Wherefore they had plenty of money and most of it, if not all, was flooding back to the source whence it had come.

Keven bought cigarettes at the cigar stand, where Brander, the manager, who had shown rather a liking for Keven, said close to his ear: "Get Garry out of here if you can. He's drunk an' Mulligan is lookin' for him."

Mulligan was a hulking figure on the river, and he and Garry had clashed. There was a strong and underhand movement afoot to oust Garry. But for the rival canneries he could not have sold his fish for a pittance.

The long poolroom reeked and smoked. A blue haze clouded the scene of jostling, lounging men, of the pool players at the tables, of the glancing colored balls. A continuous clicking sound mingled with raucous voices and laughs. Rubber boots and waterproof coats and the heavy, bright-barred woolen blouses of the North were strikingly in evidence. The odor of fish was as marked as that of smoke, and many a wet foot track showed on the floor.

Keven made his cautious way down the hall and back, without seeing Garry. He was now known to most of the fishermen as Garry Lord's upriver partner, and cordially hated. One lean-faced, unshaven gamester, who obviously got his cue into contact with Keven as he passed, called out viciously:

"I'll knock you on the knob."

"Your fault. You play pool like you fish," retorted Keven, as he passed on.

"These upriver————ought to be driv out," said the fisherman to his comrades.

It was Keven's candid opinion that eventually he and Garry, as well as the several other men from the upper Rogue, would be compelled to leave Gold Beach. Fishing for them was growing less profitable and exceedingly more difficult. Glad indeed was Keven that he had been able to pay his father what he owed him, and the good-hearted Minton. Keven's dream of saving enough money to buy a fruit farm had long been dispelled.

He made his way upstairs to the gambling rooms. No one on guard, no doorkeeper! Any person could come and go. Comparative quiet reigned up there, the noise from below filtering through the walls. Half a dozen games of poker were on. And at one table sat Garry, hunched over his cards. Keven approached.

For once his partner appeared to be ahead of the game. Five other players participated here, and one of these was Mulligan, a bullet-headed Irishman, with a shock of red hair and a face like a bull. He was a loser, and the way he glowered at Garry boded no good for that worthy. Moreover several of Mulligan's cronies also sat in the game.

Keven felt suddenly wrathful with Garry. Why did he court trouble? But it was Garry's perverse habit to tackle the worst jobs and the toughest men. Keven racked his wits. How could he get Garry to leave? Poker players did not take kindly to a winner quitting the game before an allotted hour. Here at the Sock-eye, however, all games were cutthroat and the ethics of gambling were not followed.

"Excuse me for butting in," spoke up Keven, to the players generally. Then he addressed his partner. "Come out of this, Garry."

"Wot's eatin' you, Kev?" queried Lord, in surprise. He was not very drunk.

"I've got a good reason. Come on."

"But can't you see I'm 'way ahead of the game?"

"Well, it's the first time, that's a cinch. Beat it now. There's a Grant's Pass cop hunting for you."

"Hell with him. Kev, you're annoyin' of me most scandalous," complained Garry.

"Sorry, but it's important. Brander gave me a hunch, too. He wants to tip you off."

"Go away, Kev, an' lemme alone. I'm gonna bust this bunch."

"All right then, you sap. Make me give it away," retorted Keven, with pretense of anger. "There's a big run of salmon on."

That never had failed to fetch Garry. And it worked now. He pocketed his winnings and, backing his chair, stood up.

Mulligan glared at him.

"Go wan, you little bandy-legged mud hen," he said, in loud derision. "Quit when you're ahead."

"Sure. Thet's the time to quit. I trimmed you good, for all your slick tricks," leered Garry.

Mulligan stood up to lunge at Garry, missing him only because the table intervened. Quick as a flash Garry swung a chair. The other gamesters ducked pell-mell to the floor, while the big Mulligan dodged. But he was too slow to avoid the flying chair, if he did save his head. It struck him square on the back and bounced off to crash through a window. Before the routed gamblers could rise to battle Keven dragged the belligerent and cursing Garry away and down the stairs.

Outside they ran plump into Blackwood, the sheriff, who manifestly associated their hurry with the row in the hall above.

"Hey, boys, what's the occasion for such precipitation?" he asked, with dry humor.

"Mulligan and his cronies wanted to fight," replied Keven. "You know how obliging Garry is."

"Fight! Aw, is that all? I thought somethin' unusual was goin' on. . . . Come out, an' get away from this place."

"I'm gonna lick that Mulligan," declared Garry, drawing back.

They led him up the street.

"Reckon I'd better run him in, Bell. Just for safety," said Blackwood. "And you better get back to camp."

"Aw, doggone it, I don't live at thet jail," objected Garry. "'An', listen, Blacky, there's a run of fish. Thet's what got me comin'.'"

"Garry, I lied to you," admitted Keven. "I wanted to get you away."

"You double-crossin' water dog," wailed Garry.

At the corner of the street Blackwood led them around to the entrance to the jail. "Go in, Garry. You know we're your best friends."

"Hell! Yes, you are. . . . Take my winnin's, Kev, an'

hide 'em. I'm ahead of the game an' won't never gamble no more," said Garry, then passed into the building.

Blackwood tarried to speak with Keven.

"I'll let him out in the mornin', Bell. I'd consider leavin' Gold Beach, if I were you. It's no place for boys of your kind durin' the salmon fishin'." Then the sheriff looked around cautiously, as if careful not to be overheard, and whispered. "I happen to know—Lord's a marked man. He's a great fisherman, independent, an' he bucks the combine. So don't deceive yourself, Bell. There's a hell of a lot more to this than jealous fishermen. ... Get him away. An' if you can't, go yourself."

"Thanks, Blackwood," returned Keven, and went his way. There was a dance on at another hall that evening. He had intended to drop in for a while, as he had on another occasion. Young fellows who could dance were at a premium at these affairs. Nevertheless the same aggressive antagonism asserted itself there, of the male contingent, who were mostly fishermen. The better class of inhabitants did not attend, and most of the girls were from outside. This night, however, Keven resisted any further contacts.

But he trudged down the road toward the river with contrary thoughts and mingled feelings. It might not take much more to draw him into this drinking, brawling mess, and that from indifference as well as resentment. He had kept out of the vortex of it, not so much from principle as a desire to be alone. Antagonism, however, and the shadow of the powers that controlled set harshly upon Keven Bell. It was not conducive to meekness, a virtue which he possessed only in slight degree. He loved Garry Lord and he would fight for him. Minton had spoken truth: this fisherman, who wasted his substance so prodigally, had a heart of gold. Keven felt that he could not desert Garry.

Down by the Rogue at his camp he cast off something of the oppression of untoward possibilities. It was almost like camping up the river, except for the barking of Indian dogs, the lights on the bay. Loneliness acted wholesomely upon Keven. He had been too used to hordes of soldiers, crowds of visitors, of the hard-boiled, the curious and unsympathetic. Crouched before a little

69

red-embered fire, Keven gazed into its depths and listened to the dogs, the lap of the waves, and the distant thunder from over the sand dunes.

Garry returned to camp next morning, cheery and repentant, unable to recall or frankly disavowing any dereliction on his part. Keven took occasion to repeat and emphasize Blackwood's advice.

"What? Dig out an' leave the fishin' to these muckers? It ain't in me, pard."

"Well, then, let's not loaf around so much," suggested Keven. "If we keep busy fishing we're out of mischief. Let's go to trolling by day and stick at netting by night, runs or no runs. Let's do differently from these other fishermen. They wait on the tides and the runs. On the mood of the river. But we can catch a few fish *all* the time. We'll be that much ahead."

"Keven, you're a bright guy," declared Garry admiringly. "By gosh, I'm with you. I'll stay away from town an' lay off thet Mulligan gang."

So they had a day of trolling with large spoons, taking turn about at rowing the skiff. Salmon rose few and far between; nevertheless they caught ten, which fish, at twenty-five cents each, did not aggregate a very satisfactory wage. Garry said the best feature about this trolling by day was that it gave opportunity to figure the river and thus be ready for a run of salmon by night. Certainly they could not fish all day and all night, too. But they satisfied themselves no run would be on soon. Salmon, in lagging numbers, were moving into the bay all the time. The Indians and the half-breeds kept at their daytime fishing with hook and line, probably owing to the fact that they were too improvident to buy nets.

Towards the close of the third day of trolling Garry's keen and experienced eye noted a fine sediment in the river. He peered into the water, felt it, tasted it.

"By gosh, if there ain't a rise comin' I'll eat my hat," he said. "Let's beat it to camp, get a snack of grub an' a little sleep—then come back with the net."

Garry did not have to eat his hat. That night late, having the bay to themselves, except for some trolling Indians, then netted two hundred and sixty-three salmon,

70

which they sold to the opposition cannery for fifty cents each.

This second coup of Garry's not only heralded the beginning of the big run of salmon, but also raised almost a riot among the fishermen. If black looks and harsh words could have killed, Garry and his young partner would not have lived long. On the three following nights, early and at the first of the flood tide, they made hauls far in excess of the other fishermen.

Keven had the extreme satisfaction of paying all his debts, and of adding a bonus for his father, and then had a tidy sum left. As for Garry, what might have been expected presently happened. He fell. The lure of the card table gripped him again; and when he lost he began to drink. Still he did not get so far under the influence of the bottle as to interfere seriously with his work. But he played into the hands of his enemies. Finally Keven felt forced to make a stand.

"Garry, old fellow, I'm sorry," he said, "but if you don't cut out the booze, I'm through."

The effect was instant and tragic. From amazement Garry passed to misery.

"My God, Kev, I've been sober'n a judge compared to what I was last year," he ejaculated.

"Ahuh. Well, you weren't very sober then. I appreciate that you *think* you've been, Garry. But it doesn't go with me."

"Kev, you jest couldn't throw me down."

"Couldn't I? You lay off the cards and bootleg stuff, or I'll show you."

Garry was deeply struck. His humiliation was piteous. He made no rash promises, but he seemed shocked into realization that irreparable loss confronted him. In that moment Keven knew he would never go back on Garry, no matter what he did; on the other hand, he believed a cold hard front might be efficacious.

This incident, however, seemed to mark a change in their good fortunes. They had had their windfall, out of which Keven had squared his debt and saved a little, but Garry was broke. They fished on, day and night, with a steadily growing acquaintance with the goddess of ill fortune. Still the season was young; they would have time and opportunity to recoup.

One day, on the main street uptown, Keven encountered Atwell, face to face. The erstwhile major looked opulent and important. He gave Keven a malignant look and spoke to his companion, who was no other than the foxfaced superintendent of the leading cannery. Keven intuitively felt disaster in this meeting. And when he passed on and came to a point where he could think about himself, he found he was a bundle of surging blood and rioting nerves. He hurried back to camp and to his work, irrespective of the fishing conditions. He did not like the glimpse he had had of his soul.

Nothing happened however, that day or the next. But after the third night, when he and Garry made the best haul for a good while, their fish were refused at the large factory, and they were compelled to sacrifice them at lesser price than was paid to any fishermen on the river. They saw Atwell's hand in this. But instead of disheartening them, it had the effect of making Garry sullen and dangerous, and Keven determined and fiery.

Days passed. The salmon run was at its height. Yet poor luck dogged Garry and Keven. Added to this was a fact that did not at first dawn significantly upon them. Half a dozen crews, each working with two boats, were always in front of Garry and Keven, between them and the fish. They relayed their sets, jockeyed Garry out of position, blocked the incoming tide, as it were, and slowly but surely so hampered their fishing by night that only stubbornnesss kept them at it. Mulligan and his two cronies were the chief factors, in this campaign.

"We're done, Garry," Keven said quietly.

"Done nothin'. An' if we are I'm gonna get even," growled his partner.

"Well, from now on I'm going to spend more time snooping around."

"What fer?"

"I want to find out why big steelhead don't get up the river until after October first."

"Hell!" Garry's accustomed expletive had more than its usual connotation. He knew more than he told. Perhaps he really did not want Keven to know something; perhaps

72

he thought there was no good in creating excitement and rancor over a condition which could not be proved. Right then and there Keven conceived the idea that these market fishermen kept crooked things to themselves, even if they were honest. Possibly, some years before, when the upriver men were numerous and prosperous, Garry Lord himself had broken the law.

Keven, once yielding to the urge to get to the bottom of this complex market-fishing situation, regained the thrill and interest with which he had formerly worked. Sometimes, on dark nights, while Garry sat in the flatboat, holding a net rope, Keven would paddle around in his skiff. It was admirable for this sort of thing, easy to row, noiseless, and difficult to discern. Seldom did fishermen leave their nets, which fact in no wise disconcerted Keven. He ran close, especially when he saw a net being hauled, and peered hard at the fishermen, particularly at the net and salmon. He made these movements of his appear unobtrusive and, in cases where he ran over a net, merely accidental. More than once he got roundly cursed. More than once he espied fishermen picking steelhead out of a net, to throw them back. At least they did so while he passed. But Keven wanted to look into these boats. After several encounters with Mulligan and his partners at work Keven was recognized.

"It's thet———cub of Lord's," gruffly called out Mulligan, with a word of significance.

Whereupon Keven rowed close to the boat, peering with all his eyes.

"Got any whisky?" he asked. "My pardner is sick."

"Haw! Haw!" came a derisive laugh.

But Mulligan stood up with a long boat hook. "Git out of hyar, you sneak, er I'll sink thet skiff."

"Hullo," replied Keven. "I didn't know it was you, Mulligan. Excuse me."

"About time you was knowin' me. Keep out of my way."

"Say, you're all-fired touchy. Don't want any upriver fellows around when you're fishing, huh?" taunted Keven, rowing quickly away.

But Mulligan's deep and heavy voice carried far. "I

told you, Bill. They're spyin' on us. Thet young Bell ain't no market fisherman. It's high time they was run out."

"Shet up, you loud-mouthed fool," came the reply. "We don't own this river. . . . An' don't play into . . ."

Keven heard no more, but that hardly seemed necessary. It was obvious there were reasons why Mulligan's crew did not care to be watched. All market fishermen were cranky about disclosing their methods, or having their particular places encroached upon. But was this Mulligan's displeasure? Keven rowed back to Garry and related his experience.

"You stay away from thet gang, or I'll have to kill somebody," declared Garry. "You won't do no good, an' you won't find out nuthin'."

Keven vowed he would find out something, if there were anything. He had ascertained that the hauls of some fishermen, those high in favor, were disposed of at night, right after they were made, or at latest in the very early morning. He and Garry had never approached any of the cannery docks until after breakfast, and then sometimes they had to wait. This was before they had become practically ostracized.

Whereupon Keven, sometimes late at night, left Garry to row back to camp while he went ashore, and made his stealthy way around the bay to the docks. Boatload after boatload of salmon did he espy, moored at the foot of the steps. All about them appeared regular and aboveboard. But on the third attempt, almost at dawn, he discovered another place where boats discharged their cargo. He heard the thud of fish falling upon the floor of the cannery. They were being pitched up from the boats. It was too light to risk wading out among the piles that furnished foundation for the building. But Keven listened. Some of the fish fell soddenly, indicating plainly considerable weight. On the other hand the great majority struck lightly. These were not heavy fish. Keven found himself calculating weights, according to the sound. And when he stole back into the woods, to retrace his steps toward camp, he believed he had found out something. Yet in the light of the day he had to confess to himself that he had not actually seen anything which could incriminate market fishermen. He knew he was imaginative, given to exaggeration, governed by feeling instead of logic and fact. It was imperative that he substantiate his suspicions by tangible proofs.

chapter nine

KEVEN DID NOT roll out until late next morning, and then he had to awaken Garry and pretend a cheerfulness he did not feel. Garry brooded these days.

Summer had come to the coast, and a rich thick amber light flooded down from the mountains. The gulls screamed, the cormorants fought, the fish hawks soared, and sometimes an eagle sailed across from the heights. Keven wondered how it was that he did not seem glad to be alive. Undoubtedly this strenuous labor of market fishing had broken him down for the first month, but he had now begun to pick up. It seemed possible that if the conditions here had been free from worry and disappointment he might improve in health.

"Where'd you go this mornin' early?" asked Garry at breakfast.

"I was snooping around the canneries."

"Humph. Didn't I tell you to lay off thet stuff? You ain't figgerin' these breeds an' riffraff. You're gonna git your everlastin'."

"Not if I see 'em first," quoth Keven. "Garry, I'm sure on the track of something. And if I nail it—well, believe me, old man, I'll sure be a hero up the river."

"You will like hell," returned Garry bitterly. "The only hero at the Pass is the potbellied guy with the dough. He gits the gallery, the cake, an' the girl. An' I reckon thet's what makes me sick."

"He can have her and welcome. I'll bet she'll be a mouthful."

"Ahuh. . . . Kev, look who's a-comin'."

Keven glanced around to see two men get out of an automobile back on the road. One of them was the sheriff, Blackwood, who appeared to be talking forcibly to a thickset man wearing a wide hat. They approached the river camp.

"Thet's Rollins with Blacky," spoke up Garry, and cursed under his breath.

"Who's Rollins?" queried Keven blankly. He sensed a dismaying, long-looked-for event.

"Rollins? He's the Grant's Pass constable, an' a————————if I ever knowed one."

"Well. . . . Must be looking for your fishing partner, Garry. Here's where I do get it."

No more was said while the two officers approached. Blackwood wore a serious aspect. The other, a broad-featured man, lined of face and calculating of eye, roused distinct resentment in Keven, merely by his step and look. But as they reached the camp Blackwood took the lead.

"Bell, sorry to say I've got to put you under arrest," he said.

"All—right," replied Keven slowly, as he arose. "What's the charge?"

"Assault with intent to kill," announced Rollins, in a loud voice, producing handcuffs. "Stick 'em out."

Blackwood waved them aside.

"See here, Rollins," he said brusquely. "No irons needed on this boy."

"Is that so? I'm not goin' to risk bein' hit over the head."

"Mr. Blackwood, who's having me arrested?" asked Keven quickly.

"Order from Grant's Pass chief of police," replied Blackwood, producing a warrant.

Rollins made a movement to slide a handcuff upon Keven, who gave him a violent shove.

"I'll go. What do you want next? To make a show of me?" queried Keven passionately.

"Don't get fresh with me, young fellow," rejoined the other gruffly.

"Rollins, I'm puttin' Bell under arrest."

"Wal, all right. But I'm takin' him home on the stage."

"Are you? Not till you show papers. This order is for *me* to arrest Bell. I'm doin' it. An' I'll hold him till I get authority to do otherwise."

Here Garry slouched up to give his trousers a hitch. Battle gleamed in his eye.

"Say, Mister Rollins, who's makin' this charge?"

"None of your business, you loafin' river rat."

"He's my pardner. We're workin' together. We've got some rights. Here we've gone to considerable expense. An' if you take him away we're ruined. I gotta right to know who's behind this."

Rollins ignored the query, but Blackwood answered: "Reckon you have, Lord. He told me Atwell had preferred the charge an' to push it to the limit of the law."

"Ahuh. Sure expected thet," rejoined Garry, with dark and sinister glance at the constable. Then he sat down as if suddenly helpless. Keven felt sorrier for Garry than for himself. As Blackwood led Keven away toward the car Garry spoke up: "So long, pard. Don't feel bad. This ain't nuthin'."

But for once Keven felt that Garry's habitual negative was far-fetched. He got into the front seat of the Ford, as directed by the sheriff, who evidently was the driver. The disgruntled officer from Grant's Pass stepped heavily into the back seat. Not a word was exchanged on the way up to the jail. Blackwood led Keven inside, through the office, to lock him in a cell. The ring of that lock struck somberly upon Keven's heart. Then, hearing the officers arguing, he attended to what they were saying.

"Blackwood, you can let me take Bell with me, if you want to."

"Reckon I could. An' I can keep him if I want to, so long as you have no papers. That warrant reads to me. Well, I've arrested Bell. An' so far I've done my duty."

"Curry County, heh?" railed the constable, in a temper. "Heerd a lot about your wild pigs, lumberjacks, an' your laws. Do I have to get special extradition papers from the governor to take this prisoner out of your jurisdiction?"

"I reckon it ain't so serious. That law refers to the state

line. But I'm curious, Rollins. I've a hunch this is a trumped-up charge. Bell knocked Atwell down for talkin' against his good name. Assault with intent to kill! That's bunk. An' you know it. Brandeth and Atwell are pretty strong here, but they don't run this office."

"Man, you'll not enjoy your office much longer," retorted Rollins.

"Is that so? All the more reason to run it to suit myself."

"What's the county seat?"

"Gold Beach is the county seat, if that's anythin' to you."

"Who's the mayor or the chief of police?" fumed Rollins.

"I am."

"Indeed. You hold a lot of offices, don't you?" returned the other sarcastically.

"I'm holdin' down one, without any help from grafters."

"Then you refuse to give Bell up?"

"Sure, I refuse. I've arrested him because it's customary for a sheriff to act upon an order from another office. But the charge is ridiculous an'——"

"How do you know it is?" interrupted Rollins.

"Because Bell told me what he'd done. An' because I know Atwell."

"So that's the lay of the land. You've arrested Bell to keep me from arrestin' him."

"You couldn't arrest him, just for hittin' a man. Not in my county."

"The charge is assault. With intent to kill."

"Rats!" ejaculated Blackwood, at last exasperated. "Go back to Grant's Pass an' tell 'em that. When you send me a state warrant for Bell, I'll give him up. Not before."

Rollins stamped out of the office.

For a day and a night Keven felt so warmly grateful to this stubborn champion that he scarcely realized the shame of his position. But that came soon enough. Day after day, and week after week, while he waited, he grew more dejected. The sheriff was kind to him, brought him papers and magazines, and kept him isolated, and even out of sight of other prisoners that came and went.

Meanwhile Garry Lord did not put in an appearance, a fact that sat strangely upon Keven. It began to beset him with dread. Every day he looked for his partner to call and never failed to ask for him. Blackwood told Keven that Garry had been seen trolling on the bay, but he was not fishing with a net. It was tough, Keven thought, to handle a net alone.

"Bell, look at this newspaper," said the sheriff one morning, after Keven had been in jail nearly three weeks. "There's a hitch over this warrant matter. I reckon they framed you. Atwell can't prove you did any more than knock him down."

Keven took the newspaper, which bore a Grant's Pass title and was a marked copy, evidently having arrived on yesterday's stage. With the blood beginning to beat at his temples he read about his unwarranted attack upon Gustave Atwell, one of the town's prominent citizens, about his arrest at Gold Beach, and of complications arising that threatened to involve two county governments not any too friendly and co-operative with each other. Then followed an extract from an interview with Atwell:

"The matter is not worth arguing, let alone annoying citizens of two towns who have much in common. Bell is a crippled, half-witted soldier who assaulted me because I made public the fact of his connection with the degradation of a family of five sisters, who lived near our training camp. He is certainly to be pitied. I recall the charge against him, except in case of his return to Grant's Pass, where I wish to be protected from further danger."

In slow-gathering weight of horror Keven ended the paragraph and then read it over. His hands shook the paper so quiveringly that he had utmost difficulty in concluding. "I'll kill him for that," he cried hoarsely, and with the bursting of that speech a terribly fury possessed him. He plunged face down on the cell pallet. This seemed to be the end of all things for him. Blackwood unlocked the cell and placed a strong hand on his shoulder.

"Bell, don't take it so hard," he said. "Pretty rotten, I'd say. But don't sink under it. . . . . I reckon on the strength of Atwell's talk I can let you out. I'm goin' to do it, anyhow. Go back to your fishin', an' when the season's over stay away from Grant's Pass."

Keven slunk out of the jail, so crushed that he found no heart to voice his gratitude to this sturdy-minded sheriff. He went to the Sock-eye and drank and drank, clouding his brain without mitigating his suffering. Before he fell victim to drunkenness, however, Garry discovered him and dragged him back to camp. There in the darkness of the tent he lay throbbing and spent until sleep intervened.

When Keven awoke a familiar state of consciousness was manifest. A weary, sickening, dull reluctance to see the light of day! But the sun was rising. Shadows of branches moved across the gold of the tent. He could not hold the day back. When he went outside Garry had keen and anxious eyes for him.

"You look kinda thin, an' pale round the gills," he said.

"Garry, languishing in jail is not the best thing for one's health. How are you, old fellow? You don't look so grand yourself."

"Aw, I'll be all right now," replied Garry, with confident cheerfulness. "Set down an' eat, Kev. There's fresh eggs an' ham."

Keven gazed around, beyond the campfire to the shining river, where at the moment ducks were swimming and salmon rolling. He had only to look once to realize he was human. A great crowding, blessed relief waved over him. He was outside those drab, confining four walls. He could breathe and see. Never again would he be locked in a jail. Death was preferable.

"How have the fish been running, Garry?" he asked presently.

"Fine. Second big run, steady for days. No big hauls made. Jest consistent good fishin'. Bay's full of steelhead. They're pilin' upriver to beat the band. Thet is—them thet git by."

"Garry, the nets shouldn't stop steelhead, unless a great wide-backed lunker happened to get stuck."

"No, they shouldn't," said Garry, with noncommittal air.

"I'd give my shirt to go up the river fishing," declared Keven.

"Better keep your shirt, Kev. You had only three. An' I borrowed one."

"You're welcome."

"How'd you git out of jail, Kev?"

"Blackwood let me go. Here—read this," said Keven, handing his partner the piece of newspaper he had torn out.

"Blacky is a good feller."

Garry scanned the printed page and burst into the profanity of a riverman. He indulged himself to a breath-taking limit.

"Much obliged, Pard. That does me good. I haven't been able to swear."

Garry shook his uncombed head seriously.

"Kev, you can't let thet stand," he said. "If you do, folks will believe it. Not everybody, but 'most everybody. ————tough! Boys an' girls you growed up with—to read that. . . . Kev, I reckon if another war'd bust out you'd not be in such a hurry."

"I'd fight if our country was invaded. A man could not do less than defend his home—and the women. But otherwise I'd see them in hell first. . . . God, what a ghastly place that training camp was!"

"Ahuh. I git you. Trainin' under fatheads like thet Atwell. . . . No, siree, Kev, you jest can't stand fer thet newspaper roast."

"I don't intend to," returned Keven with cold dark grimness.

"An' thet's the hell of it. What *can* you do? . . . Kev, I reckon I'd hosswhip him within an inch of his life. There'd be somethin' to make folks think, if you did thet. No rowdy stuff. No fightin', though sure thet yellow cur wouldn't fight nuthin'. But hosswhippin' him? Thet would set better."

"Garry, it'd be a good idea—if it were enough."

"Hell, man, are you thinkin' of killin' Atwell?" queried the shrewd Garry.

Keven had no reply for that. Perhaps his cold tight face made words superfluous.

"Thet'd be natural," went on Garry ponderingly. "It'd be just. But if you have any hopes fer a future, you can't do it, Kev. . . . Atwell has money an' friends. He's in with Brandeth. They've got a political pull. Look how this cannery business is run. A few men gittin' rich at the expense of the state. Of the taxpayers! Of such pore fishermen as you an' me! . . . Thet's what I hate about the good old U.S. Graft!"

"Garry, I'm afraid I've no hopes for the future."

"Kev! See here, you lay off any serious intent on Atwell," flashed the riverman, with sudden fire. " 'Cause, by Gord, if you don't, I'll kill him myself."

All Keven's blood went with a shock back to his heart. He had never seen Garry look or talk like this. Strange little flecks danced in eyes as clear and intense as blue steel. Like sunlight quivering on ice! But there was no other beautiful feature about Garry's visage. He could kill a man as easily as he could flip a salmon from the net. A tremendous loyalty to his friend seemed to emanate from him.

"Very well, Garry, I'll lay off such intent—if I had it," returned Keven earnestly. Garry must be deceived at any cost, or if not deceived, then protected. It was not his fight.

"I ain't so damn sure about you," said Garry. "Kev Bell, you're as deep as the sea out there." Then the intensity of him gradually relaxed. That vivid scorching flame died out of his eyes. "You oughta have some sense. If you haven't, I gotta have some fer you. We've been screwed good an' hard on this market fishin'. But thet ain't nuthin'. Nuthin' a-tall. You can find better an' easier work. Huntin' fer gold back up the river! Thet'd be fine. I'll take a crack at it with you next winter, if you want to. . . . Kev, you're gonna git well an' strong again. You're gonna git over this deal the Army gave you. An' you're gonna do fine—an' marry some decent girl who don't paint like a chippy an' run around with 'most no clothes on—an' you're gonna be happy an' mebbe have a boy who'll beat the socks off you fishin' fer steelhead."

Keven laughed in utter incredulity and amaze at this raving partner of his.

"Garry, you're getting softening of the brain," he replied bitterly.

Instead of a volley of curses, Garry surprised him still further.

"Nope. It's somethin' I feel, Kev, an' can't explain. My mother had a queer way of seein' things. I take thet after her. You're gonna come out all right in the end, Kev."

An unquenchable loyalty and faith and something even greater shone from the eyes of the riverman. Keven dropped his head, at last shamed before this outlaw among fishermen, this improvident roisterer, whose soul was bigger than his. For the moment Keven surrendered to a regurgitation of that which was the best of him and which died so hard. After all, that spirit which Garry seemed to believe was his might actually be his. He had been denying it, repudiating it for months. Passion and hate had engulfed it. Keven promised himself a lonely day, not along the seashore, but back in the hills, high up among the firs, where he could look down upon the river and ponder over his miserable state. But alas, the hills were far back, and the forest still farther!

"Look there! By gosh," ejaculated Garry, pointing out across where the river flowed into the bay. Fishermen were rowing by in big boats heaped high with shining salmon.

"Another run on!" cried Keven eagerly. Under any conditions, sight of fish would have stirred him.

"Sure. An' thet looks somethin' like them fellers have been goin' an' comin' all night. There's other boats goin' out. . . . Well, ding the luck! I knowed there'd be a big run. Yestiddy I had it figgered. I could have beat them yaps to it."

"Why didn't you, then?" queried Keven. "It's tough for one man to set and haul a net, I know. But you've done it."

To Keven's amaze Garry gave him a queer glance and, without another word, stalked away in the direction of the canneries. Keven did not know what to make of this.

Garry not fishing when the bay was full of salmon! Could he have gotten drunk and sold the net? No, for there it hung on their rack above the river. Keven stared. Somehow it did not appear natural. Evidently it had not been wet of late. He walked out to investigate. Limp, ragged, gray as ashes!

"I'll be damned! Rotten!" he ejaculated in dismay, and took hold of the netting. It fell to pieces, as if the twine were a thousand years old. He stood a moment, completely nonplussed. A new net, of good material, kept with faithful care, rotting in a few weeks—the idea was preposterous. It had not rotted. Keven strode along the rack, feeling the net here and there, until the truth dawned upon him. Some kind of destroying agent, probably sulphuric acid, had been poured upon that net.

His rage, then, flaming so readily, paralleled that which the foul words of Atwell had engendered. This piece of villainy had never originated in the rum-soaked brains of Mulligan and his crew. Only another link in the chain meant to fetter Garry Lord's capable hands! Keven saw through it.

Long he waited for Garry to return, brooding in the shade of the big pine that sheltered the tent. And his righteous anger alternated with grief. At length his partner came back.

"Biggest salmon ketch this year," announced Garry simply, as he sat down to wipe the sweat from his moist face. The day was hot and the shade welcome.

"Garry, what was it that ruined our net?" demanded Keven, again inflamed.

"Sulphuric acid."

"I guessed that. Who could have done it?"

"Any of our enemies. An' most of thet gang is against us. But I reckon it was Mulligan who got one of his half-breeds to do thet little job."

"But do you know? Can you lay it onto him? Have you any proof?"

"Nary proof. I went to the store an' found out thet they hadn't no acid. I asked the stage drivers an' nuthin' had come up with them."

"Did you inquire on the freight boat?"

"Thet hasn't been in lately."

"What have you been doing?"

"Trollin' every day. Ketched a few salmon right along. I sure got the hosslaugh from some of them fishermen. But we gotta live. An' I reckon we can make wages."

"All right. We'll stick at it. But what we want to do most is to get something on these men. Mulligan and his crew. Or any of them who're in that ring."

"You're talkin' gospel, Kev. I'm glad you ain't suggestin' we borrow money again, to buy another net. They'd pull the same trick on us when we was asleep. Nope, Kev, we're screwed, we're licked, we're done."

"Garry, is it reasonable to connect Atwell with our misfortunes here?" asked Keven.

"It sure don't seem reasonable. A big man like Atwell ruinin' two pore fishermen! You'd have a hard time makin' anyone believe thet. But hell! We haven't the least doubt he'd be low enough. An' this fox Priddy here—the guy who tried to git you to double-cross me. He'd steal coppers off a dead nigger's eyes."

"Garry, we can be slick enough to get the goods on them," declared Keven, fiercely resolute.

"Sure, we oughta be. But what'll we do then? I jest wanted to find out who ruined our net an' beat the daylights out of him. But thet wouldn't satisfy you."

"No. I want to rile the people up the river. And through them the whole state. Throw the rottenness of it all into the Portland courts!"

"You're talkin' big. I was in Frisco when they cleaned up thet burg. Jest one guy did thet. He was a man, Kev, believe me. . . . But this ain't Frisco, Kev. This's only a little one-hoss coast town, pretty an' sleepy, where 'most everybody is as honest an' clean as daylight. They don't know how us fishermen git jobbed—thet sooner or later the salmon an' steelhead runs will be things of the past."

"Garry, it's more important to the people upriver," declared Keven. "These folks here can get sea fish. But if the runs are blocked the farmers and townspeople all along the Rogue are going to suffer. They eat fish during the season and smoke them for winter use. Then take the fly-fishermen. They're too many to count. They come and go. They spend money. They advertise the Rogue. And it is the most beautiful and wonderful trout stream in the West, perhaps in the world. Are a few men to be allowed to kill the food value and the sport value of this river?"

"Hell, no, if you can stop them. But as I've told you before, look at the white cedars—goin' to Japan. Goin' to build airplanes—our finest lumber. Gord Almighty! Can you beat thet! All fer dirty rotten money. An' take the grand redwood forests, thet oughta stand ferever, jest because they're so few, an' so grand, an' somehow part of America. They are goin' like hot cakes, fer the same reason. Take the timber north in Washington. I was in a loggin' camp owned an' run by English contractors. Shifts of five hundred men day an' night. Cuttin' thet forest clean. Mowin' it down, as if it was hay! It's happenin', Kev, all to stuff the pockets of a few hogs. Thet oughtn't to be. It takes ten lifetimes fer such trees to grow. It's horrible waste. It'll dry up our rivers. Will the government do anythin'? Nix, no, never! These short-term guys stand with their hands behind their backs. Do they git 'em greased? You bet your life they do."

"But, Garry, people can be awakened into revolt," expostulated Keven.

"Kev, by thunder, you're a pard to be proud of," sang out Garry, as if wrenched by a poignant fact. "You've no call to be fightin' for ideals. You gave your strength, your health, your eyesight—an' fer what? Your good name was ruined by a potbellied slacker of a politics-made major. An' now the mean little job of market fishin', by which you hoped to earn an' save a little—thet's been screwed fer you. Yet you stand up an' fight fer the right! . . . Kev, I gotta hand it to you. An' all this—the thing thet you *are*—makes me feel you'll come out on the top at the last. Otherwise, there ain't no good, no justice, no hope on this green earth."

chapter ten

OUT ON THE BAY, where it narrowed to the river mouth, the green of salt water, coming in with the tide, met the darker bluish green water of the Rogue.

The gulls were screaming raucously, as they wheeled above the sandspit; the cormorants dove and fought in the shallow current along the edge; steelhead were flashing opal and rose in the sunlight; great leather-backed Chinook rolled on the surface. The tide ran in, chafing the beach, gurgling in little eddies, hissing low as it swelled on the front of the river flow. A well-defined line of demarcation, irregular and changing, showed where salt and fresh water met, to contend for the mastery. But the tide was the stronger. Slowly it gathered momentum to halt the river, and then to force it back.

This was the hour that Keven liked so well to fish. Sorely as he had been tempted, he had never let the fun and sport and thrill of rod fishing interfere with business. But hand line and heavy spoon could not wholly rob the work of its charm. While Garry rowed like a machine, Keven let his line back to drag the bright lure along the merging of currents. This day salmon ran large and plentiful. Smash! and the line would whiz through his hands. The strike never failed to make him jump. Then followed the short battle, always ending when a gasping salmon was hauled over the gunwales.

"Somethin' doin' today," said Garry, for the tenth time, and he grinned his pleasure.

"Sure is. Now, Garry, you troll and I'll row," replied Keven.

"I ain't tired yet. Reckon I'd never git tired watchin' you fish, Kev. Your ears stick up like a jack rabbit's an' your eyes shine. Then when one hits into you, my gosh, you jump like a boy. . . . Fishin' is fun, though. It was the love of it thet made me a market fisherman."

No day this season had yet compared with this one. But few boats were out, and none of the Indian fishermen. Keven had the trolling at the mouth all to himself. By the time the tide had pushed the river back, to occupy the bay, he had half loaded the skiff with salmon. And even then the trolling remained good.

"Jest happened we hit it right," said Garry philosophically. "Reckon it won't happen again, wuss luck. We could make fair money at this rate."

"I never thought of money," returned Keven with a sigh.

"My Gord, boy, do you reckon I'm wearin' myself out fer love of fishin'?"

"Garry, you're like me. You'd fish for nothing. . . . Wow!"

"By gosh, you've hung a lunker. Let him run."

"He's taking all the line. Say, what a strike! Garry, row after him. I'll bet this is the granddad of the whole bunch."

It developed, at length, that he had indeed hooked a mighty Chinook. Ordinarily a forty-pound salmon would tow the light skiff for quite a while. But this one pulled it fast and failed to tire.

"If he heads out to sea we jest ain't a-goin', Kev," declared Garry, as the fish drew them towards the outlet.

"We'll follow him to Kamchatka," retorted Keven. "Aw, Garry, we've got to catch this Chinook. I'll bet he'll go eighty pounds."

"Come down, Kev. I never seen but a couple of eighty-pounders, an' thet was 'way north of here. . . . Listen to thet surf out there."

Indeed the boom and pound of the sea could not have been anything but dominant here, except to a deaf man. With tide at flood and a fresh breeze from off shore the thunder on the beach was incessant, deep, and heart-quaking.

Meanwhile the sun had gone down over the wide ridged expanse of ocean, which Keven could see out across the narrow mouth. Already shadows were forming under the low sand dunes, and near shore on the north side the water had begun to glance and gleam darkly.

"Ain't you ever goin' to land thet Chinook?" queried Garry. "I'm 'most starved. Hoss him in, Kev."

"Ha! ha! 'Hoss him in.' You ought to have hold of this line."

"Well, I'm willin' enough, if you can't lick him."

"Thunder and blazes!" ejaculated Keven, aghast. "He's making for that net."

"Sure. Thet's why I've been hollerin'. I seen it was comin'. Better cut him loose."

"What? Like hell I will."

"Kev, if I ain't mistook thet's one of Mulligan's nets. He an' his gang have gall enough to set nets an' leave 'em. Somethin' we upriver fishermen never dared do. . . . Ahuh, your fish is fast."

"Yes, dang it. But I'll get him or bust."

"Better cut him loose Kev," repeated Garry soberly.

"Say, pard, are you afraid?" asked Keven, derisive in his excitement.

"Hell if you put it that way," rejoined Garry, offended, and he backed the skiff toward where the net buoy bobbed on the surface.

Meanwhile Keven hauled in the slack line, which led them somewhat to the right of the buoy. Keven directed his partner to row close to the buoy, so that he could pick up the net rope. Soon he was hauling on the net and at the same time taking in his hand line. With a lunge and a roar the huge Chinook came up. That flurry was apparently his last, for he turned his great, broad shiny side up, and gaped with the jaws of an enormous wolf.

"Help, Garry," panted Keven, as he tried to lift the salmon.

"Tip the skiff an' slide him in," replied Garry.

Between them they got the fish into the skiff, where it lay gasping, the most marvelous salmon Keven had ever seen.

"Oh! What'll he go?"

"Some lunker!" ejaculated Garry. "Sixty-five, mebbe seventy pounds."

The big spoon had become entangled in the net, and as

Keven extricated it, with some difficulty, Garry suddenly burst out, hoarsely: "By Gord! . . . Look at thet net!"

"What? It's all right. I've got the hook free. No damage done."

"Look at thet mesh!" exclaimed Garry, low and sharp. His blue eyes shot fire.

Keven gazed from Garry back to the net, a fold of which dragged over his knee. It appeared to be made of smaller twine, more closely knit. Puzzled, he lifted it—spread it wide. Measured the net with eye and then with fingers.

"Four-inch mesh!" he whispered.

"Sure as you're borned," corroborated Garry.

"And the law allows only an eight-inch mesh?"

"The law allows! Haw! Haw! But thet's the law, Kev."

"Garry, we've got it on them."

"Lemme look." Then Garry reached over to spread the folds, sliding them back into the water, until he came to a line of heavier twine and larger mesh. The top of the net had a border of mesh which conformed with the existing law.

"Thet top is only a blind," went on Garry. "Pretty slick, I'll tell the world. . . . This net is deep an' heavy; I'll bet there's twenty feet an' more below. Look out! A boat comin'."

Garry flipped the top line back into the water, where it disappeared, and sitting back to his oars, he added: "Stand up an' be liftin' thet salmon."

Keven, further spurred by the creaking of oarlocks, did as he was bidden, while Garry rowed. A few strokes took them out from the shadow cast by the sand dunes. Still they could easily have been seen before that, if the approaching boatman had been looking. As his back was turned, however, there was a chance that they had not been observed.

"Hey, look out where you're goin'," bawled Garry, in quite unnecessary alarm, for the fisherman was some rods off. He backed water with his oars and then turned to look.

"Can't you see when a feller's on a fish?" went on Garry, loudly, as Keven made as if he had just that instant hauled the Chinook aboard.

"Hey yourself," replied the fisherman gruffly. "Hev you been foolin' round my——" He plainly was going to say net, but he checked himself and added, "hyar?"

"Naw, we haven't been foolin' round nuthin'," replied Garry, just as gruffly. "We was landin' this Chinook an' thought you'd run us down."

Keven dropped the fish with a great flop, and then flopped down himself. No easy task had it been to hold up that weight. He gazed from the magnificent salmon to the grim Garry.

"Lucky catch, pard?"

"Ump-umm! Damn unlucky."

"But why?" gasped Keven.

'Lemme think, you dinged amatoor fishin' detective."

Keven let him alone then and tried to compose his whirling thoughts to some clarifying order. Dusk had settled down over the river when they arrived at their mooring. Flares of lightning showed the bold peaks of the Cascades. Storm threatened. The river slid by, gleaming and melancholy. Leaping ashore, Keven hurried to camp and started a fire, while Garry attended to the catch. Sometimes he made a deal with Stemm to dispose of it. Soon he came slopping up the path, to sit down before the tent and kick off his rubber boots.

"Seventy-one pounds," he announced.

"You weighed him? Say, didn't I tell you? What wouldn't I have given to catch that Chinook on a rod! Seventy-one pounds!"

"Never could have licked him. Stemm's scales weigh under, too, you can gamble on thet. . . . Kev, I'm in the need of a stiff swag of likker. But as I can't have it, a cup of strong coffee might settle my nerves."

Between them they got supper with little or no unnecessary conversation. Keven waited patiently for his partner to speak, but that did not happen until the meal was finished, the chores done, and Garry was smoking by the campfire.

"One way or another we got it on them!" suddenly Garry burst out.

"Ahuh!" agreed Keven. That was exactly what his conclusion had been.

"Pard, I swear I've long suspected that very thing, but honest—I never seen a net like thet before," declared Garry. "Might only be one. Might belong to a half-breed who was ketchin' steelhead to smoke fer winter use. Might not have any connection with the canneries. Might be a lot of things."

"Ahuh," continued Keven.

"An' then again it might not!"

"But Garry—what do you *think?*"

"Think? A hell of a lot. An' now I *know* why big steelhead seldom or never show up the river till after October first. I mean the fourteen- an' sixteen-pounders we used to ketch. . . . I think mebbe there's many such nets. I think Mulligan an' his crew are back of thet. Mebbe the whole damned ring. I think they sell every little fish they ketch—an' not to the natives up in the hills to smoke fer winter. Ho! Ho! Not hardly. . . . I think it's crookeder than hell. I think it's rottener than hell."

"My, what a stink it will make! What a row up the river! Garry, I'm tickled pink," raved Keven.

"Kev, we can't lay thet onto the canneries. It could never be proved. They'd make the fishermen the goats. But thet's nuthin'."

"We don't need to implicate the canneries," declared Keven intensely. "All we need is to show evidence *why* the salmon and steelhead run fewer up the river."

"By Gord, Kev, you're right. If we can steal thet net full of small jacks an' silversides an' steelhead, we'll raise such hell thet it'll ring all over Oregon. Blackwood is honest. He couldn't be bought. If we steal thet net with fish in it, by gosh, he'll make it hot for these fishermen. He'd stand by us. He'd blow thet news far an' wide. Then the big holler would come."

"Whew!" whistled Keven, loosening his collar. "What'll we do?"

"Watch thet net day an' night," returned Garry, his eyes narrowing to slits. "An' the first time the coast is clear we'll steal it. A net with a small mesh like thet will have fish in it—even an hour after it has been picked over. When our chance comes we'll cut the anchors loose, keepin' the buoy, an' we'll pile the net into the skiff an' beat it fer shore. All we gotta do is to keep from bein' ketched in the act. . . . Kev, we're broke an' pore as church mice, but we're settin' pretty this minnit."

It turned out during the next few days that that particular fishing locality in which Keven and Garry were especially interested was never without fishermen on it. At dawn boats were everywhere; during the day no safe opportunity presented; from sunset to dark appeared to be the time in which they were going to get their chance.

They fished early and late and, contrary to their expectations, caught as many salmon as the trolling Indians. This was killing two birds with one stone, and they were jubilant. But one morning Garry returned from the canneries to inform Keven that they no longer had any market for their fish, unless they would sell to Priddy for ten cents a fish.

"Think of thet. A dime fer a big salmon," declared Garry wrathfully. "A measly ten cents fer an hour's hard work! . . . Kev, it's plain as print. The little cannery is broke. They'll take our fish if we'll trust 'em to pay. I heerd Atwell has now got interest in the Smith factory. An' of course Priddy's offer is jest an insult. What'll we do, pard?"

"What do you think?"

"Let's shoot the whole works. Let's burn them two big canneries to the water. Then Smith will come into his."

"No. We can't do that, Garry," replied Keven gravely. "Take our fish to Smith. It's no matter whether he pays us or not. But we don't want these fishermen to see us out there, trolling day in and day out, with absolutely no market for our fish. That'd give us away."

Garry agreed, and now in settled conviction of the wrong done them, and in growing wrath, they returned to their profitless work. Garry drank steadily. He always had a bottle, from what source Keven did not know. And Keven drank, too, more than usual, 'and more than was good for him. Garry had long been without money, and Keven's was fast disappearing. Their supplies were low and they had no credit because the store belonged to the interests that were hounding them off the river.

"We can't hold out much longer. We gotta swipe thet net quick," Garry kept saying.

93

All this strain had worn severely upon Keven. He grew no longer capable of the keen, patient watching for opportunity. And once more that dark, bitter mood fastened upon him, until at last he was desperate.

One August afternoon storm clouds appeared over the mountains. The sultry atmosphere heralded rain, but it was slow in coming. Sunset had a red, smoky, sinister aspect.

"Kev, we're gonna git our chance," averred Garry, as they shoved off. "The tide's runnin' hell-bent fer election. An' there'll be a storm bustin' soon."

"High time we had one. Rain has been as scarce here as loose change with us," replied Keven.

"Row straight across," directed Garry, as he took up the coiled trolling line. "Kev, I don't see a damn boat. But the light's queer. Did you ever see the like of thet? . . . An' listen. There's thunder thet ain't from the surf."

A gold-red glow suffused the western sky and was reflected in the quiet waters of the bay. Northward, up the river, the sky was black as ink, illumined now and then by flares of lightning.

"There's one boat, with two fellers," said Garry, pointing, "Rowin' in. . . . Kev, pull easy, like we was trollin'. I tell you, our chance has come. There's been pore fishin' lately, the tide's runnin' out, an' a storm's a-comin'. There won't be no fishermen out there a-tall."

"We'll grab that net tonight even if there are fishermen on the bay," rasped Keven.

He had reached the end of his rope, the limit of endurance. Yet never had he been so passionately determined to secure evidence against these crooked fishermen.

"Pard, drink to our success," said Garry, offering a bottle. "Only a little left. Save one fer me."

Like fiery flame the liquor seemed to course through Keven. Then he watched Garry tilt and drain the bottle. His form showed black against the golden gleam of the bay. "Aggh!" he ejaculated huskily and flipped the bottle into the water. It sank, sending up bubbles.

A darkening of the afterglow, sudden and striking, changed the beautiful effect of sky and water. The lights were dying. An ominous calm, a menacing silence, lay like a blanket over the country. It was broken by low muttering thunder from the mountains and the answering roar of the sea. Then again the muffling silence. Keven's oars dipped noiselessly, as if in oil. Garry had the posture of a hawk, peering over the shimmering bay. Soon the shore line, except on the western side, vanished in the gathering gloom. Wavering and dark the sand dunes began to loom against that fast-fading dusky gold in the west.

"Pretty black under them dunes," whispered Garry. "A boat could be hid along there. But we ain't got time to look. . . . Coast is clear. . . . Turn now, Kev, an' pull. . . . There. We're in line with our landmark."

Keven sent the skiff gliding swiftly. He faced to east and north, while Garry faced the west. An unearthly glow came from the last fire in the heavens. Weirdly it lighted the surface of the bay, magnifying the floating bits of driftwood and the widening circles made by fish. Driftwood was a sure sign of a rise in the river. A faint soft breeze struck Keven's heated face. It bore the burden of the sultry, oppressed air, and a deeper rumble of thunder. Jagged forks of lightning shot down from that black pall to the north.

"Slow. I see the buoy," whispered Garry. "Left—a little. Now stop. . . . Slip the oars behind you, so you can grab them quick. . . . Quiet, Kev! Sound carries far a night like this."

Keven had thumped the gunwale with an oar. The skiff glided smoothly. Garry reached far out. Then Keven saw him catch the buoy.

"Cut her free, Kev, while I haul," went on Garry, standing up.

Grasping the big fish knife, Keven leaned forward behind Garry and slashed the anchor rope. It twanged. It let go. Garry lifted the buoy into the skiff and began to drag the net likewise.

"Let 'er swing, Kev. . . . Gee! What you make of thet?"

The net held many wiggling steelhead, just gilled, and salmon under size. Garry hauled powerfully, dropping the wet folds into the skiff. Keven laid the knife down to help. While they slowly drifted with the tide, downstream and inshore, they gathered in net and fish, to pile them at their feet. Soon they were standing on the thick folds and squirming, gasping fish.

"Here's the end. Kev. Cut the rope. . . . By Gord, the job's done."

Keven straightened up, knife in hand, his back to the shadow cast by the sand dunes. His heart beat high. Exultantly he gazed out across the pale bay toward the canneries. On the instant a flare spread across the sky, lighting the hills, the trees. It appeared to augment the unreal, opaque gleaming surface of the bay. He was about to second Garry's husky whisper of triumph when a slight noise froze him. The skiff was drifting. Garry had just lifted the trailing anchor rope aboard. Had he been accountable for that sound? A gurgling, sucking dip? It had been made by an oar. Warily Keven sought to turn.

"Look out, Kev!" shouted Garry, with piercing suddenness.

He leaped to shove Keven back. His upflung arms went protectingly above Keven's head.

"Ketched you net thieves!" rasped out a voice thick with fury.

"Aye, Mulligan—you blackhearted half-breed!" returned Garry fiercely.

A boat thumped hard against the skiff. Then came a swish. Keven saw a dark descending object, over him. A terrible sodden thud! Garry fell over the seat into the bow.

"Take thet, you upriver———!"

Mulligan's boat bumped against the skiff, bringing the burly fisherman somewhat forward of Keven, yet within reach. Mulligan lifted the long oar over the prostrate Garry. Like a tiger Keven leaped. With all his might he swung the fish knife. He drove it into Mulligan's burly neck. Hot blood squirted over his hand before he could let go. A horrible, hoarse, strangled cry rent the air. Mulligan plunged overboard, his oar striking the boat and sliding off.

Keven had lost his equilibrium. The skiff had been overbalanced. Water was pouring in over the net. Then he plunged, face forward, into the bay. The icy shock, succeeding the awful rush of fire through his veins, aided rather than hindered his desperate lunging up, to where he could breathe again and see.

The skiff had righted, but the gunwale was only a few inches above water. He dared not attempt to clamber aboard. It had been caught by the current. Keven grasped the bow and held on.

Then as he peered back a lightning flash showed the other boat, black on the white water, drifting down. There was no sign of Mulligan. He had sunk. A fiendish primitive glee danced in the cold marrow of Keven's bones.

Keven saw one of Garry's arms hanging limp over the gunwale. Holding fast, keeping the skiff trim, Keven peered about. They had drifted from the bay into the mouth of the river. Like a millrace the outgoing tide carried the skiff toward the outlet. Nearer sounded the crash of the breakers. Keven began to kick, and to paddle with his free arm. Gradually the skiff swung toward the sandpit. He could discern the pale gray point, lashed by that sliding tide.

Suddenly his feet touched bottom. He waded, desperately clinging to the bow. The skiff swung broadside. Then the tremendous current tore it from his grasp. He lunged, meaning to catch it again, and go with Garry. But too late! The current beat him. The boat gleamed against the dim white waves—swept on—disappeared. And the tide dragged at him. Frantically he plunged and clawed his way out on the sandspit, where he fell.

chapter eleven

OVERCOME BY HORROR and exertion, Keven lay on the sand, his face upturned to the oncoming storm. At length he sat up, panting, wet, trembling. The river swept by, out into the darkness whence pounded and threshed the surf.

"Oh, my—God!" he cried, in dreadful realization. "He saved—me! ... He's gone! . . . Garry! Garry!"

Even if Garry were alive when the skiff drifted out he would soon be drowned in those wild waters. Mulligan had sunk. He would drift out to sea. But the sea gave up its dead. It would cast the half-breed up with that knife stuck in his neck. Keven would be branded a murderer.

The instinct to escape arose in him. Staggering up, he gazed fearfully at the pale sand beach, across the gloomy bay toward the town. Thunder was crashing nearer. The storm would soon break. When the lightning flashed he saw boats with the dark figures of men. Fishermen at their nets! They might find Mulligan's drifting empty boat. He slunk over on the seaside of the beach until he drew under cover of the wooded hill, when he swung around to the bay shore again. As he hurried on he gathered strength. No person saw him reach camp.

It was in his mind to go up the river. He packed a small bag of biscuits, cooked meat, dried fruit. He donned his rubber coat, which had the wool lining. Then he removed it and also his wet shirt. Finding his remaining one, he put that on, and the coat over it. But he would not leave the wet shirt behind. It might somehow be a clue. What else would he take? As he stripped off a blanket from the bed, Garry's gun fell out from under the pillow. Keven heard it, then felt it. The cold steel sent a shiver through him, followed by a swift gust of hot blood.

98

He would make his way up the river trail to Grant's Pass and kill Atwell before he was caught. That was what he would do. All the passion and hate, the bitter consciousness of foul wrong done him, welled up to fix in grim, unalterable decision. Rolling the blanket lengthwise, he slung it over his shoulder. The shirt he stuffed in the bag. Then he thought of his watch, comb and brush, his little mirror, and other small articles, which he stowed in his pockets. He was ready. But he turned back once more for his tackle.

He peered through the gloom. A dim light shone in Stemm's cabin. Keven strode off silently, his nerves taut, his eyes roving everywhere, his throat contracted. He got by the few remaining fishermen's shacks.

It would be necessary to cross the river. On the opposite side a road led up some miles, he did not know how many, to the government trail. He could cross in one of the Indians' boats, but he rejected that idea because it might direct attention to his flight. The river was rising; however, it had been low, and a few inches or even a foot would not prevent him from crossing at a wide rocky island bar some distance upstream.

Flashes of lightning aided him to make his way along the shore. Drops of rain splashed on his face. How slow the storm in coming! But if it were as heavy as the roll of thunder portended, if it raised the river overnight—that might be well for him. He found the rocky bar and made out the island. The river was rising and salmon were running. As he waded across the wide shallow channel he heard the big Chinook thumping and ranting upstream. Not now did they have power to thrill him! The Rogue had ruined him, betrayed him.

He crossed without difficulty, but had trouble over the boulders and through the brush. He pressed on to come out into the road. Then the thunder crashed and the clouds burst. Heavy, warm rain flooded down. He welcomed it. His tracks would be washed out.

Exhaustion had left him. He felt strong, enduring, swift. He could have run. The blanket and bag hung easily on his shoulders. He carried the rod in his hand. The reel had been stowed in one of his pockets. Funny he would not leave them behind! He strode on, free, through the downpour, with the lightning flashes blinding him, the rolling, booming thunder deafening him. This was no passing shower, but a mountain cloudburst. The Rogue would rise as if by magic. Midnight would see it in flood. By dawn there would be no fishermen on the bay. Keven had no hope of ultimate escape. All he asked were days enough to make the long tramp up the river and to consummate his revenge. Then let what would happen! But freedom tasted sweet. He would die before surrendering, to be thrown behind bars, to languish and wait for worse than death. He might even escape after killing Atwell, to flee into the fastnesses of the Rogue wilderness, where he could never be apprehended and captured. Bloodhounds could not trail him through the fir forests and the canyons along the river.

Thus with active and grim mind he strode on through the storm. Its fury and ceaselessness seemed to beat in time with his thoughts. Hour after hour must have passed, but time was not significant. In the gray of morning he came to the end of the road. A house and some cabins marked this terminal. From there the government trail climbed to the mountainside above the river. Daylight delayed long. The rain fell steadily, though its violence had departed. The Rogue roared below. When he could at last discern it down through the firs and the mist it looked like a dark brown swirling torrent. Uprooted trees, their foliage green against the water, told the tale of the mountain storm.

Toward noon the rain ceased and the clouds began to lift. Long before he reached it, he espied the hamlet of Agness, which he recognized by the white suspension bridge that spanned the river. Here he plunged into the woods and made a slow wide detour, to come out on the trail far beyond. He began to be aware of sensations of fatigue and hunger. But he kept on, meaning to pass Illahe, the second and last little hamlet on the river, before he halted to rest and eat. Late that afternoon he came out into a widening of the valley in which Illahe was located. It consisted of a few scattered outlying farms and a few houses clustered together near the river. This detour took longer, but he did not have to climb uphill. At last he came out again on the trail. Dusk overtook him, and he felt that he had gone his limit. While there was still light enough to see he made off the trail into a pine thicket. He felt too weary to eat, yet he forced himself. He had walked forty miles or more without food or rest. When he rolled in the blanket night seemed to shut out his senses.

When he became conscious of them again the forest was full of golden light and slanting rays. The trees had ceased to drip. Birds were singing. The mellow roar of the river stole dreamily through the woods.

Keven lay like a log, his mind quick to grasp this was no enchantment of sleep. When he attempted to move there followed only a painful spasm of his muscles. They were stiff. He had driven himself to the limit and then had slept in wet clothes and blanket. It required effort to roll over and get up on his hands and knees, then to stand up. Moving about a bit, he discovered that some animal had overturned his canvas bag, to make off with his little store of food. This serious mishap struck him with panic. It would take days to reach Grant's Pass, and without food he never could make it. Then it dawned upon him that he was only eight miles from Aard's cabin at Solitude, and Aard was a man he would not be afraid to trust. Rolling his blanket and taking up the bag, he set out, dragging one foot after the other. Before stepping into the trail he glanced back and forward. Squirrels were frisking across it. The river hummed below. All seemed locked in solitude. He turned south.

Presently he came out in a sunny glade through which ran a clear stream, splashing and babbling over rocks. Depositing his things on the ground, he drank deeply, then washed his face in the icy water and combed and brushed his tangled hair. After which he sat motionless on a mossy log, conscious of nothing except that the light, the smell, the sound and feel of the woods were working upon him. Then he arose to plod on.

Soon the trail emerged on a high slope above the river. The scene somehow burst upon him, halting him in his tracks. The river was in turgid flood, bank-full, covering the rocks, swinging swiftly around the green gap above and sliding the same way out of sight below. It had been a very quick rise—so quick that only vigilance on the part

101

of the fishermen at the mouth of the river could have saved their nets and boats.

Then a shocking memory, like a blade, stabbed through him. Faithful, simple, rough Garry had died for him. And he had killed a man. The latter seemed nothing. It was self-defense, justice. No qualms of conscience weighed upon Keven. He would have done the same thing again. But who would believe his story? He would be branded a murderer and he would be hanged. He was a fugitive who would be hunted. Then his deadly project returned, stronger than ever, possessing him utterly, driving him on, the lust to kill stealing along his numb nerves, through his sluggish blood, even into his aching bones.

But spirit was one thing and physical strength another. Less than a half mile up the trail he had to rest again. He wanted to drop down and never get up again. So, toiling on, and resting oftener, he covered a few miles. The sun now shone hot; the leaf-strewn trail had become dry; from the slopes floated up the sweet fragrance of myrtle, and the pungent odor from patches of pinewoods clogged his nostrils. Birds and squirrels were unusually gay this fresh, bright, golden morning. Only when deer met him on the trail, to stand and gaze with long ears up, did he remember that he was penetrating the wilds of the Cascades. Thereafter he watched with the eyes of a hunter, because it was not possible for him to pass along blind and deaf to the creatures of the wilderness. Only there was no thrill, no joy, no consciousness of beauty, no thought of the glory of nature. Also he listened for a hoof thump on the trail behind.

The trail entered what appeared to be a green tunnel under the forest, shady, silent, drowsy in the noonday heat. Presently the hoofbeats he had been listening for vibrated on Keven's sensitive nerves. Stealthily as an Indian he slipped into the brush, to crouch in a shaded covert, his heart thumping, the roof of his mouth dry. But soon he ascertained that the horse was approaching from the north, which fact instantly released the clutch of terror.

Tramp of hoofs, merry whistles, rough gay voices of men, swelled upon Keven's ears. Soon he caught a glimpse of packers going down the trail with their pack train. Seldom were any other travelers encountered along the river. These were half-breeds, happy and carefree. Keven wondered dully how anyone could whistle, and he envied these natives of the Rogue wilderness. When they had passed on out of hearing he entered the trail again, pondering whether or not they would see his tracks. It was unlikely, for the trail was hard and dry; only a hunter on foot could have discerned the slight disturbance of dust and leaves. Keven toiled on.

He rested oftener, sitting idly on logs or stones he came to, or at the trunk of a stately fir, conscious of some strange lagging of resolve, of the will to force his weary body further.

Midafternoon found him within sight of the great V-shaped valley which marked the entrance to Solitude. Not once along this stretch did he rest. Indeed he tried to hurry, as if his desire were to reach Solitude and get it behind him. The trail descended, crossing the old flumes left by the miners who had long years before passed on, leaving these eloquent reminders of their dream, of their passion. Endlessly the left-hand slope of the valley slanted toward the blue sky, plowed by dry gullies, here bare and red where avalanche had scored the earth, there gray with long slide of weathered rock, and above sunny with wide grassy plot merging in the oak forest of the summit. Across the river, at the water's edge, began the forest of firs, so densely grown that only the spear-point tips could be discerned; and it sheered up, black and wild, to the mountain peaks.

But when Keven got round the bend to Solitude he fell victim to infinitely more than fatigue. Sight of Solitude broke his gloomy and rancorous mood. It brought something nameless back to him. Was it youth, was it love of the river, was it this most lonely and fascinating stretch on all the wayward Rogue, was it the dead joy of fishing—that he would know no more? The mile-long channel, the cliff wall, the foaming bend, the dark bench of tan oaks across the river, where under their shiny tight foliage moldered the old moss-roofed gold mill of the miners—these seemed nothing to him now. The tranquil and unbroken solitude—was that dimming his eyes? High above him in the fir tops moaned the wind, the restful sound, the

103

song of the trees. He sought to grasp the old beauty, the dream and the glory of Solitude. But for him they had vanished. He wept. His heart seemed to break. He surrendered to he knew not what. It would be better for him to plunge into the river and find peace there under the lichened shelving cliffs. He had courage to do that—but a hellish resolve had clutched him. He would be what they had made him. He had been trained to kill and he would kill. But not even this recurrent and augmenting hate could subjugate his grief.

Keven shouldered his burdens and plodded on. The trail wound among huge mossy boulders, skirted the sandy shore, went on into the brown-matted and pine-scented forest, to emerge in the open above the bench where Aard lived. Keven saw two cabins now, one above the other, and the higher, with its peeled logs, its yellow stone chimney, its wide sloping eaves and porch, appeared unfamiliar to him. But the lower cabin, old, mossy, vine-covered, nestling under a grand fir, strangely called to that vague, haunting, faulty memory. He heard the ring of an ax; he saw a curling column of blue smoke. Aard must be home. Keven meant to rest awhile, ask some food of this backwoodsman, tell him nothing, and go on to the fulfillment of his last task.

The deep bay of a hound startled him. It pealed up the slope, returned in hollow echo. How that, too, pierced into the closed chamber of his mind! He went down the sunlit, shadow-barred trail. Presently up in a green-gray notch behind the cabin he espied a white lacy waterfall. Sight of it gave him the same perplexity; likewise the succeeding low mellow hum of tumbling stream, like the murmur of innumerable bees. Again the fragrance of sweet myrtle struck his nostrils. The smell pierced deeper than other sense stimulations. He remembered that waterfall—how he had climbed to it—to the fern-choked source of the stream. Yet there seemed something more.

Keven mounted the bench, over which the giant fir stood sentinel. The trail forked. He kept to the left, coming out suddenly into the colorful open. Asters bloomed along the path, in the clean hard-packed sand on which Keven caught a trace of little moccasin tracks. The first cabin stood on the river end of the clearing. Back of it fenced gardens and orchards reached to the mountain slope. Beyond this cabin, and higher, stood the other, on the brink of the green gorge down which the stream hummed.

The hound bayed again, and a chorus of yelps and barks from lesser dogs filled the air. A voice silenced them. Keven directed his gaze back to the first cabin. Someone stood on the porch surrounded by dogs.

Keven halted to sit down on a huge log that lay between the path and the edge of the clearing. He was spent again, and it might be better to wait until Aard came out. He laid aside his burdens and removed his cap.

Suddenly a wildly sweet, piercing, trilling cry rent the silence. Keven jerked up in startled surprise. A girl came running swiftly down the path, followed by the dogs.

"Kev! Oh, Kev!" she screamed.

He was as if thunderstruck. He stared. She came flying on winged feet, her dark face and dark hair shining in the sunlight.

"Oh, Kev! I thought you'd—never, never—come back," she panted, and reaching him on the run, without giving him a chance to look at her, she clasped her arms round him and held him close, her head over his shoulder, her face against his. "But, thank God—you did come. I *knew* you would someday."

Keven essayed to find his voice, but in vain. He doubted his senses. Yet he felt a clinging of tender arms, though strong as steel, of a throbbing, heaving breast, of hot tears wetting his cheek. They affected him even more strangely than the surprise of this onslaught. For a moment he was as if almost paralyzed, his thoughts hopelessly jumbled.

Then she released him and stood erect, her hands on his shoulders. He could see her now—strong, beautiful face, smooth and clear-skinned with scarlet showing under the dark golden tan, eyes piercingly black for all their brimming with tears, and hair like an Indian's.

"You nearly broke my heart, Kev," she said, smiling through her tears.

Keven racked his clouded brain. He stammered: "Aren't—haven't you—mistaken me—for someone else?"

"Kev Bell!" she cried reproachfully, and she shook him ever so slightly.

"You have my name pat. But who——"

"Don't you know me?" she interrupted, deeply hurt and shocked.

"I—I'm afraid not."

"Oh, Kev, you are teasing me."

"Indeed, no, Miss."

"I am Beryl," she said simply.

Beryl! That name knocked at the gate of closed associations: "Beryl! . . . Beryl who?"

"Aard, of course. . . . You *are* teasing me. It's mean of you—almost as mean as your going by here last May without stopping to see me."

"I'm sorry, Miss——"

"Miss! How can you call me that? How can you sit there sober-faced, making me feel ridiculous—when I—I'm dying to be kissed?" she protested, in doubt and fear, yet obviously so overjoyed at his presence that she could scarcely refrain from embracing him again. She blushed, too, at that bold conclusion.

Keven gazed at her more bewildered than ever, though he realized now that this was no case of mistaken identity. She knew him if he did not know her. And he was involved somewhere, somehow. In these few thrilling moments her face had grown strangely familiar.

"Well, I wouldn't let any girl die for want of so simple a thing," said Keven, sparring for time. "But I—I see you are earnest. And I just can't place you."

"Oh, it must be true, then," she cried poignantly. "You don't remember me!"

"Ought I to?" asked Keven.

"Indeed you ought, unless you've become a fickle, faithless soldier."

"I assure you I'm not that. But if you had said a crippled, broken soldier, you'd be right. . . . I was injured by the bursting of a gun. The breechblock blew back into my face. It was many weeks before I recovered enough to know what had happened. Then I lay in a camp hospital for months. I'm nearly blind in one eye. My lower jaw was blown off. See the scars on my lip and chin? Then I suffered other injury to my head, and so my memory fails

106

sometimes. That must be why I don't remember you—if it's true that I should."

Keven did not expect that his lengthy explanation would bring about any other result than to calm this magnificent young woman and earn palliation if not forgiveness for his offense. But it did far more. Her face blanched, her eyes dilated and softened, expressing unutterable sorrow, her red lips quivered. And her hands went with exquisite tenderness to his chin and cheek, and then over his brow, finally to run in sudden wild rapture through his hair and to lock back of his neck. Then she kissed his cheek and drew back.

"Kev, does *that* help—you to remember?" she asked, with a break in her rich voice.

"I—yes—that is, the way you mussed my hair—somehow I—I sort of remember that," he replied, in tremendous embarrassment.

"Kev, it's not that you've forgotten me," she went on earnestly. "I was horribly hurt. But then I didn't know how you'd suffered. I will come back to you presently."

"If you'll let me ask you questions, perhaps that might help."

"Ask away. . . . Kev, you smiled then for the first time. Oh, you poor soldier boy!"

"You're Aard's daughter?" began Keven.

"Of course. I was born in that cabin. My mother died last winter."

"I remember Solitude better than any other place on the river," went on Keven. "I have been here twice, fishing. Once for what must have been a good while. Only a little over four years ago! But now it seems so far away and long ago. . . . You must have been here when I stayed with Aard that last time."

"Yes, Kev, I was here," she replied wistfully. "I spent every hour of the livelong day with you—and often far into the night."

"Did—I——?" asked Keven haltingly, almost afraid to go on. "But weren't you a—a mere child?"

"I was not. I was sixteen years old and large for my age," she returned emphatically.

"Did—did I make love to you?"

107

"Terribly. . . . No girl ever had such wonderful love made to her."

Keven felt as if a gulf were about to open up and swallow him. She held her head up proudly, as if she had been vastly honored. Poor Keven was in a quandary. He could not doubt her. Simplicity and honesty breathed from her.

"Did I kiss you, Beryl?"

"Did you?" She trilled a happy laugh of incredulity. "You teased me, coaxed me, begged me for one little kiss. . . . And when I gave in you took ten thousand."

A thrill shot through Keven, and something snatched away his breath.

"It seems I must have been—wild and bold," he continued, gravely trying to meet her black eyes. "I hope—I—I didn't lay a hand on you."

"Kev Bell! Your memory *is* gone. A pretty fresh boy you were. You laid two hands on me—and if you'd had a third that wouldn't have been enough."

Keven bowed his head under this startling admission. He felt the slow hot blood sting his cheeks. What had he done to this girl—when she had been a child of the wilderness?

She touched his head with gentle hand and smoothed his hair.

"Don't feel badly about *that*, Kev," she returned, in shy earnestness. "You weren't all to blame. . . . I—I loved you. And you did me no harm. . . . Only you made me worship you—made me so I could never look at another boy—made me wait and wait for you to come back."

"Did I promise to come back?" asked Keven.

"Yes. But the United States was forced into war," she went on. "You did not wait to be drafted. Dad had the newspapers from Portland, Grant's Pass, Seattle. I read of you going to training camp. But I never knew where. Always I expected to hear from you. We thought you had gone to France. That nearly killed me. I could not stay here at Solitude. It drove me mad. . . . Then I read of your accident. Scared and sick as I was at that, I was terribly glad you'd never gone to war. I waited and prayed—knowing you'd come back to me some day. . . .

Oh, how long—the weeks, the months, the years! No news! No letter! . . . Still I trusted and waited."

Keven writhed under the enormity of this thing that was befalling him.

"You say—you couldn't stay here? Where'd you go?"

"I went to Roseburg, to my aunt's," she returned. "There I attended school. Vacation times I came home. I ran wild. I fished, I hunted, I chopped wood, I worked. I helped build a log cabin. But I couldn't be happy. I longed for you. . . . Then when Mother died Dad fetched me home."

"Tell me something more about what I did, when I was here that last time," said Keven, determined to damn himself utterly and forever in his own sight.

"Oh, there are a million things," she jubilated, in contrast to her former pathos. "We climbed the trails. We used to watch the deer in the oak groves. Once we were treed by wild pigs! How funny that was! We gathered flowers and ferns. We used to wash the sand for gold. I have a little vial full of gold dust that we washed. But the river was your god. I was jealous of the river. You loved it best, and then the water ouzels and the steelhead. . . . All the time since you've been away, while I was home, when I heard the ouzels in the mornings and evenings I would cry."

"Water ouzels? These little elfish Rogue River birds that build their nests under the cliffs, so when their young ones hatch they'll fall in the water?"

"Yes, yes, Kev," she cried eagerly. "We used to try to get to those mud nests sticking on the walls. But we never could. . . . Don't you remember how I first took you to the rock ledges where the steelhead lay? No one ever knew them but Dad and I. But I showed you. Don't you remember one lovely morning that I saw a big steelhead rising? And I showed you where. You cast and cast. You tried every fly you had. And at last I let you try one I had tied myself. It was buff and black. The old sockdolager rose up and fastened to that fly. Then he leaped—a monster. Sixteen, perhaps eighteen pounds. And he took you down around the bend. You ran, you waded, you swam the river over and back again, while I flew and

109

screamed along the bank. Oh, don't you remember, Kev? . . . How I met you at the head of the rapids where you lost him? Your rod was broken and so was your heart. . . . It was then, Kev, that I let you—no, that I gave you my first kiss."

A door seemed to jar and shock back on the dim threshold of that closed chamber in Keven Bell's brain. He saw again that monster rose-and-silver trout, leaping and tearing down the swift river. He saw again a girl, black-eyed and blackhaired, flying barefooted over the sand and stones, screaming in wild abandon.

"Beryl, I remember—I remember!" he exclaimed, his eyes closed in a rapture that had its inception in the past. The next instant the girl was on his breast, weeping, crying out her thanksgiving for his deliverance from oblivion. Instinctively, unconsciously his arms closed round her. And when he opened his eyes there he stood with a dark head on his breast, with fragrant hair at his lips. He could not realize it. The dogs wagged eager tails and gazed up wonderingly at this stranger. Then Keven looked up. Was that waterfall, like downward-flying lace as white as snow, anything real and tangible? Did cloud ships sail across the blue sky and drop moving shadows along the mountain slope? Was that scent of sweet myrtle a delusion? Were the purple asters swaying in the breeze flowers of a dream? Was he only mad or dead?

It was she who released herself.

"Dad is away from home," she said. "He goes to Portland sometimes. He said he would stop over at Gold Beach to see you. Oh, won't he be glad!"

The horror of the fate that had overtaken Keven swept over him again.

"You are pale—tired. You look so strange," she said tremulously.

"I'm all in, Beryl," he replied, suddenly weak. "I wasn't strong—and I walked too far. Then I slept in my wet things and it cramped me. I'm starved, too."

"Oh, dear! And here I've been wearing you out with my fury!" she exclaimed self-accusingly. "But, oh, the joy of having you back! My Keven! My soldier home from the war! . . . Come. I shall rest you and feed you and nurse you till you are the Keven of old."

110

She led him toward the cabin. He espied an Indian woman peering at them from the porch. The dogs trotted on ahead, assured now that all was well. The blue smoke curled up from the stone chimney. Keven caught the odor of a wood fire and baking bread. He seemed powerless to resist, though he knew he could flee like a madman into the forest.

chapter twelve

KEVEN WOKE TO the sweet, wild, plaintive notes of a water ouzel outside the open window of the cabin where he had slept.

He lay listening, marveling. A faint murmur of the brook came up from somewhere. These two wilderness sounds belonged together. Sunlight and shadows of leaves lay across the bed. He gazed around the cabin. It had not been used as a habitation of late. It smelled like the pinewoods. A chair and table made of boughs were the only other pieces of furniture. An open fireplace and chimney of gray stone occupied the center of the back wall. A ten-point set of deer horns stood out prominently. Ornaments of reeds, shriveled and sere, hung on the peeled yellow logs. Outside the open door, on a wide-roofed porch, lay a black hound asleep.

At the same time Keven looked about him, curious and thoughtful, he became conscious that he did not feel well. His body ached and his head was hot. The tremendous exertions to which he had driven himself, the exposure and starvation, and his overwrought condition of mind, had knocked him out.

But what was he to do? The answer struck harshly. He had to go on, the moment he was able. A day's rest perhaps would fit him to travel. Yet—this Beryl Aard! He groaned and writhed. Last night, before slumber had claimed him, bit by bit he added to the regurgitation of memory. To him she had been a pretty wilderness girl, tormenting in her charm and reserve. He had not meant or done her any harm. He had not! But he had made love to her, in a boy's teasing, passionate way, never thinking that she might take him seriously. Then he had gone home to fall victim to Rosamond Brandeth. Next the war, with its disruption of ties, of work, of life! He forgot the little girl who lived at Solitude. He had forgotten her as fickle, careless youth forgets. Then had followed the shock to his brain, his impaired sight and memory. How terribly now to come strangely face to face with Beryl Aard—to find her a woman, strong, good, beautiful, waiting for him through the years, loving him with that faithful love all men dreamed of and so few ever encountered! He was a fugitive. If he was not a murderer, if the slaying of that half-breed fisherman was just, he had yet murder in his mind. He swore he would kill the man who had ruined his good name, had made honest labor fruitless.

"I've got to beat it away quick," he muttered. But could he sneak off like an ungrateful cur? Could he invent some urgent excuse to get up the river? Never had he been in such an appalling situation. But of what avail to torture himself? He had no choice. He was lost. He wanted only to beat down the malignant Atwell—mash his smug face, kick his fat belly, strangle him with bare hands. The lust of it obsessed him. Beyond that idea he had not thought collectively. Only chaos there! But he had persuaded himself that he would find satisfaction in this last bitter blow to the society that had wrecked him.

There came a light footfall upon the porch. The hound awoke to beat the floor with his tail. Then someone knocked.

"Keven. . . . Are you awake?" followed the query, in Beryl's rich voice, eager, expectant.

"Yes. But that's about all," he replied.

She entered carrying a box-lid tray with his breakfast. She wore white, that brought out vividly her dark beauty. She appeared taller in white, not so robust, so full-bosomed. Her brown ankles were bare. On her feet she wore deerskin moccasins. She set the tray upon the table and moved it to his bedside. Then she looked down upon him with dark deep eyes he found hard to meet. They were fearful.

"Are you hungry? You couldn't eat last night."

"No. I'm just sunk," he replied, and his voice did not appear strong.

She felt his cheeks and brow with a cool hand, and smoothing back his hair she sat down on the bed.

"You have fever. Try to eat a little," she entreated.

"I'm not very presentable," he replied awkwardly, yet he was thankful that he had forgotten to remove his blouse.

"This is Solitude, Kev," she replied simply.

Whereupon Keven struggled to a sitting posture, placed a pillow to his back and the tray upon his lap. Blackberries and cream, ham and eggs, toast and coffee, discovered to him that he was famished. While he ate she watched him gravely. She was studying him with all a woman's keen faculties, hiding her feelings. Yesterday it had been the past upon which she dwelt; this morning she was concerned with the present. The force, the charm of her, frightened Keven. What could he say to her?

"You were hungry," she said. "Kev, I think you have fever."

"Might have any old thing, but I reckon it's only a cold. I'll get up after a little and mozy around."

When she took the tray her hand came into contact with his, and again her touch gave him a magnetic thrill.

"Kev, you look ill—troubled," she said, standing beside him.

Slowly he sank down under the blanket, as if he wanted to hide. But he met her eyes, and something in them inhibited his cowardice.

"I am, both, I guess. . . . Beryl, I learned to drink in the army hospital. It deadened my pain. At Gold Beach—my partner was a hard drinker. We were always cold and wet. So I drank more and more. I reckon it gave me false strength. I've had no liquor for two days. This morning I need some badly. . . . But I don't want it. . . . I shall—never—drink—again."

"That makes me very happy. I hate drink," she returned. "Before I came home I saw a good deal of it at

113

Roseburg. My aunt kept an inn, out of town along the river. It's a pretty place. Motorists stop there. Often I used to serve them sandwiches. They usually had flasks. That Major Atwell, who spoke so vilely of you in the paper, he came there with a girl named Brandeth, from Grant's Pass. Did you know her?"

"Rosamond Brandeth? Yes. I used to know her," replied Keven steadily. What next would this girl reveal?

"He got her quite tipsy," went on Beryl. "It disgusted me so. . . . Then, after that, Major Atwell came frequently, alone. He tried to make up to me, Kev."

"He did? Well," replied Keven, conscious of a raking sting in his veins, "I heard Atwell was a devil among the women. . . . How did he make out with you?"

Her red lips parted, showing her white even teeth, and she laughed. "He didn't make out at all. The minute I realized he was after me—I'm a stupid little country girl, Kev—I never showed myself again. Soon after that I came home for good."

"Beryl, you read what Atwell said about me assaulting him?" queried Keven.

"Dad told me. I'm ashamed to admit I was tickled. But I was wild with rage over Atwell's implicating you in—in the Carstone scandal. We heard of that two years and more ago."

"Then you didn't take it—seriously?" gulped Keven, swallowing hard.

"I knew you could never be mixed up in anything like that," she replied, with sweet directness.

"Ahuh. . . . I—I'm glad to tell you I wasn't."

"Kev, is that what's troubling you?"

"Yes, a little. Atwell had me arrested at Gold Beach. I was in jail a month. He had hatched up a case on me. But it fell through. Somebody upstate must be wise to Atwell, for he couldn't get the papers necessary to move me out of Curry County."

"In jail—a month!" she gasped. "Soon after you arrived there?"

"Yes. And afterwards I was no good."

"I wondered why you didn't write me. How often I rode to Merrill, in hopes I'd get a letter! None ever came."

114

"Garry and I did well at first," went on Keven. "We were market fishing. But there's much antagonism toward upriver fishermen. The fishermen at Gold Beach worked against us in every way. Finally they destroyed our net. Then we took to trolling. And last they either refused our fish or offered a miserable price. And, Beryl, no less a person than your Major Atwell backed those fishermen, egged them on to drive us out."

"Slacker Atwell, they call him in Roseburg. Don't call him mine. I loathed him," retorted Beryl, her face hot, her eyes snapping. "So he's been hounding you? The beast! I'd do more than assault him, if I were a man."

Keven found her championship incredibly sweet. It stirred him to Homeric eloquence, to betrayal of his secret, to gratitude that was reverent, to the utter impossibility of deceiving this girl.

"Beryl, my trouble is—I killed a man," burst out Keven, meaning to tell all.

She gave him a horrified stare and sank to her knees by his bedside.

"Kev! . . . You can't be serious?" she cried, wringing her hands.

"It's true. I killed a fisherman named Mulligan," replied Keven hoarsely. "Jabbed my fish knife in his throat. . . . But I wasn't—I'm not sorry."

"My God!" she wailed, and her face went deathly white. "Kev, what have you done? . . . Oh, darling—darling—how awful!"

She clasped him with fiercely protective hands. She bent over him blindly, convulsed of face, choking in her realization.

Keven lifted her up, shook her, pulled her twining arms from round his neck. "But it was self-defense, Beryl," he began, in hurried passion. "I'm no murderer. . . . He was beating down my partner, Garry. I think he killed him. . . . Brace up, Beryl. It's not so terrible—the truth isn't. Listen. Let me tell you the whole story."

His vehemence, his physical violence, checked her terror. She sank back upon her knees, her hands at a pulsing breast which seemed to house too big a heart, and she fixed great tragic eyes of love upon him.

Keven began with his attack upon Atwell, and went on

115

with the flight down the river, the market fishing, the jail episode, the underground process which wore him and Garry down, their resort to hook-and-line fishing in order to live, its utter failure, and then the discovery of the net with the four-inch mesh, and at last the terrible fight on the river in the dusk of the gathering storm, and his escape.

"Oh, Kev—thank heaven it's not—what I thought," she whispered. "You frightened me so."

"But it's bad enough anyway. I can't prove my innocence."

"Truth always comes out."

"It does not," he said bitterly.

"You should give yourself up," she replied earnestly. "Your innocence will come out. You have friends to fight for you."

"I'd die before I'd go to jail again," his voice rang out. "Atwell is too strong. He and Brandeth run the fisheries. They'd frame me. They have money, political pull. The matter of the four-inch nets would kill their interests at Gold Beach if it came out. They'd stop at nothing. I'd have no chance. They'd *hang* me!"

She shrank as if he had stabbed her. "Don't—don't! . . . Keven, are you honest with me? If your enemies are so strong, why then were you rushing to Grant's Pass?"

She fixed him with accusing eyes before which he quailed.

"You were not coming here to hide," she hurried on. "You were not only escaping. . . . Kev, you have something on your mind. Some deadly intent. . . . You mean to kill the man who has ruined you!"

Keven could neither deny nor confess. For him there seemed a monstrous inhibition in her love, in the incredible fidelity she had given him. And he was suddenly struck to the heart by his own falsehood. He could not tell her because he could not bear to make her suffer. How much more agony would his planned revenge heap upon her innocent head? He was stunned. He felt as if he were beating his head against a wall. Presently he would become as weak, as unstable as water.

She leaned over to grip his hands.

"Listen to me, Kev Bell. You are out of your mind. To

kill Atwell would be fatal. Foolish! It's beneath you. It would wreck me. . . . Oh, I beseech you, give it up. Think of your old father! Think of my faith in you—my love for you. . . . Stay here at Solitude. I know a place high up the mountain—a cave by the stream. You could live there for years and no one would ever know. I could see you every day. We could roam over the mountains. You could hunt. You could trap fur, you could prospect for gold. There *is* gold in these hills. It would be safe sometimes for you to come down to the river and fish for steelhead. Only the packers and the mail rider go by Solitude. And we always know the hour they pass. Dad would keep our secret. This Indian housekeeper of ours is dumb. You would be safe—and we could be together. . . . And all the while Kev, the truth of your innocence would be working out. Something will happen to save you. Oh, trust me, darling, for I know. I feel it here."

Keven had closed his eyes, blinded by the tragic loving spirit shining upon him. And as she went on in heart-arresting eloquence there seemed to be a gathering knot within him. It swelled, it multiplied, it possessed his soul and the very springs of his being. It took the shape of a diabolical Hydra-headed twining fetter against which was arrayed all that was good in him, all that hope would not let die. There came a vital wrench. Something black and hideous seemed to loosen and pass out of him, leaving him free.

"Beryl, I will stay," he whispered, "and you can hide me. I meant to kill him. You have turned me."

She laid her head on his breast.

The hound on the porch outside jumped up with a deep-throated bay and dashed off the porch. Then rang out a wild chorus of yelps and barks.

"Dad!" cried Beryl joyfully, leaping up to run to the door.

"Are you sure?" asked Keven, who had been rudely jarred from a tranquility so new and marvelous as to hold him prone and silent.

"I know what the dogs say, Kev," she answered. "There, it is Dad. He's alone. There's nothing to alarm you."

"Suppose he has—bad news!"

"*I* think not. . . . Kev, my prayers have been heard."

"Please bring him here, but don't tell him anything except that I'm here."

Keven propped himself up in bed, as if to prepare himself. Aard would have the news from Gold Beach; and Keven shuddered at what that might be. He nerved himself for the worst. How long Beryl seemed! The moments dragged. Then he heard voices, approaching steps. Beryl flashed into the cabin, radiant of face. Then the tall form of Aard darkened the door, and his spurs jingled. Keven had expected to see a grave dark face, with piercing, searching eyes. But Aard, for once, seemed surprised out of his habitual imperturbability. He took one swift glance, as if to assure himself that his daughter had spoken truth, then he strode in, long arm extended.

"Kev, you dod-blasted steelhead ketcher, I'm glad to see you," he greeted Keven heartily, and he wrung his hand until it was numb.

Keven was the one with the piercing, searching eyes.

"Hello, Aard. I reckon I—I'm glad if you are."

"Wal, I'm 'most as glad as Beryl. What ails you, Kev?"

"Collapse, I guess. Walked too far and slept on the cold wet ground."

"You look sort of hollow-eyed," rejoined Aard, "but not so sick as Beryl made out."

He sat down on the bed, holding Beryl's hand, as she stood beside him, excited and quivering, her black eyes devouring Keven.

"I'm not sick. Just sunk, Aard."

"That's how they got you slated in Gold Beach. Sunk! I'm right glad, Kev, to see it's exaggerated."

"What?" asked Kev, huskily.

"Your drownin'."

"My—what!"

"You're reported drowned, Kev, along with Garry, Mulligan, an' a couple of fishermen whose names I don't remember. They found your skiff yesterday. It had washed up on the beach. Nothin' would do but I had to identify it. But Stemm had done that before me. Black-

118

wood wanted to be sure. . . . So the old river didn't get you after all?"

"Aard, it seems not. My mind's a little hazy on what did happen."

"My daughter's not hazy about it, that's sure," laughed Aard. "Because it fetched you to Solitude."

"Dad, tell him—tell us all you heard," implored Beryl.

"Nothin' much, though I am surprised at Garry Lord lettin' the Rogue ketch him. A ten-foot rise of water went rollin' down the river. I remember the same kind of flood years ago. It ketched some of the market fishermen at the mouth, when the tide was goin' out. That made it bad. Mulligan sure was drowned. They found his boat out at sea, an' it had his coat an' hat, also some salmon. Two other fishermen were swept out with their nets. Andy Huell had a tough fight with the flood. Told me he was bein' swept over the sand bar. He jumped an' waded out of danger. Lost his boat. For that matter a dozen boats are missin'. Most of these, though, had been pulled up on the riverbank. . . . What's your story, Kev?"

"Mine? I—I have—no story," faltered Keven. But there was a story in Beryl's pale rapt face, in the deep relief in her eyes.

"But you sure was in that flood!" expostulated Aard mildly. "Was Garry with you in the skiff?"

"Yes. Poor faithful Garry!"

"Wal, then, enough said. I know how you feel. I'm doggone sorry. Garry was a man. . . . Kev, you're goin' to stay with us now? It's about time, an' I reckon, the way things have broke for you, Solitude's about the best place on earth for you to land."

"Perhaps it is. Beryl says I'm to stay. I—I have no home. But I won't be a burden. I want to work."

"Sure, after you get well," replied Aard kindly, as he rose. "Beryl has her way, as you'll find out. You can help me with my traps this winter. An', waal, somethin' might turn up."

"Come, Dad, I'll help you unpack," said Beryl. "If you didn't fetch all the things I wanted there'll be war." At the door she turned to Keven. Then he saw her eyes were full of tears. "Kev, you rest and sleep. Don't feel so—so badly

119

about Garry. Forget it—all. Solitude will make up to you—for everything you've lost."

They went out, and once again the hounds bayed to sight of their master. Kev lay still, his hands nerveless upon the blanket. What was it that had happened? He was free from the shadow of the hangman's noose. Yet, magical as that was, there seemed to be still more. Spent by emotion, he gradually relaxed, though he strove still to think, when the effort was torture. In this hour he must fix, forever on his consciousness, the stupendous truth that life was worth living. For him! It could never have been any other way. He had been only little, miserable, base, overcome by misfortunes. He had lost belief in man and faith in God. How terribly he had been rebuked! The faithlessness of a shallow woman rendered as nothing by the fidelity of a noble one!

There was significance in all that had happened. He matched the sacrifice of Garry Lord against the treachery of Gus Atwell. There was always the balance—good to outweigh bad. Humble, penitent, Keven stood upon the threshold of a new life, he did not know that. It might be that he could never again know the vigor of a strong, unimpaired body. His strength, his youth had been sacrificed on the altar of patriotism for something that seemed futile and false. But at least he would no longer be afflicted with a morbid centering in self.

chapter thirteen

LATE IN THE afternoon Keven awoke for the second time that day. He had no idea when he had dropped off to sleep. But it was not the glorious gold-red rays of sunset that had awakened him, nor the deep lilac haze which filled the ravine outside his window. Fangs in his vitals— the gnaw of alcohol! In the past he had known it, only to feed the brute. A man who imagined drink brought permanent ease to pain and mental distress only misled himself. The day of retribution had to come.

He got up laboriously and, pulling on his trousers and shoes, he went out. Solitude seemed to leap at him. The great V-shaped cleft, where the river turned into the long stretch, was veiled in deep dark blue, above which stood the sunset-flushed peaks. The Rogue flowed pink and white. And below him the sun touched the rapids at the sharp bend, turning the turbulent waters to topaz.

That evanescent moment had waited for him. A change came as the sun sank, and the river ran a glancing red. He saw wild ducks winging rapid flight round the curve, black against the fading light of the sky. From the ravine at his left pealed up the wild plaintive notes of a water ouzel.

Keven directed his heavy steps down over the mossy rocks to the brook. Here under the arch of firs and pines it was dark, cool, moist, melodious. The water was so clear that pebbles and sand appeared to be uncovered. He sat down to form a cup of his hands, and scooping them up full, he drank. The water was cold and tasteless. Time had been, not so many years back, when Keven had loved the pure fountains that poured down from the dark, stony, fir-shaded dells. Water did not satisfy now, but he drank and drank. "To hell with whisky," he muttered softly. It was as if some former self that he had known long ago had come to stand there and speak. "To hell with war!" he went on. And then he thought he would make a clean sweep of things. "To hell with the painted, shallow, giggling, man-imitating salamanders with the plucked eyebrows! To hell with their joy riders! To hell with the grafters and the flashy, gross, material world they preyed upon!"

Cold and clear as the water fell his voice. And that seemed final. Late in the day, he thought sadly—too late! But it came to him, nevertheless. The usual things that men worked for could not be his. Success, money, position, all these which in common with his kind he had dreamed of and meant to achieve, were merely chimeras. And when he climbed up out of that singing ravine he left something distorted behind. It seemed, too, that when he

121

gained the bench, to view the towering peaks once more, fading from rose to gray, and Aard's cabin where on the porch Beryl stood with the hounds—it seemed that the problem which fronted him was unsolvable and inscrutable. It staggered him. He must dismiss it from mind and try to live objectively and to do what little he might be able to do for these simple good mountain folk.

That decision went scattering with the glad look in Beryl Aard's eyes. He had forgotten that she loved him. But dense as he was he could not but see it, once again in her presence. Even the hounds saw it, for they gazed with solemn, jealous eyes from Beryl to him.

"Kev, you are a bad boy," she said reprovingly as he approached. "Come up and sit down. . . . Curry, behave!" One of the long-eared hounds rumbled in his throat. "This is Keven Bell. He's a great hunter, as you will learn."

"Hunter?" queried Keven ruefully, as he sat down in one of the comfortable rustic rockers. "I feel as if I could never walk far again, let alone pack a gun."

"Kev, Dad told me you looked as if you hadn't had enough to eat," replied Beryl hesitatingly.

"Reckon he guessed right the very first time."

"What have you been eating?" she went on, in anxious solicitude.

"Not much of late but fish, bread, and coffee. We started out pretty well. He had supplies and we bought some vegetables. Garry was a good cook. But when we got poor—well, we went to loose ends. Many a day with only one meal!"

"No wonder. Listen. We have peaches, apples, blackberries," she returned, with a half-teasing smile. "Crocks of milk in the springhouse. Thick cream! We have chickens, turkeys, pigs. We bake our own bread. Brown bread we like best. I can bake, I'm telling you, Mister. We churn our butter. We put up jars and jars of preserves. It's getting almost time now to make peach butter. We have steelhead, whenever I catch them. I hope you remember that is *every* time I go fishing. We smoke all the steelhead we don't use. And smoked fish, the way these Indians fix it, is sure good. Then the frost has already come up on the high slopes. Wild grapes! And venison. And sometimes bear meat or wild pig, when Dad shoots one. And we have——"

"Beryl, I am overcome," he interrupted, laughing. "I'll eat myself to death. . . . But I must question one of the many items. You said steelhead whenever *you* went fishing, didn't you?"

"I certainly did."

"Beryl!"

"There, the jealous fisherman comes out!" she retorted, clapping her hands. "But, Kev, I can. I know when to go."

"I don't think I could ever forgive any fisherman who never failed. Steelhead! Those queer, changeable, finicky, aristocratic trout!"

"Kev, I tie my own flies and I know where to drop them on the river."

Nothing she had yet said compared in thrill to this simple statement. She nodded her dark head sagely. Then Aard came out on the porch, in bare head and shirt sleeves. What a splendid type of mountaineer!

"Wal, son," he said, "Beryl can make good her brag. She's the darnedest best or luckiest fisherman on this river."

"Dad, it's not luck. Don't I know the birds and the wild animals just as well? If I told you where all the mink and otter and raccoon lived we'd soon have none."

"Aard, do you trap a lot?" asked Keven.

"Wal, I try a lot. This spring I took five hundred-odd hides to Portland. Mostly mink. Otter gettin' scarce. But still there are some left."

"Five hundred!" ejaculated Keven. "Trapping sure is good around Solitude."

"Pretty fair," returned Aard complacently. "It's out of the way. But few hunters ever get in here. An' no trappers. So I have it all to myself. Hope you will pitch in with me. I can guarantee better wages than market fishin'."

"Thanks, Aard. I'll pitch in, you bet," returned Keven enthusiastically. These people struck him just right. With that promise he burned his bridges behind him. Up to then he had felt a vacillation about staying here at Solitude. He had oscillated like a compass needle between the absolute salvation in the prospect and perturbed unwillingness to do Beryl further wrong. He was only half a man. But he shied from that strange personal thought.

"Kev, I hate trapping," spoke up Beryl. "I've come across traps of Dad's sprung, with a foot or leg of some poor wild creature that had chewed itself free."

Keven looked blank at that. Assuredly he had never heard of such a thing. It might prove a bar to happy work in that line.

"Wal, we have to live, Beryl," said Aard dryly. "An' we have to wear warm skins and furs. I notice you're not so all-fired pitiful about cracking a steelhead over the nose."

"But, Dad, that's merciful!" she expostulated, flushing. "Besides a fish has no feeling. There's no comparison."

Keven decided this girl had a mind of her own and a temper to match it. He hastened to change the subject to that of fruitgrowing.

"Sure, that'll beat trappin' someday," Aard agreed. "You see I've ten acres in apples already. Oregon apples sell high. They're just a little slow down here. But this bench catches the sun. It's 'most as good as the land upriver. I only wish we had more of it. There's a fine plot up on the mountain. Good water. You might homestead that land, Kev. Then we'll develop it."

"Can you still homestead national forest land?"

"They say you can't, but the breeds do it, right along. I homesteaded this place twenty years ago, before the Cascades were included in a government reserve. They've tried to scare me off. They can't. I've never received a patent for this land, but I own it an' I can prove that. . . . Also, you can locate a minin' claim for about twenty acres, an' so long as you do your assessment work you can't be put off. You can get hold of a piece of land that way."

"By Jove, I'll do it," declared Keven.

"Say, Keven Bell, that wonderful bench just above the shelving ledges where the steelhead lie—that's mine," declared Beryl.

So they talked on, while Keven's eyes roved everywhere. He discovered that the Aards appeared remarkably comfortable for folk isolated in the mountains, fifty

124

miles from railroad and motor road. The house, though made of logs, was really not a cabin. He could see into the living room, which was large, light, colorful, plainly but comfortably furnished, and most homelike. The big open fireplace took Keven's eye.

Then there were many more evidences of considerable prosperity. The gardens were trim and neat, well cared for and enclosed in high picket fences. There were a barn and outsheds, chicken coops and pigpens, and two thriving orchards, which ran up a gradual slope to the timber. He heard running water that had been piped down to the cabins. The springhouse Beryl had mentioned very likely was down in the ravine. Aard's horses grazed along the trail, where probably the cows did likewise.

Keven tried to recall what this property had looked like four years ago. And he was sure Aard's prosperity had come since he had last visited Solitude. He conceived an idea that the trapper had other means.

"Aard, I haven't anything to wear except these fishy rags on my back," Keven remarked presently.

"Wal, hop a hoss an' ride down to Illahe. There's a store where you can buy plain stuff."

"I haven't a red cent," confessed Keven, in shame, yet earnest to acquaint them with his actual condition.

"Wal, that's nothin'," replied Aard practically. "Beryl can let you have what you want. She's banker, treasurer, bookkeeper, an' general all-around boss of this camp."

"Kev, I'll ride down to Illahe with you tomorrow," said Beryl, pleased at the prospect. Then her face fell. "But I forgot—you're really not able."

"I might ride a very gentle, easy-gaited horse, if you have one."

"Put Kev on the bay mare," suggested Aard.

"She's gentle, but sometimes she takes a notion to buck," returned Beryl dubiously. "We'll try Sam. He's only a mule, but——"

Then the conversation was interrupted by a call to supper. They went in, and on the way Beryl gave Keven's arm a little happy squeeze. She radiated something that convinced Keven she was overflowing with an unspeakable, all-satisfying happiness. If he were responsible for that—what a responsibility! It gave him a melancholy

125

pleasure, that faded quickly before the thought of only added pain to her in a future. What could he do?

Keven sat down to a bountiful meal that despite his hunger proved tasteless and unsatisfying, because of the craving of his stomach for alcohol. It was an unpleasant and disgusting realization. But he did not despair. That craving must and would begin to grow less and less until it left him entirely. He knew because he meant to starve it to death.

Dusk had fallen when they went out upon the porch, and the valley was full of purple shadows. Bats were wheeling over the cabins. There was an intense, all-pervading silence, which seemed unbroken until Keven caught the low murmur of the river. The miner who had named Solitude must have taken this beautiful hour of the evening to express the utter significance of the place. The feeling fell so strongly upon Keven that for the moment it obliterated the almost always present sense of his sorry state.

"Do you smoke, Kev?" asked Aard, lighting his pipe.

"I used to. Coffin nails."

"What are they?" Aard continued, amused.

"Cigarettes."

"Dad, there's nothing funny about it," spoke up Beryl. "Most of the women who stopped at Aunt Lucy's in Roseburg smoked cigarettes. They inhaled the smoke and blew it out through their noses. Struck me as a dirty kind of habit. How could you smell the pines, the firs, the myrtle, the lilac, if you cluttered up your nose with vile smoke? Really that thought was what made me realize how great a pleasure I get out of smelling the woods. . . ." And then she asked quickly, "Kev, could you like a girl who smoked?"

"Well, I reckon I could, if she had an overwhelming number of fine qualities to offset that one bad habit," replied Keven. "But most girls who smoke also drink, and when they drink——"

He did not complete his statement.

"That Brandeth girl drank," said Beryl, without any particular expression.

"Wal, liquor is bad enough fer a man," interposed Aard.

"Beryl, since we're speaking of a very modern thing, tell me, do you like cars?" queried Keven curiously.

"You mean the railroad cars?"

"No. Motorcars."

"I didn't mind riding in the stages. They were so big and felt safe. But small cars scared me stiff."

"You wouldn't like to drive one? A spiffy little roadster?"

"Me drive a car? Good gracious, no! I'd rather chop wood."

That made Aard chuckle. "I tell you, Kev, she's no mean hand with an ax. Grew up with one."

"It's a rather unusual thing for a girl, I'd say. Beryl, how'd you ever come to learn it?"

"We were poor when I was a kid," replied Beryl, with that simplicity which grew so upon Keven. "Dad was always away in the woods. Mother was not well. So I had to chop wood."

"Where'd you go to school?"

"I didn't go," laughed Beryl. "My school was the woods."

"Beryl, you had some schoolin' those days," corrected Aard. "Your mother was well educated. An' I hope you don't think your dad is an ignoramus."

"But it was the four years at Roseburg," explained Beryl. "I just ate up books alive. I didn't get on well with the boys and girls. I was so homesick for Solitude that I nearly went crazy. So I studied."

"You must have. I don't think there's anything I could teach you, unless of course how to fly-fish for steelhead," said Keven teasingly.

"Why, Kev Bell, I could fish rings around you," she replied vehemently. "Four years ago, too. You haven't had any trout fishing all that while. I have—every summer. Don't you think I haven't learned a lot. But it's to know where steelhead lie. That's the secret. You never knew. You'd wade in like a cow drinking and scare all the trout out of their wits. That's why I never would fish downstream behind you."

"Wouldn't you?" replied Keven feebly.

"No, I wouldn't. You used to make me—till I just quit. Oh, you were a high-and-mighty fellow, Keven Bell. You wanted all the river to yourself. For three whole days I tagged after you, carrying your trout, and trying to raise one for myself. Then I rebelled and the fourth day we quarreled."

"What day was it you showed me where the big trout lay, and I hooked him, and he dragged me a mile down the river?"

"That was that fourth day," she replied demurely. And Keven, realizing this frank girl would tell anything and everything, desisted from further teasing. But it had come back to him—the memory of the delicious pleasure he had derived in that way. She spoke lingeringly of days as if they embodied whole endless, unforgettable summer months. And as such they began vaguely to return to Keven, engendering a pensive sadness.

"Aard, I can't earn my keep by fishing," said Keven. "Lord knows I'd love to fish the rest of my life away, with Beryl, along the river. But I must work. Have you work I can do or learn to do?"

"Wal, now, let me see," replied Aard, puffing his pipe. He seemed never to hurry, to be disrupted out of his tranquillity. That was what the river and the forest had done for him. "You mustn't pitch in too hard. I take it you're not a well man. Let's give nature a chance. . . . Kev, if you don't mind my bein' personal, haven't you drunk pretty hard?"

"Not hard, as drinkers go. But too much for me," admitted Keven. "I got in the habit not through love of liquor—for I really hate it—but to dull pain. . . . Never again, Aard. I am through with that forever."

"Good. I was just goin' to say you wouldn't be welcome here at Solitude if you drank. An' I reckon my daughter stands by that. How about it, Beryl?"

"Oh, Dad, don't—don't be hard upon Kev," she replied. "I'd not say he wouldn't be welcome under any circumstances. But we don't need to speak of it. Kev has had a horrible ordeal. He is ill yet. He will get well here with us. Solitude needs no false stimulation."

"Wal, I reckon Kev has got it in him, an' if you can't fetch it out, your Indian blood isn't red any more."

"Indian blood!" ejaculated Keven, astounded. "Has Beryl really Indian in her?"

128

"I'd say sometimes she's all Indian," rejoined the father. "But for real Indian blood, yes. Beryl's mother's mother was a half-breed. She had a child by an Englishman, a gold-huntin' wanderer. So Beryl's about one-eighth redskin, an' sure comes honestly by her love of the wild. Kev, I was proud of that drop of blood in her mother. 'She was a woman. If I'd fetched her here to Solitude years sooner she'd be alive today. . . . Wal, Kev, to get back to talk of work," resumed Aard. "Now, let's see. The garden an' the orchards—a man's job all by themselves. There's a fence to repair an' fence to build. These pesky deer can jump over the moon. One big buck comes down most every mornin'. He plays hell with my garden. I'd have shot him long ago but for Beryl. *She* says he knows her. Wal, I reckon you'd better knock him over one of these fine mornin's an' we'll have some deer meat. We've got to kill pigs this fall. We've got a lot of shakes to split. There's the winter firewood. An' with you an' Beryl sittin' up at nights before the burnin' logs—wal, it'll take ten cords or more. An' from now on to November we've got to ketch steelhead to smoke for winter use. That job of course you won't like. Haw! Haw! . . . All of which is outside the big job. An' that's trappin' fur."

"By cracky, I don't have to worry about plenty of work, but whether or not I can make good," exclaimed Kev.

"Take things easy, Kev, We're in no hurry here at Solitude," said Aard.

"Dad, it's good you added that. Kev might get a wrong idea. You should also have told him how from November till spring we are shut in."

"Is the winter hard here?" asked Keven.

"Not down in the valley. The snow melts off the south slopes. But up on top it's sure winter for a few months."

"Kev, sometime soon I want you to help me order books for winter reading," said Beryl. "We mustn't tie trout flies *all* the time. Or sit before the blazing logs, holding hands, as Dad hinted."

"I didn't hint no such thing," vowed Aard stoutly.

Keven caught the reiterated sense of long-past acceptance of him, in a close regard that was indeed thought-provoking, not to say agitating. What would Aard say if someone proved to him that Keven Bell had made love to his young daughter, had won her, and then had gone away to espouse another girl and to forget Solitude? That was a bitter, sickening pill for Keven to swallow.

He managed a laugh that was not wholly sincere. "Now if you're going to poke fun at me I'd better say good night. . . . But, Aard, you and Beryl make me feel so deeply that I can't even try to thank you. God knows I do. I was at the jumping-off place. . . . I hope I can come somewhere near your expectations."

"Kev, I reckon you'll pull out by the skin of your teeth," replied Aard enigmatically.

Presently Keven leaned out of the window of his cabin to take a last look at the splendid black slopes, so still and wild, at the winding river, half in shadow and the other half shimmering under the stars. The river song seemed sadder. From the depths of the ravine came the soft flow of running water.

"I ought to want to fall in love with this strange girl," he mused broodingly. "My God, I know I shall—if there's man enough left in me."

He shrunk from the thought because he had nothing to give, except gratitude, and like attributes of spirit. Materially perhaps no half-breed along the river was so poor as he. He must henceforth be dependent upon some kindly man like Aard, or else return to one of those hideous army hospitals. Anything, even death, would be preferable to that last. But to love this Beryl Aard—as only a ruined, broken, hopeless man, still young, could love— that would be the culmination of all his sorrows. Yet how could he help it? When in her presence, this mocking, introspective, moody Keven Bell turned into a shadow. And it was only when he left her that he came back to the one self he acknowledged as true. Then the pang seemed keener. Night was cruel to him. And that serpent of fire within coiled and gnawed.

chapter fourteen

KEVEN SLEPT ONLY after long hours that exhausted, and then specters visited his bedside. But daybreak at Solitude, the slow coloring of rose and blue, the gold creeping down, the changing, speaking river—these made the night with its horrors as if it had been naught.

That fought the demon of his unrest, gave him courage to undertake the one thing instinct told him was best. To move, to see, to feel, to smell, to hear, to eat—these faculties that had to do with his physical being, these senses that were opposed to thought and remembrance, to intellect and realism, to all that was not primitive, these pointed the only way. That morning Keven gasped for whisky. His mouth, his throat, his esophagus, his stomach, his intestines burned for the cooling draught that was an infernal lie.

Beryl never guessed it. She was blind and feminine enough to pivot before him in her riding jeans and to ask gayly: "Do you like me—this way?"

Keven had a gay compliment ready, but though he saw her lithe and supple, sturdy as a boy, though with feminine contours, he could not thrill at her beauty or feel her appeal.

"Sam isn't a stubborn mule," said Beryl, when she led Keven out to the barn, where Aard had saddled the mule and a white horse. "But he falls asleep on the trail. And when he does he stops. So just give him a dig."

They mounted and rode out of the clearing into the trail, with Beryl leading. At once it struck Keven that with the silence and shadow she changed from the lighthearted girl who had greeted him that morning into one indefinitely different. She talked no more. She seldom looked back. She touched the leaves, the pine needles, the mossy

131

trunks, the lichened rocks, the ferns, with slow lingering, loving hand that was careful not to destroy. Her dark head had the poise of a listening deer.

Keven was grateful for this, while he wondered at it. For he was having a bad time of it. He saw all that Beryl touched. He saw the shadow-barred trail and the gold-splashed glade, the thick amber moss that covered the trees, the ferny, cool dell down which a sparkling stream-let leaped. And when they emerged where the trail ran along the open shore he saw Solitude in all its sublimity. The dark green slopes, the darker green river, sliding, whirling, foaming around the shaded bend, the grand bronze and fern-festooned cliffs, the black rocks that were sections of a splintered mountain—these seemed alive under the purple mantle of the lifting mist, gleaming in that subdued and supernatural light like the strange glow of low clouds before a storm. He saw all this spell of Solitude, but without delight or gladness.

Some few miles down the trail Keven made a twofold discovery: first that he was perceptibly tiring, and second-ly that it would be wise not to risk going on to any place where drink was procurable. This was confessing a grave possibility. He hoped he would not utterly fail to be a man, but he did not wholly trust himself. Why should he imperil the resolve he had made? If he fell on this occa-sion he would never be quite the same again. He had the spirit to do anything for Beryl Aard, but he was now concerned with the physical man's abnormal demands. So he planned an innocent ruse to deceive Beryl, without betraying his susceptible state.

Coming to an open glade in the forest, he called to Beryl and then slipped out of his saddle to sit down upon the ground. She cried out in alarm, and leaping from her horse, she flew back to kneel beside him.

"Kev! Kev!" she cried, putting her arms about him.

It was all he could do to meet those eyes, wonderful with sudden betraying fear and love.

"Beryl, I'd better not try to go farther," he said, smiling.

"Oh, is there anything the matter? You said you had not ridden for years. . . . A stitch in your side, maybe? *That* is terrible, I know. Or have the stirrups twisted your feet under too far? They're heavy, and I was afraid they'd tire you."

"Yes, I guess I've the stitch, all right, and the paralyzed feet, also a knee or two, and one hip. But that's not all," he said jokingly.

She studied him with most earnest gaze, and spoke with red lips quivering.

"Kev, you wouldn't deceive me?"

"How—how do you mean?" he queried.

"You haven't any organic trouble? Heart disease—or anything like?"

"No, I'm not as bad off as that," replied Keven, glad he could tell the truth.

Suddenly she drew his face close against her breast and held it there tight. He felt the swell of her bosom, the throb of her heart.

"Oh, if anything happened—to you!"

She let go of him then, still pale of cheek and dark of eye, unaware of the betrayal in action and word, or utterly disregarding them.

"You rest, then we'll go back," she said.

"Is it all right for you to go on alone?"

"Yes. I often ride to Illahe."

"Well, then, I'll stay here and rest. You go. I'll be okay when you get back. Will you buy me the things I need? Here is my list."

She scanned it carefully. Then: "Kev, there are no shoes here. Have you any but those awful things your feet are falling out of?" she asked, in most practical solicitude.

"Beryl, I told you I had only what I wore on my back," he replied, trying not to be stiff.

She was too earnest, too honestly practical to catch any hint of pride in his voice. She was concerned only with his needs.

"You'll need hunting boots, as well as moccasins. What size?"

"Number eights."

"And size of hat?"

"Seven. You see I have a big foot and small head, instead of the other way round."

"Likely they won't have anything that'll fit," said Beryl.

"I send to Portland for what I want. It comes parcel post. But that takes two weeks and more. We can't wait. . . . You'll need gloves, too. And, well, I'll buy what *I* think you need."

"Thanks. You're very kind," replied Keven meekly. "Only don't make it so much I can't pay back."

"Are you sure you'll be all right?" she concluded dubiously, as she turned to mount her horse. "Sam will not stray far. I won't be long."

Then she went clattering down the trail to disappear in the green forest. Keven felt relieved, yet somehow resentful with himself.

"By thunder, have I come to this? A liar and a beggar! Yet a blind man could see she—she cares for me."

His first impulse was to crawl into a pine thicket near by and hide. Not that there was anything or anyone to hide from, except himself! He composed himself finally and found a comfortable posture, with his head on a mossy mound. He then applied himself grimly to enduring his ordeal. It was there, the damnable desire, but he could stand it. He found that he could. As moments dragged on into an hour he became conscious that it grew no worse. He got used to enduring it, with stoicism, with defiance, and then it strangely seemed to diminish. Presently he fell asleep.

Something startled him back to consciousness. The lacy foliage of a fir tree filled his gaze.

"Kev! Kev! Wake up!" called Beryl gayly. "Oh, I'm so glad. You were sound asleep. . . . Behold me—packer for one Keven Bell!"

Keven stared at her, where she appeared to rise head and shoulders out of innumerable bundles. "What'd you do, child? Buy out that store?" he queried, aghast.

" 'Most did. Come, Sleepy-eyes. Sam's right there. Get on him. We've got to walk the horse home."

"I think I'll walk a little myself, and lead Sam. So go ahead, Bright-eyes."

A mile or so was about all Keven cared to accomplish before mounting again. Beryl forged ahead. The mule, however, when he was no longer led, soon caught up with the horse. Early afternoon found them turning the bend into Solitude.

Beryl rode her horse up to Keven's cabin and, dismounting, she began to untie the bundles and deposit them upon the porch. Keven got off to help her, not unaware of her blushes and giggles. She was a most bewildering girl.

"There, Kev. You carry the things in and unwrap them. I don't want to be around," she said, with a kind of repressed glee, and led the horse and mule toward the barn.

It took half a dozen trips for Kev to carry all the bundles inside, and not once did he go unburdened. "I'll be jiggered!" he muttered. But it was impossible not to feel a curious pleasure. Slowly he began to open the parcels, to lay each article on the bed, and after that was covered, the rest on the floor. What an assortment! She had bought out the country store. Those particular things he had listed were only a small part of this purpose. She had not lived in the Rogue River wilderness for nothing. The embarrassing feature of this deluge, however, was the fact that she might have been the wife or nurse of a sick man, and mighty keen as to his needs. Nor had she neglected the things most useful and dear to the man of the open: a hand ax and a flashlight, a buckskin shirt embroidered in beads, a cap and a sombrero, and last, but indeed not least, a tin box full of native-tied steelhead flies. Then more necessary, perhaps, certainly more commonly practical, a wash basin and pitcher, towels and soap, clothesbrush and a small mirror.

All this array delighted him, in spite of his silly pride. "Darn it, she's a thoroughbred and a sport. . . . Who ever thought of me, like this, except my mother? . . . No use, I'm going to love her. I've got to."

He made this speech with dimming eyes. He tried to deceive himself. But he had no illusions. His gratitude, his realization of the simple goodness of this woodland girl, were not love. Was his heart dead? He thought he had loved Rosamond Brandeth. But he had been only a boy just smitten with a pretty face. He realized that he had never loved her—that now he despised her. As a woman she was a candle to the sun, compared to Beryl Aard.

Keven then applied himself to the task of practical application. He shaved, he donned clean new clothes.

135

One of the several flannel shirts was a gorgeous one, barred in black-and-white check, with dots of red, and this one he chose. The boots fitted fairly well, and would do when his blistered feet got well. He buckled on the gun belt. Thus arrayed, he went out to find Beryl, uncertain whether he would scold her or hug her. But she could not be found. Aard, however, was at work in the orchard, where Keven joined him, eager to work, if not strenuously capable.

When hours later Beryl called them to supper it was none too soon for Keven. He again felt ready to drop.

When he stepped into the Aards' living room, the sun, shining its last that day from the river gap, flooded through the window. Keven encountered Beryl, quite unprepared to see her in a white dress, which, simple and modest as it was, completely changed her. Keven stared in undisguised admiration.

Beryl clapped her hands at sight of him. "Dad, look at him. Kev Bell, you handsome backwoods riverman!"

"You—you're not so bad yourself," replied Keven confusedly.

Poor as were the words of his compliment they brought damask roses to Beryl's cheeks and unmistakable delight to her dark eyes.

"This dress! You should see me in my good one," she exclaimed. "But that must wait till Dad takes us to Portland. . . . Dad, when will that be?"

"Wal, if we have a good winter trappin', why, I'd say next spring," replied Aard.

"If it depends on *that,* Dad Aard, I don't care to go," retorted Beryl.

"All right, you stay home an' keep house. Kev an' I will have more fun, mebbe."

She shot him and Keven a glance that gave manifestation of what a magnificent blaze her eyes might be capable of if she were really angered.

"Wal, son, did you buy out the store at Illahe?" went on Aard, as he seated himself at the table.

"No, I didn't. Beryl did. I couldn't ride all the way. She went on and did the purchasing. . . . Heaven help her when she gets a husband—unless he's rich."

136

"Heaven help her, indeed, if she *ever* gets him," was Beryl's startling rejoinder.

"Haw! Haw! Haw!" roared Aard.

Keven stared down at his steaming plate. He would have to be careful how he bandied wit with this girl. He felt at a loss just how to take that sally of hers. Silently then he waived reply and applied himself to the supper. After a time, however, he looked up at Beryl, to find her eyes downcast.

Emboldened by this, Keven glanced at her then, and from time to time afterward, but he could not catch her eye. There was a heightened color in her cheeks, almost a red spot. Twice when she rose to go into the kitchen his gaze followed her. In the white dress she looked slight, compared to the stalwart girl she appeared in rougher garb. Keven found himself becoming critical.

Later in the bright lamplight he had better opportunity to observe her unobtrusively. She was a little over the medium height for women, compactly, beautifully built, though not on delicate lines. She had a firm strong hand, brown, well shaped, and a rounded superb arm, upon which the muscles played. She stood erect as an Indian, lithe, almost pantherish in movement, broad-shouldered, deep-chested, giving singular impression of tremendous vitality. He had no fault to find with her feet and ankles, for they conformed to the rest of her splendid physical equipment. If Beryl Aard could not wade over the slippery stones of the swift Rogue and climb to the peaks of the mountains, he very much missed his guess. Once before he had compared her with the erotic Rosamond Brandeth; and when he did it again all the finality of that decision swung immeasurably to Beryl's benefit.

chapter fifteen

NEXT MORNING, bright and early, Keven went to work. Standing and bending were much harder for him than sitting in a boat rowing. Moreover he missed the stimulus of liquor. On the other hand there was a remarkable inspiration in the mere surroundings of Solitude. He felt it without looking. The resistless sense of loneliness, of wild solitude, of nature in its prodigality of forest and stream, of primitive life, began to insulate his nerves and almost imperceptibly to come between him and the thinking, brooding, introspective man. Vaguely he recognized this as good for him, and aided it all he could.

Beryl did not let him forget her. From time to time that first day she appeared much interested in how he was progressing, and visited him while he worked under Aard's direction. Invariably, however, she would wander away into the shade of the firs, or to the bank of the ravine, or down toward the calling river. Keven was quick to grasp that she was an unconscious worshiper of nature. A butterfly, a colored leaf, a flower could instantly obsess her. He liked her all the better for this. But while she did stay near him, attentive to his task, her humor seemed paramount.

"Kev, you might become a great fisherman—under expert advice, if you would heed it—but you'll never make a farm hand," was a final example of her remarks.

"My dear Miss Aard," replied Keven, standing erect to fix her with grave eyes. "I *am* a great fisherman. As for the rest, beggars can't be choosers. At that, I like this kind of work better than rowing all day and half the night, wet and cold, covered with fish slime."

"You're so slow and awkward, Kev," she objected.

"You bend as if you were afraid of breaking a wire in your back."

"I am. That's my spine. You forget my body stopped the recoil of a cannon. I will never again be a man such as you could admire."

Quick tears dimmed the fun in her eyes, and she turned away. He had hurt her. And this would ever be so, if she continuously kept making remarks, however innocent, that threw his oversensitive mind on his frailty.

"Wal, son, don't mind Beryl," spoke up Aard, who had heard the byplay. "She's a girl an' a woman an' a mystery. She's full of the Old Nick. . . . As for your condition, I reckon you exaggerate it. You're a better man than you think. Just now you're run down. You're starved. But even so you work pretty good. Forget about everythin'. When you tire out go lay down. Soon we'll have these little jobs done. Then you can fish an' hunt, an' later take to the trappin' with me. By that time you won't know yourself."

Aard was always helpful. He radiated quiet strength and assurance, like the great dark mountains under which he had lived so long. Keven could not help being influenced for the better. Aard was a man to look up to.

Keven stuck on the job till just before sunset, when he repaired to his cabin to clean up and rest. The call to supper interrupted a dreamy contemplation of the river.

"I called you three times," announced Beryl, when he presented himself at the other cabin.

"You did! I'm sorry. I get sort of absent-minded sometimes."

"You go into a trance. Anyone might think you were in love with one of those Grant's Pass girls. . . . Rosamond Brandeth, for instance, with her bobbed hair and her painted face, and her silky finery—what little there is of it!"

"Anyone might think anything if she hadn't control over her mind," retorted Keven, hiding the start he had sustained. Had Beryl heard gossip? "It happens, however, that I am not suffering from such affliction."

But Beryl was not suspicious or in possession of facts embarrassing to Keven. The magnificent flash of her black

139

eyes seemed merely jealousy of his absorption. She stirred so many conflicting sensations in him.

After the meal he said, "Beryl, I've just strength enough left to drag myself to bed. Please excuse me."

Considering the variety of her moods, Keven rather expected her to pout or to tell him tartly to go, if he would rather sleep than have her society for an hour before the fire. But she said nothing and walked with him through the dusk to his cabin. It was the gloaming hour, with the last of the afterglow on the river, and everything was permeated with the wonderful peace and silence of Solitude.

"I put a bag of fir cones and pine needles in your cabin," she said. "They're nice to start a quick little fire. They smell so sweet when burning."

"Thanks, Beryl, that was thoughtful of you."

She touched his arm and looked up at him, her face in shadow.

"It makes me happy to realize you're actually here at my beloved Solitude," she said. "To see you can work! To know you can rest! ... Dad says you are already improving. I think so, too, and that is well. ... Good night."

She left him then, and Keven went into his cabin, to start his little fire, before which he sat a few moments, marveling, thoughtful and sad. How could he prevent the recurrence of his poignant state of consciousness? Work was one way—sleep another. So he went to bed.

Two weeks sped by, bringing the end of summer and the beginning of the colorful days of autumn. The Rogue Valley was famous for its blazing beauty of foliage, but Solitude was magnificent beyond comparison with any other place along the river. It flaunted its frosted maples and oaks, the madroña, the myrtle, and the manzanita, the ferns and rock vines.

Keven's application to his tasks, which precluded all else for this period, was not in any sense slavish, though too hard and exhausting to be enjoyable. But more than duty to the Aards drove him; he realized he was toiling and sweating the pangs of rum from his body. At first it was something he felt he owed Beryl for her faith, and then something deep and still unconquered in himself.

140

The dawn came when he awoke without any particular craving, and that focused thought on things he had persistently kept out of mind.

"After all it was nothing," he soliloquized. "I wasn't a drunkard. Whisky had no great hold on me. And now it's over with."

Then no longer could he blind himself to other facts. His appetite had imperceptibly come back; he was gaining weight slowly but surely. This astounding circumstance added to his freedom, carried him to the trembling verge of possibility, of realization, of hope. What could he do with such feelings, which seemed so antagonistic to the facts of his permanent disablement, so ridiculous in the face of his broken heart and ruined life? Yet they persisted, and would continue to persist, until he lost himself in that vague sensorial perception which had grown upon him.

"Wal," remarked Aard, at supper, "we sure eat up those jobs. Firewood an' shacks must wait for snow. We have to snake the wood from on top. Reckon it's up to you an' Beryl to ketch about a ton of steelhead for smokin'. An' right now some venison would go fine."

"Kev, have you as much as looked at the river lately?" inquired Beryl.

"I'm always looking at it."

"Seen anything?"

"Nothing unusual," replied Keven, almost nettled by her demure tone, her mysterious smile.

"It's full of steelhead. There's a run on."

"No!"

"Yes indeedy."

"Have you been fishing?" asked Keven eagerly.

"Not yet. I wouldn't be so mean as to go to the river without you."

"You're very good, Beryl," he replied constrainedly. "Why not? Your father says we need the fish to smoke."

"I'd hate to make you feel badly," Beryl admitted.

"That wouldn't make me feel badly," went on Keven, puzzled. "I'd be only too glad to see you go."

"Yes, you would," she protested. "I always make Dad very tired, and I'm sure I'd make you sick."

"How so?"

"I'd catch a lot of steelhead. Then, when you saw them you'd rush down to the river. And when you couldn't catch any you'd be wretched."

"Is that so?" returned Keven spiritedly. "Well, to be honest, maybe I would *if* I couldn't get results. But, Beryl Aard, I can raise and catch steelhead in the Rogue as well as anyone."

"Most likely, up the river. But this fishing down here is different. You never did catch any—except a couple of little ones. Five pounds or so. And I don't keep that size. Here at Solitude you must know the river. Where they lie—what they take. And if I remember rightly you just wouldn't listen to me."

She was not teasing, but deliberately in earnest. And the fact was she thought poorly indeed of Keven's fishing. Whatever else Keven might have been reasonable about, he certainly was not reasonable when it came to fishing. He recalled flashes of illumination, after some particularly tragic and blundering loss, when humility overcame egotism, and he had thought himself the most asinine of all anglers who ever cast a fly. But far indeed was this humility from him now. He would teach this amazing girl of Solitude something about the one thing he did know.

"Beryl, you don't honestly mean you could beat me fishing?" he queried frankly.

Her merry laughter pealed out. And Aard chuckled over his pipe.

"Beat you! Why, Kev, I could do it with my left hand and never get my feet wet."

"That last *is* impossible in the Rogue. And as for beating me, why child, you are crazy."

Beryl smiled adorably at him and then at her amused father.

"Dad, the war you predicted is on. Will you be stakeholder and judge?"

"I reckon I'll have to be, though it's a risky job, considerin' how much I like you both."

"You really have the nerve to bet?" asked Keven, admiration and respect wrung from him.

"Yes, I'll bet you. What is more, I'll let you set the

142

conditions. One day, or two days, or three. You can choose where you want to fish."

"Say, don't rub it in," retorted Keven, feeling the fun and thrill of a promised contest, such as many and many a time he had entered in the past. "We'll draw lots. . . . Aard, hold these two pine needles in your hand. One short and one long. Whoever gets the long one has the choice. . . . There. Now draw, Beryl."

She drew the short one, which not one whit diminished her smiling assurance.

"I hate to do this, Aard," said Keven, waving the long needle triumphantly. "It's like taking candy from the baby. . . . Beryl, I'll go up the river and fish down."

"Splendid. Just where I want you to go," she returned, with elation. "Oh, Kev, I feel so sorry for you. If only you'll be a good sport and not get mad!"

"Do you wish to make any conditions?" asked Keven condescendingly.

"Only one. Not a single word about flies and leaders until after the contest. Do you agree?"

"Certainly. Now I'd like to make a condition. That I give you odds."

"No. I'll not consent to that, though if I did, Mister Upriver, it would make your defeat more crushing."

"Very well. Now what will I bet you?"

"Let's make it the same for both—the best tackle we can buy."

"Whew! There's nothing sky-high about your gambling. Not at all! I'll go you, though. . . . Aard, you have got all this data in your mind?"

"Sure. All you have to do now is set the time to start."

"After breakfast," replied Beryl promptly.

"That's what I expected of a lazy, luxurious girl," agreed Keven. "But I always used to be on the river at daybreak."

"What for?" asked Beryl.

"Why, to fish, of course."

"I hope you're not one of those early-birds-catching-the-worm sort of fishermen. Steelhead don't rise till the mist is off the river. Down here in these canyons that's after sunup."

For the first time Keven had a vague notion that this Aard girl might really know something about the science of trout fishing, but like all fishermen he scouted such probability for one of the gentler sex.

"Well, good night, Beryl," he said, rising to go. "I want to look over my tackle and rig up. . . . It's too bad we'll never be friends again."

"Aren't you of a forgiving nature? . . . Good night, Isaac."

"Isaac! Why call me a jayhawker name like that?"

"Don't you know Isaac Walton?"

"Sorry to say I never met the gentleman," returned Keven, from the door.

He repaired to his cabin, and after lighting his lamp and kindling his little fire of cones he got out the tackle Minton had sold him on credit long months before.

"Fine chap, Minton. Doggone, I'm glad I paid for this tackle. And gladder that I hung onto it," he said to himself.

Whereupon he spent a pleasant hour of task and anticipation, after which he went to bed. He got up early next morning, to put on the discarded market-fishing clothes, and to spend another half hour trying to select flies for the day. At length he decided to take them all.

While he was at breakfast with Aard, Beryl came out of her room, carrying a queer-looking limber rod, evidently homemade. It appeared to be jointed out, however, and looked whippy. Beryl in short skirt, heavy woolen stockings, and hobnailed shoes looked as businesslike as her tackle.

"I've had my breakfast, Kev," she said. "You'll find me when you come down the river. Good luck."

"Same to you," replied Keven. "Don't fall down, don't get wet, and don't lose your tackle."

"Where'd that antediluvian tackle of hers come from?" asked Keven, after she had gone.

"It was made by an old friend of mine who lives on the Umpqua. I gave it to Beryl. That yew wood is too limber for me."

"Yew? Never heard of it. Split bamboo is the only wood for rods."

"I reckon the rod don't cut much ice, nohow. It's part your leader and party your fly—then most the way you work 'em. I'll give you another tip, Kev. Use small dark flies with some buff in them. Or gray with tan wings."

"Haven't any such flies," replied Keven.

"Wal, you ought to, if you're buckin' up against that girl. An' another thing, stay out of the water."

"Aard, are you too telling me how to fish the Rogue?" queried Keven, with a hearty laugh. "Well, you want to be around when we get back."

"Don't worry, son, I wouldn't miss that for anythin'."

Soon Keven was on his way up the trail, trying to adjust himself to resurging sensations. He walked a mile or more and then made his way down to the river. It appeared a little high, but was clear. The places he had in memory were gone, and he was too eager to begin fishing to look about him.

Almost at the outset he made a remarkable and humiliating discovery. There did not seem to be any co-ordination whatever between his theory of casting, the skill he fondly had believed was unforgettable, and the actual physical accomplishment. His casting was atrocious; in fact, he could not cast at all. He hooked the bushes on his back throw, the trees, and himself. But he persevered and waded on downstream. Presently he raised a nice trout, that leaped on a slack line and escaped. Keven recovered the hook to find that the point had broken. He was convinced it had been done by the trout. This was his first bad luck, and it augured ill. But he persevered, and the harder he tried the worse things became. He could not wade out far, owing to the depth of the water; he could not remain in it long, owing to its icy nature. The most annoying feature of his return to fly-fishing, after four years and more, was the way he snagged the brush behind him. Several flies were lost this way and leaders broken. He tried to woo patience which would not be wooed.

At a likely pool, the first where he saw steelhead rising, he slipped off a rock, like an elephant, and spoiled that place. At another spot he cast his favorite fly, and cast and cast, until he did get a smashing strike. The fish felt heavy. He was about to whoop when it got off. Again Keven found the point of his hook broken.

Then out of dim past associations brightened the one that had to do with a fly-fisherman's jinx—the breaking of hooks on rocks, on the backcast. Keven remembered, after it was too late. Then he essayed to send his backcast high, with the result that he hooked branches over his head. After breaking half a dozen leaders this way, and decorating the trees with gaudy counterfeits of insects, he found himself humiliated by having to climb to recover a fly that was a killer upon the upper Rogue. After hard work he got out on the branch, which promptly broke with him, letting him down ten feet, half in and half out of the water. It was not only his feelings that got hurt.

The day wore on. So did Keven's temper. And then to cap the climax he hooked a little steelhead that darted downstream and could not be held. Keven let it run and ran himself. He had long been unused to running over slippery rocks, and he lost his balance. Trying frantically to regain it, he only made the plunge longer and harder, which ended him heels up and head down, crack against a rock.

He saw stars and had a terrific pain in his jaw. The iron contrivance, which did such poor duty as a lower maxillary, came loose from where it hinged on the bone, causing such pain as he had not suffered in a long while. After a time it eased and Keven went on fishing, discouraged now, hopeless, miserable—the poorest, unluckiest fisherman in the whole world.

He kept on downstream, casting here and there, hoping for a rise and knowing he would not get it, until he could travel no farther that way. The water was deep, and a cliff impassable. Keven retraced his steps and climbed up the wooded bank, and went on down, searching for a place to get back to the river.

He had to climb over logs, driftwood, rocks, and he was forever snagging his line. Human nature could endure no more. He became furious. He swore. Not only angry was he when he tore through that thicket, but hot, sweating, and scratched.

To Keven's utter amazement he grasped the fact that

he had reached the bend at Solitude. The great boulders trooped like huge beasts out into the wide stretch above the rapids.

Suddenly he spied Beryl. He had absolutely forgotten her, and his first sensation was a thrill of surprise. Something checked his impulse to halloo. He watched.

"What in the dickens is she doing?" he muttered.

She stood on a low rock, back from the edge of the eddying pool, apparently quite shallow there, and she was moving the limber rod sidewise toward the shore and below her. Then she whipped the rod, back and forward, to send her fly out a little way. It could hardly be called a cast. Keven laughed under his breath. Poor kid! She was deluding herself. Yet how earnest, how absorbed! She bent forward slightly, every muscle and nerve evidently taut, and she drew that tiny fly sidewise, with delicate, almost invisible vibrations of the rod, across the water. Keven's eyes were keen. He saw the fly, and it surely resembled some crippled little winged thing struggling to escape. Suddenly Keven saw a boil on the still water, then circles, ever widening. She had raised a trout.

Keven climbed up on a high boulder, the better to see. Beryl repeated that queer performance. Incredulous as it appeared, she manifestly had raised a big steelhead and expected to do it again. Her posture, her caution, her delicate manipulation proved that. Then Keven saw a broad bar of white and pink rise out of the shady green water. What a steelhead! He rose, he turned, he poked at the fly, and refusing it he turned back again, sending the telltale circles widening over the eddy.

"Hey, Beryl," he yelled, "that's a lunker. But he won't rise again. Rest him awhile."

Keven jumped down and ran around and over the jumble of rocks to a point near where Beryl was fishing. She stood blankly astounded, her rod up, and she stared at him.

"Get back. You'll scare my fish," she called peremptorily.

"Scare? He's already scared. He won't rise again—not for a while anyway. Come here and let me give you a fly. . . . Gee, he's a corker. I saw him," babbled Keven in his excitement.

147

"Will you get back away from the water?" she queried sharply.

"What?"

"What! Can't you hear?" Beryl actually stamped her foot. "Get back! Vamoose! Chase yourself! And hurry before you scare my steelhead."

"You poor child," ejaculated Keven pityingly. "So that's how you fish? I was afraid——"

"Get back or I'll throw a rock at you," screamed Beryl, suddenly scarlet of face. "You're deliberately trying to scare my steelhead—so I can't catch him. He'll go ten pounds. And you don't see many that big till October."

"All right, throw a rock. Throw two rocks," retorted Keven, growing exasperated. "I was only trying to help you."

"Help nothing, you ninny," cried Beryl, and stooping suddenly she picked a round stone from beside the boulder and threw it with remarkable speed and precision right at Keven's feet. He had to jump quickly to escape a crack on the shins.

"Well, you—you—darned little fool!" burst out Keven. He wanted to swear, but as he could not do that he substituted a wholly inadequate epithet. And he stood stock-still in his tracks.

Beryl picked up another rock.

"I'll hit you next time," she said, and she looked her threat.

"Very well, you sweet, gentle, dovelike creature!" exclaimed Keven, and he moved back from such dangerous ground, to a point behind her.

Quite suddenly he came upon a shallow runway between some stones, in which lay a number of steelhead, showing their rainbowlike sides, curling broad tails, and speckled fins. They had been strung on a forked willow branch. Keven had never been so surprised in all his life along that Rogue River.

"For heaven's sake! Where'd these steelhead come from?" he yelped.

"They're mine," replied Beryl, stepping out on the flat boulder.

"Yours?"

"Yes, *mine!*"

"Where'd you get them?"

"I put salt on their tails," she rejoined sarcastically.

"Beryl Aard, do you mean to tell me you caught these fish?"

"You bet I did."

"On that flimsy two-bit rig?"

"Yes, you darned big fool. And I'll catch another and the biggest yet—if you go away somewhere."

Keven could not believe his eyes. He counted the fish. Nine there were; three around four pounds, and the others graduated up from six and seven, to one almost eight. In all his fishing Keven had never seen a string of trout to beat that. He gazed and gazed; and then when the indubitable fact dawned upon him that these were real fish and that Beryl had certainly caught them he meekly went back and sat down.

All of a sudden then he recalled their wager, and the bantering which had led up to it. She had made good her boast. Then he was stunned. It was indeed with chastened spirit and wondering awe that he turned his gaze upon Beryl again.

She was poised precisely as she had been before becoming aware of his presence. Instead of looking ridiculous now she struck him as keen, vibrant, perfectly balanced, and absolutely master of that flimsy rod and trailing fly. She made it dance on the water.

There came a wave, a smash on the surface—then a sweet, wild, high-pitched cry of elation.

Keven leaped up, beside himself with excitement, and ran back to the point nearest her. A shuddery, sliddery, tussling sound pierced his ears. He looked in time to see a huge opal-colored steelhead plunge back into the water. Beryl's rod bent like a buggy whip. The reel screamed and the line hissed. Then out in the middle of the great pool the steelhead began to skyrocket in extraordinary manner. Keven lost his head completely.

"Hold your rod up," he bawled. "Let him run. . . . Don't give him the butt. You'll break his off. . . . Oh, drop your tip! . . . Wind! Reel in, fast—faster. . . . Oh, hell, can't you hear me? You'll lose that grand fish. . . . Wind in! Let him run! Elevate your rod! . . . Drop it quick!"

"You shut up! You'll make me lose him!" cried Beryl furiously.

Keven never heard her, or at least did not heed. No mere girl could handle a monster steelhead like that on a flimsy little willow wand. He must rush to her assistance. His intentions were indeed chivalrous. But just as he reached the rock his treacherous feet slipped from under him. Again if he had let himself fall and have been done with it, all would have been well. Instead, however, he reeled and swayed to recover balance, with the result that at last he plunged down to collide with Beryl and knock her off the rock.

When he got to his knees, dizzy with pain, and so furious with himself that he could have yelled, Beryl was climbing back on the rock, drenched to the skin, water pouring from her in little streams.

Tears, too, were streaming from her eyes. Her hands were outstretched, holding the rod, which was broken in the middle. The line trailed limply on the water behind her.

"You broke it! My beautiful little rod!" she wailed.

"I didn't," protested Keven, laboriously getting to his feet, his hand to his shaking chin.

"Yes, you did! You bumped me—off the rock."

"That rod was—no good anyhow," panted Keven, manfully struggling under odds of pain and passion.

"No good!" she cried, slowly coming out of tragedy into wrath. Her eyes began to burn away her tears. "It was the best rod in the world. You made me break it—you big lummox!"

"You don't know how to handle a fish," avowed Keven heatedly. There was no use to try to be reasonable with this girl.

"Don't I? That's what you think. I'd have landed him—if you hadn't come butting in here. . . . A twelve-pounder! But I could bear that, only for my precious yew-wood rod. You broke it—and my heart, too."

"I only wanted to help you."

"Help? Ha! Ha! A lot of help you'd have been, with your crazy upriver methods. You kept yelling: *'Wind in! Let him run! Elevate your rod! Drop it quick!'* What kind of talk is that? Idiotic, I call it."

"There's a style of fishing you don't understand, Miss Aard," retorted Keven loftily.

"Thank heaven!" she retorted fervently.

"There's a difference between a real pothunting fisherman and a classy fly-fisherman."

"You bet there is. You're that last—and you'd starve to death down here. . . . Classy? That's sure the word. You're a conceited jackass of a fisherman—to make me break my rod, lose my fish, and then blab, blab, blab class to me. That's funny. Ha! Ha! Ha!"

"Don't you laugh at me, Beryl Aard," he shouted.

"I'll swear at you next—you city fisherman—you *dude* fisherman," she raged, evidently wholly unable to express her feelings unless she did resort to profanity.

"You, you country-jake fisherman!" stammered Keven hoarsely, now quite beside himself.

"*There!* You pile insult on injury," she flashed in ringing, high-pitched voice. Her eyes blazed like glowing coals. Then, swinging a vigorous arm, she gave Keven a terrific slap.

Not only the violence of it staggered him, but the blow fell on the side of his face which had been hurt twice before that day. The agony struck him almost blind. As he sank to his knees his shaking hands fumbled at his mouth. The bent iron bar, which served as a substitute for the missing section of jawbone, had been knocked loose, to protrude from his lips. He stuck it back, and then shuddering, straining, he fought to keep from fainting.

Beryl plumped to her knees before him.

"*Kev!* What was that?" she asked in slow horror.

"My—iron—jaw," he whispered huskily.

"Oh, my God! I didn't know. . . . Kev, you're white as a sheet. What did I do?"

She clasped him with strong hands, which lifted his face, suddenly to grow gentle as they felt his cheek. She scanned it with infinite tenderness, and then her eyes, blue-black from shock, pierced his to read the very soul of him.

"I hurt you terribly," she said, in awful self-accusation.

Keven tried to joke. "You hit like the breechblock of that bursting gun."

"Oh, why—*why* didn't you tell me?" she moaned, in agonized accents. "I'd never have struck you then. No matter how—how brutal you were!"

"I have a little pride left. God knows, I must have seemed crippled wretch enough."

"Hush! Do not talk like that,'" she cried, her voice breaking. "I'd have loved you the more." In a passion of repentance and unutterable tenderness she kissed the bruised and swollen jaw, whispering between her kisses: "Forgive me, Kev, I didn't know. . . . You made me see red. . . . I'd die for you! . . . Darling! Forgive me. . . . I love you so."

When those warm sweet lips at last pressed his own something loosened within Keven's cold and sick heart and ran along his veins, swelling and mounting, at last to flood his being with stinging ecstasy. His eyes closed to hide the whirling gold-and-blue world above. He crushed her wet head to him; he bent it back, blindly to seek her lips. "There's—nothing—to forgive," he mumbled. "Beryl —darling."

She vibrated to that, as if shot through with an all-pervading current. Then she became very still, without breath or quiver.

"Kev—say that again," she at last whispered imploringly.

"Beryl—darling. . . . I—I didn't know I loved you."

"I was afraid you didn't—any more. . . . Oh, Kev—oh, Solitude!"

Keven opened his eyes to behold her, arms spread wide and high, her rapt face uplifted to the sky.

Just then a stentorian voice roared down from the trail.

"Hey, thar!"

Beryl lowered her arms; she lifted startled eyes; she stared.

"Oh, Lord! There's Dad!"

Keven espied the tall figure of Aard framed in gold-green foliage.

"Is that how you kids bet on fishin'?" he yelled.

His big voice, deep with mirth, rolled down the river, to clap against the cliffs and come echoing back.

152

"Oh, Dad—I won!" screamed Beryl, waving her broken rod.

"Won what?" Aard shouted.

Beryl's gay, sweet wild laughter rang up to the skies. Then she cried: *"Everything!"*

chapter sixteen

THE OCTOBER DAYS had come, gray at dawn, etching the leaves with hoarfrost, lifting the clouds of mist, opening to the blue and gold above, windless and still and solemn, wearing through the long smoky hot afternoons to the gorgeous effulgence in the sky, and on to dusk, steeped in the melancholy of solitude.

Keven and Beryl climbed the trail back of the cabins, she leading the way, silent and pensive, with the spring of the deerstalker in her stride, he following, rifle in hand, with vigor in his step and glowing tan in cheeks no longer hollow.

The trail took the course of the brook, as it tumbled down, sometimes amber-gleaming in the sunlight and again dark and cool, streaming with mellow murmur under the shade. They reached the waterfall, where the brook leaped out of a gray notch to a wide flat ledge, over which it poured in a white sheet, lacy and snowy at the curve, to thin out into a downward-darkening smoke as it disappeared in the glen.

Above the fall stood the firs, great brown-barked trees, branchless far up, rising to lofty height, to spread a mingling canopy overhead. They stood far apart on the slanting slope, blackened at the trunks, where forest fire had scorched but failed to burn.

A hawk sailed in zigzag flight among the treetops, vanishing like a fading gleam, emphasizing the apparent

153

lifelessness of the forest. The trail climbed to a level bench where the firs thickened and the ferns began to encroach upon the brown-carpeted earth. It swung over to the brow of the ravine, deepening here to a wide timber-choked canyon, up from which floated the music of stone-retarded running water. Far under the grand, dark ever-greens flamed the maples, gold-leafed and scarlet and yellow-green, here subdued in shade and there blazing in the rays of sunlight.

Beryl paused to gaze, and Keven, with eyes roving everywhere, halted to catch his breath. The forest seemed a vast cathedral, a colorful green-roofed hall of the wilderness, giving strange sense of protection, of age-old watchfulness. The ravine sent up its cool fragrance to mingle with the pungent piny odor of the firs.

A crash in the brush startled Keven. He wheeled. Beryl was pointing at a gray-blue bounding object that vanished as if by magic. The crack of hoof on dry branch was the last they heard.

"Buck," said Beryl. "I'm glad you didn't shoot."

"Gosh, I forgot I had the rifle," he whispered.

They climbed on, and the forest grew denser, wilder, blacker, and the underbrush closed above their heads. A gloomy silence prevailed in this primeval forest, where a snapped twig caused a start, and a voice would have been sacrilege. On they walked, and wound through the woods, up and up to a changing region. The firs no longer lorded it over all, though, as if in defiance of their lessening hold, they spread impenetrable thickets of their offspring on the north slopes of ravines. Pines began to appear, and gnarled oaks, and here and there the wondrous smooth-barked red-and-copper madroña, with its wide-spreading branches and its shiny foliage.

Higher still they entered the zone of the oaks, an open forest, patched with sunlit glades of golden grass, upon which the bronze leaves were rustling down. The ground was dry as tinder and reflected the strong heat of the sun. Manzanita with its yellow berries and myrtle with its faded flowers floated warm on the still air.

Keven and Beryl wandered on with lingering, ever-slowing steps, at last to halt upon an open brow of ground, where a monarch oak, noble and old, bleached at the top, invited the rest. They sat down, backs to the wide trunk. Far below shone the river, winding along the bottom of the valley, which from this elevation appeared so deep and vast. Its roar soared up, voice of the wilderness, low and continuous.

There was life in this oak forest. Frost had kissed the acorns. Wild pigeons fluttered among the leaves; robins, halting to rest on their way southward, gave forth plaintive notes, as melancholy as the autumn. Squirrels revealed their cautious movements to keen eyes; jays squalled and crows cawed. And far down through the aisles between the oaks listening deer, sleek and gray, passed with graceful step.

Long Keven reclined there against the tree trunk, feeling Beryl beside him, watching with wide all-absorbing eyes, and again listening blindly, and still again narrowing his lids down to make the forest kingdom resemble what it might have been at the dawn of man upon the earth.

The forest spoke, the river called, the clouds sailed across the blue above. The smell of the hot dry earth, the sweet myrtle, the faint pungency of the piny mountain slope below and intangible drifting odors filtered into Keven's blood.

He had the sensation of sinking through space and the immeasurable past back to the primal day when these things had been inculcated into the flesh and bone that had been father to him. He wavered there on the verge, never quite attaining the savage state that his being yearned for. The instant his unthinking self gained that vaguely haunting happiness of a bygone age, then his consciousness intervened. He would deny it, and become again a man who reveled in his senses, only to smell and see and hear and feel his way back to realization of his state. Never could he utterly win that bliss for more than a fleeting instant. But as he had dreamily felt it stealing over him these endless transforming weeks, so now he grasped its significance, its truth, its glorious power to uplift and satisfy and save.

"Beryl, what are you thinking of?" he asked at last, no longer able to deny his intelligence, his thinking self.

She gave a little start. From whence had his voice dragged her?

"I wasn't thinking," she said dreamily.

"What were you doing?"

"Nothing."

There it was. He had expected that. Keven divined he must approach Beryl differently, if he were ever to get at this aloofness of her. He understood it. He believed she had by nature and training penetrated deep into this strange state of feeling of suspended consciousness that so baffled him.

"Are you happy?" he went on.

"Oh—so happy," she replied softly.

"You like this? To climb high up the mountain, to look far down, to be under the trees?"

"Love it better than anything except the river—and you. But you are the river, for you came with it."

"You have an oak leaf in one hand," continued Keven, "and pine needles in the other. You have been smelling them. I watched you on the way up. I saw you touch the firs with caressing hand. How many times you stopped to look and listen! You turned your ear to the falling water. You see every living creature of the woods before I do. You choose to sit in the sun instead of the shade. You stuck a long golden leaf in your hair, as an Indian might a feather. . . . A hundred things like these you've done. Were you conscious of them?"

"No, Kev, I wasn't," she replied. "I'm surprised at you. I'll have to be careful—if you're so observant."

"Dear, I'm terribly serious. I want you to help me to find out something."

"About me, Kev?"

"Yes, and through that, about myself."

"I'm an open book for you, Kev."

"You are not. You are a marvelous mystery. I don't want you any different. I only want to climb to heaven with you. . . . Beryl, only a little while ago—well, you know what I was. Then came freedom from that craving for liquor. Then came love! . . . If I was tortured before, I am tortured more now. I *feel* health, strength coming back. I sleep, I eat. My nightmares have gone. I can *see* better out of this half-blind eye. . . . There, I'll hold my hand over my good eye. . . . Beryl, I can see you—and not so dimly. So you and the river and this solitude have

156

done something to my spirit, and through that to my mistreated body. I can't explain it. I only feel. And I am tortured because it may be only a dream, a delusion."

"Ah no, Kev. It is life. It comes from my beloved Solitude."

"But what comes?" he entreated, in perplexity.

"I—I don't know exactly," she replied thoughtfully. "But I know how I feel when I'm away. I long for the river and the woods. I don't want you to think I haven't learned things and have not enjoyed the time away from home. I have. But out there in what they call civilization I see and I think. Here I see, but don't think, I guess that's it. Roseburg and Portland, one a town and the other a city, I enjoy for a while. I liked my work at Roseburg, and especially school. But I saw the haste, the waste, the madness of people. For money! For excitement! For speed! I saw their selfishness and greed, their misery and sorrow, their sacrifice, and oh, the good and courage of a few. Then I would long for the river, and the firs, for my Solitude. And when I got back something stole over me again. All that—that which troubled me faded away. I forgot."

Keven felt that she had told him much, yet the illusive thing held aloof. He must probe his own heart, perhaps, if he were ever to disclose it. But there was arresting sweetness in this glimpse of Beryl Aard's soul.

"In a word, then, Beryl, there is peace comes to one here. And after that, this other thing—this illusive spell, which you and I were under till I broke it."

"Kev, since you make me think, I'll tell you something nice I just thought. You are a very bright boy! . . . But let's go back to our spell. Let's climb higher, where we can see. This is nothing. Let's go up, Kev, up to a place I know, and forget."

"Yes, darling, I'll be happy to, but just a word more. Please."

"Well, go on, you dream-killer!"

"Doesn't this wonderful spell you speak of come from physical things? What thrills you the most?"

"Smells. The smell of the pines and the firs. The smell of burning leaves—of campfire smoke. The smell of sweet myrtle. Dad always sent me some in letters. My heart would leap. Then I was back here at Solitude. Oh, I love to smell everything here at home. Even a skunk! ... Isn't that dreadful? But it's true."

Keven laughed at that, but continued: "Now, Beryl, when you look out there and down, what do you feel?"

"Nothing, till you make me think. I just see."

He was silent awhile, because realization of this girl's nature and of his extraordinary good fortune inhibited further speech. If Beryl had Indian blood, which indeed she had in some degree, what was it in him that struggled to meet her on her plane, to understand and feel with her, to get under that smooth, golden-tanned, blue-veined skin of hers? And the answer seemed to be the heritage of a primitive day.

"Come on, enchantress," he said at length, merrily seizing her hand. "Let us climb on up—and back! But beware of making me love you more."

Midday found them on the heights, and Keven, at least, was spent and fagged. Purposely he had not looked back or down for hours—but always up the changing slopes.

Beryl led him to a ridgetop of the mountain, the last slow rise of which was black with mantle of firs. Up to this border a meadow almost on end had led, grassy, dotted with purple asters waving in the breeze. The air was thin and cool. Keven panted. He saw the heaving of Beryl's breast. There were dewy drops on her forehead. They flung themselves down on the ground beneath a huge slanting slab of gray-green mossed rock, which marked the edge of the forest.

"Look, Kev, look with my eyes," cried Beryl. "This is my throne. I've climbed here twice a year since I was ten."

Keven had fortified himself; he had learned how to look. This last ridge of the mountain ran westward, so that when Keven gazed straight he faced the west. He saw only heavy pearl-white clouds, moving almost imperceptibly, closer than he had ever been to clouds, across the deep dark-azure sky. Then he looked down.

The grassy slope rounded its descent for a way, then fell precipitously a thousand feet, to check its headlong flight in an open cape fringed by firs. A troop of deer dotted the meadowlike promontory. And as Keven gazed a golden eagle sailed wide-winged and grand below him, so that he looked down upon its bright-flecked back.

That little halting bench did not prepare Keven for the blue gulf below. It seemed as if he were falling sheer. How far down the firs, now mere needles of green, millions of them forming the thick black slopes of the canyon! But still deeper down a forest as of flaming fire leaped out of the void. A riot of yellow, of scarlet, of orange, of cerise, of purple, seen through smoky veils, blazed the truth of autumn. He swept his gaze farther down, holding his breath in anticipation of the river, but he saw only bits of gleaming brook and dancing white cascades like the wings of a white moth. This canyon, that seemed to penetrate to the bowels of the earth, was only a side canyon.

Up the colored mosaic of slope Keven's gaze traveled to the black dense belt, on and up to the crags and the bleached firs, grotesque and deformed, and higher still to be riveted on the peaks and domes of the mountains beyond. It was an endless field, with notched horizon as far as the sky, and leagues and leagues of unbroken forested slopes. Here was the mountain kingdom from which the numberless springs and brooks and streams sent their pure waters down to the farther river.

Even before Keven sighted the Rogue he heard it, and instinctively he closed his eyes and turned his ear. Low and far away, deep down and faintly clear, its mellow roar! He had not before heard it like this. And he pictured its long green sweeps, its white rapids, its broad still reaches under canyon walls, its majestic curves. But when he forced his eyelids open he saw, far, far down, only a winding broken blue ribbon with knots of white. He rubbed his eyes. Could that be the Rogue? That strip of spotted blue, smiling out of this incredible void!

But gradually he realized that it was his river—that he was gazing from a great height into a valley ten miles wide at the top, and sheering down over endless slopes and shadows of forest, over wooded basins and black canyons, over labyrinthine mazes of gold and red and magenta, of bright spots in the green, to the ragged iron cliffs, and to the tiny blue-and-silver thread between.

He watched then and no longer thought about what he saw. Even Beryl's head, finding his shoulder, seemed a fragrance and a caress of the senses. Her hand sought his, clung and rested there.

The gulf in the green earth yawned beneath; the mighty slopes flowed down; the river wound its way to be lost; the lilac haze spread across the valley. The white clouds sailed to cast their shadows. And the soaring golden eagle black-barred the sky. Low and far away roared the river. Up to the cool heights wafted the woody smells, like enchantment in their power. And the past of man merged in the present, strange and vague to peering eyes, yet strong and attainable in the scents of the earth.

chapter seventeen

KEVEN RODE WITH Aard down the trail toward Illahe, leading pack mules, which were to be loaded with supplies for Solitude.

The sun did not break through the mist or dispel the frost until the riders were well below Missouri Bar. Opposite a still reach of river Aard halted his horse and pointed down.

"Let's watch a little," he said. "I see steelhead risin', an' if I don't miss my guess, here's the run Beryl is lookin' for."

"Gosh!" ejaculated Keven, as he watched a ring widen on the smooth dark waters. "That was a lunker."

Aard took his interest in studying the pool. It soon became manifest that a great school of steelhead were resting and rolling here. Below was a stiff fall, difficult for salmon and steelhead to ascend, and still farther down extended a long series of rapids, rocky and shallow, with no eddies. Keven became all eyes and had a great longing to ride back after his tackle; but was ashamed to mention his desire to his employer.

These steelhead were spread up and down the still deep pool, and they showed close to the rocky walls, in the middle of the river, and everywhere. They rolled on the surface, they lazily broke water, and then a big one leaped, to thump back solidly. Keven whooped. He saw broad silversides turn just below the surface and vanish. They were big fish. When they rolled they flapped the water with wide tails. Then another jumped, shining pink and pearl in the light. The pool would become smooth for a moment, then suddenly show boils and splashes and ever-widening circles.

"Wal, that's the run of big ones," observed Aard. "Let's see. It's October eighth. Took 'em eight days an' nights to run up this far. . . . Kev, did you ever wonder about these big steelhead never gettin' started upriver till after the canneries shut down October first?"

"Humph! Sure, it's funny," replied Keven.

"Wal, not so damn funny for us upriver folk," replied Aard shortly. "I reckon nothin' can or ever will be done about it, but it sure ought to be. . . . You'll have some good news for the lass. Mebbe she won't be tickled! Reckon this bunch will hang up at Missouri awhile an' then come on to Solitude. Both steelhead an' salmon make good stays at Solitude, which accounts for the grand fishin'."

"Aard, that's a tackle-busting run of trout," replied Keven dubiously.

"Ahuh. An' the next batch of smoked steelhead will come high. . . . Wal, git up, Baldy, we can't loaf here all day."

They rode on, while the clouds of mist melted into the green and blue, and the sun shone hot, and the dry scents began to float drowsily, and the blazing golden-purple glory of autumn mantled the river.

Below the long white-running stretch of rapids, where again the river slowed and stilled, Aard halted to point.

"Kev, there's the other an' better side of the story," he said.

"By gosh, yes. Little salmon going back to the sea!"

exclaimed Keven, thrilled. Showers of tiny glittering glades and slivers of silver glinted in the sunlight. All along the whole stretch! Millions of baby salmon going down to the sea, to the home they knew only by instinct!

"Yes, that's the hopeful side. It always cheers me up," went on Aard. "Man is a greedy, destructive cuss. But nature is prolific an' resourceful. Those little salmon will come back when they are matured—some of them will get by the nets. An' so the cycle goes on. It's a blessed an' mysterious thing, son."

The trail led up off the open slope into the woods, where it wound, sunlight-streaked and shadow-barred, under the trees. It zigzagged in to head the canyons, where dark shades alternated with amber light, and the brooks trickled over the mossy rocks. Moss and fern were singularly expressive of Oregon. In every dell and glen they encrusted trees and roots, stones and logs, with their furry and lacy beauty.

Deer crossed the trail, to crash into the brush, mountain quail ran and twittered and whizzed through the golden aisles; and the gathering autumnal congregation of birds fluttered in flocks with sad requiem to the death of summer.

They reached Illahe about the middle of the morning, but owing to various delays did not get packed until afternoon. Keven, while waiting for Aard to do a last errand, espied two khaki-clad fishermen clambering wet and weary and fishless up from the river. As they approached he had an eye for their tackle. One of them slopped down on the step while the other went into the store. A barefooted, freckle-faced urchin edged closed to the fisherman, drawn by the shiny rod and reel.

"Sonny, your Rogue River is no good," declared the man.

"Oh, yes it is, Mister. You jest don't know how to ketch 'em," replied the lad.

The angler laughed and addressed Keven. "I suppose all you natives, young and old, think the same about city fishermen."

Keven laughed himself. "I've got sort of that way myself."

"Excuse me. I took you for a native," said the man, turning to look at Keven. He had keen blue eyes, a sunburned face, and a ready smile.

"No offense. But really it's a compliment," returned Keven, smiling.

"What are those flies in your hat?" queried the other, in sudden interest.

"They're homemade," answered Keven, removing his hat. "Bumble Bee, Black Gnat, Tan Upright."

"Who tied these?" asked the fisherman curiously, as he fingered them.

"A girl friend of mine," said Keven laconically.

"Trout don't rise to these things, do they?"

Keven laughed at that incredulous query, for once upon a time he had vouched precisely the same thing.

"Rise? My dear sir, steelhead not only rise to these, but they pile out on the rocks after them."

"Aw, go wan!" ejaculated the fisherman, for all the world like a boy, and he grinned like a boy. But he was eager, hopeful, too.

"Straight goods," returned Keven. "Last Monday I caught nine steelhead on that Tan Upright. Largest, seven pounds. It's a pretty good fly, but she—my friend—ties a still better one. Buff and black, with a white wing and a tiny sliver of red. She calls that one Solitude. It's sure dynamite."

"Have you got one with you?"

"No, I'm sorry. I lost the last one. She wouldn't give me another. We had an argument about steelhead—she's a great fly-fisherman—and we fight a lot about tackle, method, theory, and so on. You know fishermen."

"Lord, yes. Crankiest people on earth. . . . Would you sell these flies?"

"No. You're welcome to them. And I'll give you a tip about fishing the lower Rogue, if you want it."

"Young man, we want it as badly as we need it," rejoined the other heartily. "My friend and I are from Portland. First time on the Rogue. We've fished the Stilliguamish, the Umpqua, and other famous rivers. Caught trout, too. But this Rogue *is* a rogue, believe me. Beautiful water. But we just can't raise fish."

"I had the same trouble. Was born on the upper

163

Rogue. Fished from the time I was a kid. And I thought I was a great fisherman till I struck the lower Rogue. I was beaten to smithereens by a girl."

"You don't say!" said the Portlander, who after the habit of his kind was heartily engrossed. "She must be some fisherman."

"I'll say she is. . . . Now let me give you a tip. Try those flies. Locate some steelhead. *Don't* let them see you. Keep back from the shore and out of the water. Wading is okay, after you have exhausted the water close in. And the result of that will surprise you. Most steelhead lie along under the bars and rocks, close to shore. Cast a short line and draw your fly in. Make it dance or jiggle, like a fluttering bug."

"You are most kind, young fellow. I sure appreciate it. My friend, too, will be pleased. We have had rotten luck. By the way, what's your name?"

"Bell. Keven Bell."

"I see you've been in the service," the other went on.

"Yes, sir," replied Keven, surprised. "But I didn't get to France."

"You were lucky. I thought you had been at the front. Excuse my being personal. By profession I am a dentist. And it's a habit for me to see things a layman wouldn't."

"I got hurt though, without going to the front," replied Keven, and then briefly told of his accident and its consequences.

The fisherman exclaimed his sympathy and interest and then introduced himself.

"I am Dr. Allan Ames, and my friend is Dr. McIntire, an eye specialist. It is very evident you have not had proper medical attention. May I call him out to meet you?"

"Why—certainly," stammered Keven.

The other doctor was a stout little man with a merry face, also sunburned.

"Doc, shake hands with this young man, Keven Bell. . . . He has done us a favor, giving us some killing flies and good advice about the river. We certainly must return the kindness. It seems he saw service at an army training camp, where the breechblock of a gun nearly blew his head off. Lost part of his lower jaw and injured his eye. He has not had proper treatment. Let's look him over."

These kindly gentlemen took Keven to the more secluded porch of the inn near by. And when Keven removed his iron jaw Dr. Ames swore and his colleague stared his amaze.

"What a hideous contraption!" went on the dentist. "How could he ever have worn it?" Then he made a careful examination of Keven's mouth and jaw. "Compound fracture, with a section of bone missing. Unhealed tissue, and ulcerated stomatitis. . . . Bell, you've had rather a bad time of it, haven't you?"

"Yes, Doctor. My mouth is sore always, and now and then it gets fearful. So I can't eat."

"I'm glad to tell you that can all be corrected. You throw this iron junk away. I'll give you some medicine to use, and mail you more. Then when your mouth gets well come to my office in Portland and I'll fix you up."

"Wouldn't it cost a good deal?" asked Keven anxiously.

"Yes, it'll be expensive. You'll have to have a gold-and-platinum piece to fit in there, with teeth, of course. It must be heavy, so that its weight will hold it in place till the muscles grow accustomed to it. . . . Your case is really not so bad. I've seen far worse."

"What would it cost?" asked Keven eagerly.

"I don't know precisely. But don't worry about that. I'll do it as cheaply as possible—say around five hundred dollars. It will be worth a million to you."

"Thank you, sir. I'll come, just as soon as I can raise the money."

"Don't wait too long for that. I'll trust you. . . . Now, Doc, take a look at that bum lamp of his."

Whereupon Dr. McIntire bent over Keven and made close scrutiny of the injured eyeball, using a small magnifying glass.

"Not so bad, I'd say, on superficial examination," he said cheerfully. "Partial paralysis of the optic nerve, probably. Young man, you need a glass to do the focusing for that eye. I'll give you a shield to wear until you come to Portland. Don't strain that eye any more."

165

Then he went inside, to come out presently with a black eye shield attached to a rubber band.

"I always stick a few things like this in my kit, wherever I go," he said, adjusting the shield. "There now—doesn't that make the good eye feel better?"

"I think I can see better," replied Keven, as he gazed about him. "And I must keep this thing on?"

"Yes, when the light's bright. Early morning and late evening you needn't wear it. But as Doc here said, don't wait too long. I may help that eye to recover. At the least I can relieve the pain and the strain."

"Gentlemen, I surely thank you," replied Keven gratefully. "Give me your address. I will go to Portland as soon as I can."

Keven took leave of them presently and, returning to the store, found Aard waiting with the last mule packed.

"Hey, what's happened to you?" he ejaculated, gaping at Keven's transformed features.

"Aard, so I look very bad?"

"Turrible. Like someone blacked your eye and kicked in your chin."

Then with eager excitement Keven imparted his good news.

"Doggone my picture! That's just fine. It'll make Beryl so happy she'll be wild. . . . Kev, I reckon you should go to Portland soon. Anyways before the snow sets in."

"But, Aard, I must earn the money first. That'll take long, a year or more. All the same I'm happy. I just don't know——"

"I'll lend you the money," interrupted Aard dryly.

"You will not—you bighearted backwoodsman," declared Keven forcibly. "My word, Aard! You've already done more for me than I can ever repay."

"Wal, it's between friends. An' you're doin' a lot for me."

"Humph! I'd like to know what."

"You're makin' my lass happy. She's been a different girl since you came."

"You think so, Aard, really?" queried Keven, strangely moved.

"Hell, I know it," replied the trapper gruffly. "Let's hit the trail."

All the way home Keven dwelt upon this incident whereby two strangers, in return for a simple kindness, had changed his world. He saw the river, the foaming rapids, the steelhead shining in the red light of the westering sun, the yellow flare of the woods, the dark fir slopes, with an eye which seemed to have magnified its powers to discern the beautiful in nature.

Solitude was veiled in its transparent shadows of pink and lilac, of golden rays that pierced through the trees.

Keven was in the lead, with the line of bobbing pack mules between him and Aard. The hounds bayed till the welkin rang. Beryl came running out onto the cabin porch. Her red lips had opened to cry gay welcome when she caught sight of Keven's face. Her own lengthened and turned pale. She took a hesitating step and halted.

"Howdy, Solitude," said Keven, and he knew his voice was gruff and strange, because of the removal of his iron jaw.

"Kev! . . . You've—you've——"

"I should smile I have—if you mean got my face pushed in," interrupted Keven.

"Oh! A fight?"

"I reckon."

The swift changes of feeling in Beryl were unutterably sweet to Keven, and sometimes he could not resist inspiring them. But this grew tragic.

"Someone hurt you?"

"Well, I guess. 'Most as bad as you did that day when you slammed me one."

"Who struck you, Kev?" she cried, white now, with eyes beginning to blaze.

"Ask your Dad."

"Did he dare!"

She seemed to rise up in majestic royal wrath.

"Oh, Lord, no, Beryl," shouted Keven, suddenly confounded. "I was only teasing. Honest! I felt so good I had to see if—if you . . . Well, I feel awful good."

Then he related his experience with the doctors and concluded: "All because I gave one of them those three dinky flies of yours!"

"Kev Bell! You will make me angry someday," she said gravely, with a slow recession of the white from her skin. "I'm very, very happy for you."

After supper, when Aard had gone early to bed, Beryl left Keven before the fire and went to her room. Presently she returned and laid a goodly roll of bills upon his lap.

"There, Kev. Go to Portland at once," she said.

"You too? Darn you Aards!" He fingered the money, spread it out, counted it, and then turned to her in surprise. "Five hundred dollars! . . . Beryl, where did you get so much money?"

"I earned it and saved it."

"Well! . . . Forgive me for being so inquisitive. That seems a good deal of money—to me. . . . Beryl, I thank you with all my heart. You're just the best girl ever. But I can't take it."

"Why not, Kev?" she asked softly.

"I—I suppose because I'm not sure how or when I could ever pay it back," he replied.

"If our situations were reversed I would take it from you," she said, with ever so slight a lift of head.

Keven divined he was skating on thin ice.

"That is different, Beryl. You are a woman and I'm a man."

"Why is it different?"

"I suppose because custom has made a man feel he could help a woman, but he could not take money from her."

"Oh, I—see," she said curtly. But she did not see. She grew white to the lips.

Though Keven's objection was not so grave as he had apparently made it seem, still it affected him seriously. He divined, however, that this would never do. He must make amends and swiftly.

Wherefore he stood up and gazed straight into the proud hurt eyes, bent so darkly upon him. Most certainly they changed what he had intended to say. Smilingly he returned the money.

"Beryl, you save this till I earn enough to pay for that dental job. You'll need it—for you'll be going with me."

She actually staggered back.

"Going with you?" she whispered, utterly bewildered.

"Why, sure. At least I hope you will," he hastened to respond. He felt his own face chill and tighten, while he saw hers change and glow and suddenly flame dusky red.

"Keven!" She tried to stem the tide of shy and unexpected joy which stormed her, and tried in vain. Her eyelids fell to hide strange radiance that yet filtered through her long lashes. She was overwhelmed. Then with a gasp she fled.

chapter eighteen

THE DARK GRAY dawn came with a breath of frost from the high peaks above the singing river. October was well on its way.

Keven took to the tunnel-like trail through the forest; and, rod in hand, with the spring of a mountaineer in his step, with dancing blood, and his mind full of vague winged expectation of the long, long hours to come, he brushed the asters aside and trod the fallen leaves.

At the head of Solitude Valley, where the river turned north to seem lost in the gloom of the walled canyon, Keven struck off the trail and descended out of the woods to the open bank. He saw his own footprints, three weeks old, in a strip of sand which ran between the brush and the boulders of the riverbank. Deer tracks showed their cloven marks, and otter and mink and other wild denizens of the forest made their patterns, but Keven's were the only ones contributed by man.

He sat down on a flat rock at the edge of the water and dropped his leader in to let it soak thoroughly before attaching a fly. A familiar pleasurable sensation ran along his veins. The long, long day was all before him, and here ran the glancing river. From far above the dark bend floated a very faint, almost indistinguishable song of running waters; from far below where the river wound out of the jealous clutch of Solitude came the same voice though of different note and melody.

The gray curtain of mist overhead was as dense as fog; it hid the mountain slopes; it had not yet begun to rise or move. The light under the cloud bank was dull gray, and the river reflected it, except in places where a thin cold vapor rose off the surface. A tiny whistling sound pierced Keven's ears and increased as he tried to locate its source. Then a flock of wild ducks bore down to swoop up over his head and whistle on. They had white barred wings. He saw them streak down to the ledge pool above Solitude and make long sliding splashes as they alighted.

No other signs of life were manifest. The river might have been empty of steelhead and salmon, for any disturbance on its somber gliding surface. They might be there in the favorite resting places and then again they might not.

Keven picked up his leader and stretched it, before attaching it to his line. Then he applied himself to the task of choosing a fly. He had many, but only a few favorites, any one of which he was loath to start in with so early. All the long, long day ahead! So he selected a Coachman.

There beside the rock lay the strong sharpened staff which he used to aid him in wading across the river. He noted that the water was half a foot lower than when he had crossed last time. This would render the task far easier and lessen the risk. Whereupon he waded in boldly, soon to discover that though the water was low and without swift current there, it was far colder than before. It made him jump, and he was at some pains to go slowly, lining his marks on the bank, so that he could keep to the shallows. It was no fun to wade the Rogue in October. When the water edged up from his knees to his hips it was all he could do to step cautiously; and when he reached the center of the river, to be immersed up to his waist, the icy touch was breathtaking.

On the opposite bank he laid aside rod and staff to

exercise briskly. His hands were numb and his legs shaking. Presently his blood was running free and warm again. Then, rod in hand, he stepped to the river, facing downstream, and was about to begin casting when a moving object caught the tail of his eye. A big buck, with magnificent antlers, was crossing the wide bar below. Keven watched him disappear in the brush.

Keven made his first cast, and time was annihilated. When next he looked up, the valley had lightened; dark blue rifts showed in the rising canopy of mist; the river seemed strangely, vastly changed. He marveled at it. Again he sat down, just to look and listen. Spots of color stood out of the dark green; the gray shadow in the notch where the river disappeared had turned to purple. And at the moment there awoke the wild sweet rising and falling notes of a water ouzel, herald of the sunrise.

He resumed fishing, and eventually changed his fly to a favorite he had named Beryl. He had tied it himself, to his sweetheart's vast amusement. It was not a thing of beauty and therefore no compliment to the vivid Beryl, but somehow he just had to name it after her.

On his first cast with this new fly he raised and hooked a steelhead; and there came another change in the world. With a five-pounder on his string the long, long day had begun.

Some time after that a broad bar of pink and silver flashed under Keven's fly. That bar was a foot deep. Another cast again raised this giant of a steelhead. He rose boldly, he showed clearly, but he missed the fly and turned to leave a hole in the water. Keven let out gaspingly the breath he had held for tingling seconds.

Then with the lust of battle and for capture seizing him, and the sheer unrealized joy of his environment, Keven set himself to outwit that king of trout. He raised the wary, lazy gorgeous monster many times, but all in vain. Curiosity was not hunger; play was not feeding. And at last that deep dark eddying hole under the golden ledge of rock became blank.

Keven went on. Anything had the power to gain distraction. The color or ripple of a rising trout would set him to vigorously casting, until he either caught the fish or put it down. He watched two playful otters for a long time, as sure that they saw him as he was that he saw them. Halfway down to Solitude the singing of the river swelled to deep and murmuring music. Small trout, crayfish, water spiders all came in for serious attention. He just watched them, after the abstracted manner of an Indian.

All at once something drew his interest from the level of the flowing river. The valley burned gold and purple; clouds had melted away in the radiant blue; the mountain slopes seemed bursting in full autumnal glory, the dark green boldly infringed upon by the reds, the scarlets, the cerise and magenta, and the dominating splashes of gold. And there under it all wound and murmured the river in an endless solitude. It descended upon Keven like a mantle, it enveloped him, it bore the warmth of the sun and the fragrance of the forest. He looked and looked, felt it all as one in a dream, and went on fishing.

Like a boy in the serious pursuit of his most cherished pleasure he went on fishing, and everything was an event. A yellow leaf fluttered down from the high slope to alight upon his arm. A yellow oak leaf, with tinge of bronze and hint of green. It suggested the dry colorful aisle of the oak forests, high above the river, where the deer browsed for acorns, the wild pigeons fluttered, and the doves mourned. He put the stem in his mouth.

The river sang on, glided on, ever the same, yet ever changing. It shaded from green to gold, and then to a deep rose. The rapid below appeared crested with fire. But again, as so many times before this day, a rising steelhead claimed Keven's attention. He caught that one—and another—before he noticed that the color of the river had again changed. It was purple, deep rich purple like the shadows in the bends of the fir slopes. And presently he found it hard to see his fly.

Looking up, he stood aghast.

"What! Night already?"

The hounds bayed Keven welcome as he staggered into the dusk of the clearing under his load of trout.

Beryl ran out onto the porch, her white apron showing against the dark background.

"Oh, Kev, you had a fine day!" she cried. "How many?"

"Nineteen, I think," he replied lightly, as if that were nothing for him.

Straightway Beryl underwent that strange transformation inevitable to a true fisherman. She touched several of Keven's string of beauties with the toe of her boot.

"Under five pounds, Kev. You should have let these go."

"What? Why, they'll weigh six, at least."

"Ump-umm, my boy," she returned, shaking her head. "You can't see a steelhead right. Your eyes magnify. It's the habit of a novice."

"Novice! Me? . . . With nineteen to my credit?"

"Kev, you're still a city fisherman," she replied.

"What did *you* do today, may I ask?"

"Oh, I had a lot of work before I went out. But I didn't lose much. You know steelhead won't rise when the mist is on the river. Dad went down to Missouri. So I followed this afternoon."

"Did you catch any?" queried Keven, as if forced.

"We had a good day, especially after the sun was off the water."

"Humph! How many?"

"Thirty-four," replied Beryl nonchalantly.

"Thirty-four what?"

"Why, steelhead, you goose. And I let *my* little ones go."

"How many did you catch out of that thirty-four?"

"Sorry to top you, Keven. I got twenty-one."

Keven gazed up from his string of fish to Beryl. It was not yet so dark that he could not see fairly well. She seemed calm and demure, but he felt that she was bursting with glee. How she liked to beat him! A strong, sweet, almost overpowering passion stormed his heart. But for his wet fishy clothes he would at last have yielded to the hunger which consumed him and have snatched her to his breast.

"Beryl, I don't love you any more," he said gravely, and moved away toward his cabin.

He had gone a number of steps when a trill of laughter rent the silence. Keven felt that, too, in his very veins,

173

and thought somberly that an hour of reckoning for him was at hand.

"You're just in time to change for supper, Kev," she called after him.

He did not hurry, nevertheless, and pondered more than usual. The day had been one long enchantment. He had come back to life, to realism, to love. When he presented himself in the bright cozy living room, sight of Beryl made his heart leap, while he set his lips grimly. Beryl had on that marvelous white dress. It might have been a simple inexpensive one, as she claimed, but when she had it on he could not take his eyes off her. In it she appeared to lose the ruggedness which attended her in heavy outdoor garb. She seemed slender, when in reality she was not slender. It gave her grace, yet not only did it not deny her bounteous contours, but enhanced them. Then it brought out in vivid relief her rich coloring, the brilliance of her dark eyes, the luster of her hair. She smiled at Keven a little wistfully, as if she hoped he might find her pretty.

"Wal, son, it sure was one of the Oregon days," remarked Aard, taking his seat. "Set down, an' don't stare at Beryl as if she wouldn't last in that dress. I don't blame you much, though. She's an eyeful. . . . Fishin' does things to me. Tires me out an' starves me half to death."

"Yes, it *was* an Oregon day," replied Keven, breathing deeply as he sat down, still with his gaze riveted upon Beryl.

Presently she observed that his long day on the river, and his wonderful luck, had not given him much of an appetite.

"Sure, I'm hungry, Beryl, but it's getting harder all the time to eat without half enough teeth," he replied. But though he spoke jokingly he seemed to have gotten into a current which was rushing him somewhere. Beryl evidently sensed his mood and it influenced hers.

"Kev, you better take my advice an' not put off your trip to Portland till spring," interposed Aard.

"It's easier to take advice than money," returned Keven seriously.

"Wal, sometimes, yes. But you've come to be like a son to me, an' what's mine is yours."

"Aard, my feelings for you and—and Beryl—don't

174

square the deal," said Keven stubbornly, though he was glad the subject had been broached.

Beryl's downcast eyes were fixed upon her plate. The rosy gold had fled from her cheeks. Nevertheless Keven's deliberate gaze drew her own. Curiosity and fear overcame her modesty. Suddenly she blushed scarlet. Perhaps there appeared more in Keven's eyes than he realized.

"Kev, seems to me you worry a lot. Let well enough alone. You've got husky and strong. That was the main thing we wanted, wasn't it? Solitude has done much for you."

"More than I ever hoped for," murmured Keven.

"Wal, it'll give you peace someday. But not till you stop frettin' an' fightin'."

Aard spoke to Keven, yet his kindly words seemed to embrace Beryl. They finished the meal in silence.

"Wal, one pipe will about do me tonight," said Aard, as he stirred the smoldering fire and threw on some pine cones. "Kev, you miss a lot by not smokin' a pipe. Sure, Beryl says tobacco is dirty an' she wouldn't kiss no man who used it. Reckon that accounts. But nothin' soothes me like smokin'."

Keven took the other chair, which happened to be the big old armchair, vastly more comfortable than presentable. Beryl, with her apron on, helped the Indian woman clear off the table. Every time she returned from the kitchen her dark eyes sought Keven's, as if she were impelled against her will. And every time Keven sustained a thrill. He felt drawn on, desperate. The situation seemed intolerable to him. He would have it out with Beryl this very night.

"There's some whoopin' big steelhead in the river now," said Aard. "But we oughtn't ketch any more till we've smoked what we got."

"We'll help. . . . Gosh, I hate to miss any of this run," replied Keven.

"Wal, I reckon they'll hang around a week or so. River's low now. . . . Did you raise any wallopers today?"

"One. He was three feet long and a foot deep. I raised him a dozen times. But he was only playing with me. If I

175

had hooked him I'd be somewhere on the way to Gold Beach right now."

"I had hold of a couple of elephants. Couldn't do a thing. The first one went downstream an' cleaned me out. The second went upstream. Busted my rod. How Beryl did laugh! That girl gets an infernal joy out of my fishin' misfortunes."

"She sure does. I suppose it's just the natural cussedness of the born angler."

"Reckon so. She can afford to enjoy it. For she's a wonder with a rod. Kev, she nailed an eleven-pounder today, right in the middle of Missouri, an' she licked him without movin' out of her tracks."

"Eleven pounds! Lord, how does she do it, Aard?" ejaculated Keven, in mingled admiration and despair.

"Wal, she uses light stuff an' she lets a fish run. We men can't help horsin' a fightin' steelhead. It's the nature of the male. Beryl has a trout gettin' tired before he knows there's anythin' very wrong."

"I can't let them run. I want to stop them," admitted Keven.

"Same here. I reckon we'll just have to swallow Beryl's gift an' luck. Because it's both. Don't ever overlook luck. Some fishermen have it. Some haven't. I'm an unlucky member of the family."

"So am I."

"This afternoon, whenever I happened to look at Beryl, she was playin' a fish. Every time. An' it 'peared I must have looked a hundred times. She must have let more go than she kept. I keep tellin' Beryl the small steelhead are best for smokin'. But she keeps on lettin' them go."

When Beryl came in a little constraint fell upon the group. Aard smoked out his pipe in silence, then, rising, he knocked the ashes out and laid it on the mantel. Beryl stood at the open door, gazing out into the blackness. The river music floated up, mellow and sad. Aard threw some more cones on the fire, and then a couple of oak fagots.

"Shut the door, lass. Can't you feel the cold creepin' down from the hills?"

"Cold! . . . I thought it was so close indoors," returned

176

Beryl, as she complied with his wish. Still she kept well back from the lighted lamp.

"I know what you mean. I felt that too," said Aard, with dry humor, and he winked at Keven. "Sort of sultry thunderous atmosphere around. Like lightnin' was goin' to strike soon."

"Oh—not like that—at all," exclaimed Beryl, in confusion.

"Kev, what do you think it's like?" went on Aard. He was more than full of mischief.

"What's like?"

"Wal, the atmosphere around."

"Very cozy, comfortable, just wonderful—if only——" He did not complete the sentence.

"Ahuh. . . . Wal, I'll turn in an' I bet it'd take a fifty-foot raise in the river to wake me. So don't you young folks feel afraid to talk, fight, wrassle—anythin', so long as you come out of it. . . . Good night."

"*Dad!*" ejaculated Beryl hotly.

"What do you know about that?" added Keven, after Aard had gone to his room.

"*I* don't know anything," retorted Beryl.

"Come sit down. Why do you hang back there in the shadow? Lord knows you're pretty enough to want to be seen."

"It depends upon whom I'm with," rejoined Beryl, slowly coming forward to take the chair on the other side of the table. The large white-globed lamp hid her face, not by accident, Keven felt assured. Quite unaccountably he was furious with her. He could see her shapely feet and ankles.

"I overheard you and Dad talking about me being a lucky fisherman," began Beryl. "That's just like two men. Because I beat you to a frazzle you put it down to luck. But neither of you——"

"Oh, Beryl, stop kidding me," interrupted Keven, with more force than elegance. "Once for all you've got me trimmed as a fisherman. I'm not in your class. I'm only a dub—a hick-town fisherman. . . . Now does that satisfy you?"

"Satisfy me! No—it doesn't," replied Beryl, somewhat

177

mystified and shocked. "What do you want to talk about, if it's not fish?"

"I want to think," he snapped.

Whereupon silence ensued. Keven gazed piercingly into the opal heart of the fire, as if that would set his mind working. It seemed to be whirling with thoughts, none of which were coherent, or at least what he wanted. But he did not know what he wanted; and that was why it was imperatively necessary for him to think, so that he could find out. It had to do with Beryl, though, and himself, and this insupportable situation. He cudgeled his poor brain.

Presently Beryl's voice came as from a distance.

"Pardon. What did you say?" he replied.

"I said you'd been thinking a whole half hour and must be having a very good time."

"I was. Ha! Ha!" returned Keven hollowly.

"Well, I'm not. Perhaps you'd enjoy yourself still more if I make myself scarce."

"Perhaps. Oh, I don't know, I'm in a funny state. I want to think, but I can't."

"Kev Bell, I'm having some thoughts, if you're not."

"Indeed?" queried Keven flippantly. He was at his wit's end.

"Yes *indeed*. And they're not flattering to you. . . . Kev Bell, I—I don't understand you. If you're just miffed again with me because I beat you fishing——"

"Cut that out," cried Keven, stung. "I never thought of fishing. Not once. I'm sick of fishing. I hate the river. I'll never—never go again."

He heard her gasp.

"You hate—you *hate* my river—my beautiful, singing river?" she asked in a low shocked voice.

"Yes, I do," he replied harshly. But his conscience tortured him. He spoke so only because he was sore, uncertain, distraught.

"Oh, Kev!" she cried, mortally hurt, and she rose to her feet, white as her dress. "So *that's* it! I knew something was wrong. . . . You're tired of Solitude—of *me!* . . . You're going away?"

"Ha! Ha!" laughed Keven wildly. But this was getting somewhere. If he could only get his hands on her!

"You—you add insult to injury," she flashed. "Good night."

As she stepped to pass Keven he snatched at her too late, but he stuck out a foot to trip her. His move only checked her. Then violently he pulled her off her balance. Staggering, with angry cry, she fell full length into his arms. Only her feet rested upon the floor.

"How—dare you!" she cried, in furious amaze, and she struggled. "Let me up."

Keven wrapped his arms around her and crushed her to him, so that for the moment she was helpless. She strained to free her arms. She was as strong and supple as a panther. A giant could not have held her long. But this precious moment was enough for Keven.

"Beryl! I love you so terribly—it's killing me," he exclaimed huskily.

All that fierce, hard muscular contraction of her body relaxed as if by magic. She sagged limp and heavy upon him.

chapter nineteen

"LIE STILL—maybe now I can think," commanded Keven, as Beryl made weak and ineffectual efforts to move.

"Let—me—breathe," she replied, in panting whisper.

Then Keven loosened the coil of his arms, though not enough to let her get up, which evidently she was trying to do.

"Beryl, I love you so terribly—it's killing me," he repeated, passionately.

"But—that's no reason—to hold me—so—so disgracefully," she panted.

"Yes, it is. . . . What do I care how I hold you?"

"Please, Keven," she implored, and slipped off his lap to her knees. This brought her head down to his neck, where she buried her face.

"Now I *can* think!" he ejaculated.

"Kev, let me up, I beg you. This is undignified—not to say shameless."

"Dignity—shame—and all the rest can go hang. . . . I love you!"

"But—you're hurting me," she went on, almost weeping. "I can't stand it—long. You'll break something."

"Promise me you won't run off," he asserted sternly.

"I—promise," she whispered.

Then he released her.

"Bear!" she exclaimed, and leaned back on her knees to get her balance. Her bosom was heaving, her face dusky red. Then she got up, smoothed down her disordered dress, and sat down on the arm of his chair. Slipping her right arm round his neck she leaned to him.

"Kev, say that again—then you can think all night long and I won't move," she whispered.

"Say what again? I'm out of my head."

"You are at last—thank heaven. . . . I mean that about—what was killing you."

"Beryl, I love you so terribly—it's killing me," he complied, even more passionately than before.

She appeared to wilt against him. Then a slight quivering ran all over her. It wore away and came again. She moved and he no longer felt her warm moist cheek. In its place soft lips pressed.

"Don't kiss me, Beryl. Not yet! If you do that I—I'll eat you up. I want a million kisses."

"Begin," she retorted, with all the sweet witchery of a woman.

"No!"

"Yes. I want two million. . . . Kev, darling, I've waited so long."

"Good God! Don't reproach me. Don't say such things. . . . That you love me *at all!*"

"At all? . . . I love you with every last drop of my heart's blood. . . . I will love you so with its last beat."

"But I—I must think," cried Keven, almost yielding to transport.

"What about? If it's me—all right."

"Of course it's you. Everything is you."

"Very well then," she whispered softly.

With Beryl surrendering to his arms, sweet as he had dreamed she would be, Keven felt an exultation that had no need of thought. But he could not give in to it. He had to find himself. Instinct had guided him truly. Love of Beryl had driven him, and in its betrayal there was illumination. His shame, his bitterness could not long abide in its white light. But he longed so passionately to think out a solution to his problem. And he could not think as he had striven to. There was no longer any problem. Beryl lay in his arms, not only a willing prisoner, but a responsive one. Her cheek was again on his and now he felt her tears.

The oak wood burned like golden pearls on fire with life and love. Keven could peer into it penetratingly, only to see the shimmering glow.

It inspired no flaming thoughts.

"Oh, Beryl, I can't think. Nothing comes," he burst out.

"Don't try, then. Talk to me—and if you can't do that—love me."

"But I must talk!"

"Go ahead, darling. Maybe I can help to ease your mind. Dad had it right. You worry. Tell me your trouble, Keven."

"It's—I—I can't *stand* this—this situation here any longer," declared Keven.

"Neither can I," she laughed, with a deep note in her voice, as she rubbed her cheek against his. "But what do *you* mean, Mister Contrary?"

"I want things settled between you and me."

"They appear to be settling very well," she rejoined demurely. "Here I am on your lap—at last. . . . But I feared I'd never get there."

"Don't be funny, you little Indian devil. This is horribly serious."

"Kev, nothing can bother me *now*," she whispered, with sublime assurance.

Whereupon Keven plunged: "You love me?"

"I worship you," she said steadfastly.

"You must have me?"

"I'll die if I don't."

"Poor crippled beggar that I am!"

"Hush!" She put a soft hand over his lips. "No more such talk! You have grown well and strong. You are incredibly improved. Soon those—those injuries will be repaired—perhaps wholly cured. You are my handsome, wonderful man. . . . And indeed you are not a poor beggar."

He felt the lift of his heart. This girl of Solitude would yet make him what she believed him. Such love, such faith, such hope! They quite overpowered the morbid giants which so long had rent him.

"Beryl, will you—will you marry me?" he asked hoarsely.

"Yes."

"When? How soon?"

"Tomorrow."

The word was spoken with cool sweet nonchalance. She had risen to the occasion of his needs. She had intuitively longed to let all restraint fly to the winds and give up to the joy she was creating in him. But he only held her tighter. He longed to call her every tender and passionate name known to lovers.

"Beryl, I thought *this* would be hard, if I dared think it at all. But it's easy. . . . Will you lend me the—the money for the Portland trip? For *both* of us! You will have to go."

He felt the jerk of released blood as it surged through her.

"Oh, Kev—yes—yes."

"Will you swear you'll let me pay that money back, if only a dollar at a time?" he asked, in terrible earnestness.

"I swear."

He held her then in an eloquent silence. After all, how simple she had made it for him! Why had he not had courage before? Presently he resumed. "We'll go to Portland. We must figure our expenses very carefully. I want to put aside enough to buy you the finest outfit you ever saw. This will be to knock 'em stiff in Grant's Pass. Oh, you will knock 'em, Beryl Aard. . . . What a surprise for

182

Dad! No doubt he believes me dead. I've never written him. I just didn't know what to tell him. But now we'll go home, as soon as the doctors fix me up. I'll have to buy a new suit. I must not disgrace my beautiful wife. . . . Oh, it'll be great to go—I never guessed what it'd mean, till now. To see Dad—to see my friend Minton. To show you off to Rosamond Brandeth and Gus Atwell! Maybe that won't be grand? It'll be revenge enough. . . . If my old pard Garry was only alive! What would he say at sight of you?"

"Kev, it'll be a—a honeymoon," whispered Beryl rapturously.

"So it will be. I've never dared think of that."

Then they became lost in dreams. Suddenly Keven roused out of his, to lift Beryl's head.

"Is it a bargain?"

"Oh, joy!" cried Beryl. "Listen to him! It is my salvation."

"You will never regret?"

"Never, darling."

"Very well. . . . Beryl, did you hint that you were starved for kisses?"

"I didn't *hint*. I said so."

"Kiss me first. Then we'll see."

"I've already kissed you," she said shyly.

"That was of your own accord. This is a deal between us."

"Oh, I see." Then she pecked at his ear with tight lips, and just brushed his cheek, then after a pause, tenderly and lovingly kissed that sunken line of his jaw.

"Kev, do you remember," she began, feeling the injured place with fingers as tender as her lips, "do you remember that horrible time when—when I struck you?"

"Remember? Huh, I should smile I do!"

"Have you wholly forgiven me?"

"Of course, honey. I didn't blame you for lambasting me one. I must have been damn exasperating."

"You were. But I've never forgiven myself," she murmured, "I——"

"See here, you're falling down on the job already," interrupted Keven.

"Wha-at job?" she asked, giggling.

"Why, the rest of your future. It will consist solely of kissing me morning, noon, and night. . . . My God, I love you, Beryl. . . . It's changed my whole life. I'm young again. And if I were a whole man once more I'd be happy. Think of that! *Happy!* I'd ask no more than to be with you and work."

"I'm happy *now*. . . . I can confess that for a year or more before you came back I—I was afraid you'd forgotten—not me exactly, but that you loved me."

Full confession on that score trembled on Keven's lips, but reluctance to hurt Beryl kept him silent. What was the need to tell her now? He was not sure that he should not. He wavered and the moment passed.

"It seems to me what matters now is the absolute certainty that I love you. No girl ever before meant so much to a man. You have saved me. I was broken, wretched, ruined. My mind was clouded. And as sure as heaven, if I had got by Solitude I would have killed Atwell and then myself."

"God would never have let you get by Solitude," returned Beryl solemnly.

"You believe in God, then?"

"Of course. God is all around us here," she replied simply.

"We'll have lots to talk about when we come back home. Married! Man and wife! . . . Beryl, call me husband."

"How can I—yet?"

"I want to hear how it sounds. All this is so darned incredible."

"It's very real to me," murmured Beryl, whose heavy-lidded eyes were closed. *"Husband!* . . . How does it sound?"

"It'd be wonderful if you weren't so awed. Beryl, after all, I'm only an ordinary mortal."

"You!"

'Well, then, what have I been to you and what am I now?"

"You were my first and only boy friend. Then my sweetheart, my soldier-hero, my absent master, my returned lover—and soon—my husband."

Keven saw that there was no help for the dream and the glory that dwelt in Beryl Aard's mind. How could any man have deserved it? But it was there. It had dragged him out of the depths. Suddenly in a passion of realization, of gratitude and love, he fell to kissing her.

"Oh. . . . Kev! . . . There! . . . No more! . . . Mercy! . . . Darl—ing—I—I didn't mean . . . Oh, Kev, you're strangling me. I——"

But he did not desist until he was exhausted and she lay white and spent back upon his shoulder. More than all else, that had been what he craved. The bliss of this indulgence, the all-satisfying surrender to it, and the supreme proof of his mastery quickly merged into a feeling of his responsibility, his opportunity.

"Beryl, I—I had to do that," he exclaimed hoarsely, as he slowly recovered. "But I promise I'll not have another brainstorm—anyway, not till after we're married. . . . Now, open your eyes, precious. . . . Sit up. We've got to get down to brass tacks. We're having a great old understanding. But there's more."

She was not so quick to respond.

"What're you—going to do? Finish me at one—fell swoop?" Her tone was plaintive and she was smiling. But her wide eyes gave Keven a glimpse into the depth and mystery of a woman's soul, before which he trembled.

"You would tantalize me. . . . Now, Beryl, come out of your trance. Let's finish each other for good. We'll leave for Portland tomorrow, and we've planned as far as Grant's Pass. We'll have our fling there. Buy all the stuff we've got money left to buy. New tackle for you to fuss over this winter—books to study and read—oh, everything."

"And a rifle for you, Kev. Do you know you're making me so, so happy I—I——"

She could not find any adequate words to express what she felt.

"Am I? Good, but I haven't started yet. . . . We'll be away about two weeks. Let's see."

"That's just fine. It'll be Indian summer then. No one who ever spent an Indian summer in Oregon would miss another."

"Indian summer is all right. But I've got to work. I'll

have a wife, you beautiful dreaming creature. You'll be moving over into my cabin then. It'll have to be fixed up comfortably."

"Indeed it will. We must get no end of things," she said with keen enthusiasm.

"But, honey, we must not go in debt," declared Keven earnestly.

"Debt? Did I say anything about that? I suppose you think I'll make a wildly extravagant wife?"

"Lord, I hope not. You'll sure make an adorable one. But, Beryl, stop making me think of you only as *that*. Let's start right. We'll be poor. And we must live on my labor. Can't you understand?"

"I'm trying hard, you dear old goose."

"Well then, no going in debt. Promise?"

"Yes," she replied, with dark eloquent eyes studying him.

"That trip will cost us all the five hundred dollars you have—which you'll lend me. . . . Gosh, we'll have to stretch it. But those Portland doctors will be easy on me."

"Kev, I'm afraid five hundred won't be enough."

"It'll *have* to be."

"Dad would lend you a little."

"Now, Beryl! . . . No!"

"Well, then, he might give *us* a little wedding present."

"Ahuh. . . . Beryl, you may belong to Solitude, but you have plenty of eternal feminine. . . . When we come home I'll go to work in earnest. At whatever Aard gives me to do. Trapping first——"

"No, Keven, darling, you won't take up trapping," she interrupted calmly.

"But, Beryl, your father's a trapper," expostulated Keven.

"Is he? Well, you're not going to be one."

"What have you against trapping?"

"It's horribly cruel."

"Yes, I suppose it is. But beggars can't be choosers. . . . I'm sorry, but I fear I'll have to do it without your consent."

"No, you won't."

186

"See here, woman, who says I won't?"

"I do. . . . There, I see battle in your eyes. Let's put that question off till we come home. Sufficient unto the day."

"A good idea. But don't be too sure. . . . The thing is I'll go to work. Beryl, we have very sweet and beautiful prospects. Only perhaps you have not thought so far ahead as I have."

"I've thought pretty far, Mister."

"Oh, you have. Well, how far?"

Here, however, she averted a blushing face.

"Beryl, honey, listen," he went on, most earnestly, drawing her face around. "Solitude will be home. And I know I will love it more and more. Our wants are few, when you come to think of them. Thank God, you are a girl of simple tastes. But you will not be marrying a market fisherman, or a wood chopper, or a trapper, even if the facts contradict that for a while. I will develop a fruit farm here. Many men have been successful up the river. Why not here? The point is that I shall not want to keep you stuck in the woods all the time. When we can afford it, I will take you out. You'd like to see Frisco, wouldn't you, and Southern California?"

"Yes, but I'd not care a rap if I never did."

"The winters are long here."

"Surely. And they're lovely. Just you wait."

"Could you be happy if we *never* left Solitude?"

"You bet I could——if *you* could."

"Beryl, it's no question of what I could do. I want only you. But there's another angle to it. You're an educated girl. You mustn't make me let you stagnate."

"Stagnate! Here on my beautiful singing river? . . . Kev Bell, you don't realize. You don't know me."

"Doggone you, anyway," returned Keven good-humoredly. "I'll have to get down to the brass tacks I mentioned."

"Ahuh." She imitated him dryly.

"You want babies, don't you?" he launched at her abruptly.

This query sent her back to her hiding place on his shoulder.

"Beryl!'" He repeated the query.

187

"Yes, of course I—I do," she whispered.

"How much do you want them?"

"Oh—very—very much."

"Very soon?"

"Not—so—very."

"How many?"

"Oh, Kev, I think you're dreadful. Such things to ask a girl!"

"It's tough, I know, darling. But you see, you're not making a very good matrimonial venture. I want to *know*—right before we start. Please don't mind. Surely we can talk about anything. It'll be a help to me, Beryl."

"Well, you funny dear, it seems wild conjecture. But if you want my real deep dream . . . I'd like to have two children at least, a boy and a girl, before I'm thirty. And then, perhaps another afterward."

"Good. I'm absolutely in accord with you there. Well, the reason for all this embarrassing quiz of mine hinges on possible children. What's your idea of school for our little Beryl and Kev to come—and possible George Washington Aard Bell?"

She laughed merrily.

"Keven, there's a country school at Agness. Surely in a few years there'll be schools at Illahe and Marial."

"Did you go to Agness?"

"No. My mother taught me. And as I told you I had four years of school at Roseburg."

"That last is okay. And surely you could teach young kiddies. But after they grew up, say to six or seven, I'd want them to have the advantages of good schools."

"I agree, Keven."

"Then in case we have such marvelous fortune—say a couple of youngsters—would you be willing to live in Roseburg or Grant's Pass, while they went to school? I mean only a few months—or at most a part of each year."

"Yes indeed, I would, provided you lived with us."

"Well, I guess. If I couldn't, I fear our little Bells would grow up Rogue River Indians. . . . Beryl, you're the most satisfactory sweetheart I ever had."

"Kev Bell, how dare you! You swore you never had a sweetheart at all before me."

188

"When did I swear that?"

"It was one afternoon, nearly five years ago. We were down by the river. We'd had an awful row. Well, we made up, and it was then——"

"Beryl, pray spare me any further details," he interrupted ruefully.

Beryl laughed.

"Beryl, to be serious again, you've changed my whole world this night," said Keven gratefully. "I shall have no more black spells. I shall have no more worries. You're as good, as sensible, as clever as you are loving and beautiful. And that is saying a mighty lot. My God, the sheer luck of it! After all the agony of those two years in a hospital—and my failing and sinking afterward—the sin and degradation that I actually faced—to meet you again, to find in you such a faithful sweetheart as no man, much less me, could deserve—to be checked, softened, saved—what else can I call it?"

"Kev, darling, don't praise me so," she replied, and she pressed his head to her breast, then released him and rose to her feet. "I am only human. Lately I've had my doubts, my fears. But since you *do* love me and you *do* share my feeling for Solitude all is well. I could not be happier. . . . Look, it is late. Where have the hours flown? Let us go out and listen to the river—then say good night. Tomorrow I must be up early to pack for our adventure. . . . Ah, Kev, it is almost too good to be true."

They went outdoors. The night was dark. The great black slopes sheered up to the strip of blue sky, studded with white stars. There were no rustlings of wind in the leaves, no chirpings of insects. The air was cold. Keven drew Beryl into his arms.

"Now I can hear only your heartbeat," she whispered, from his breast.

"Listen to that. It's all for you. I'll listen to the river for us both."

Through the incredible stillness the low murmur of the river seemed to have a supernatural significance. That voice could not come only from gliding waters. It was a gentle and singing sound, full of mystery, like the pale-gleaming, starlight-reflecting water from whence it came. There was something else out there. Keven felt it, and the

189

thing that had been vague became clear. Spirit! All was not merely physical—rocks and trees and waters. The same spirit which dreamed and murmured under the watching stars actuated this throbbing, quivering girl. The last shadow of materialism faded out of Keven Bell forever. The evil that had been done him passed like a black specter into the gloom of the forest. He absorbed the meaning and the strength of Solitude. He accepted the love of this girl as something as infinite as the Nature which had created her.

chapter twenty

NEXT MORNING, early as Keven arose, it was not early enough to be ahead of Beryl. He heard her gay voice rousing Aard and the Indian housekeeper. Keven packed his one good suit, and when he got that far he scratched his head in rueful perplexity.

"Doggone!" he soliloquized. "No white shirts or anything. No civilized hat. Down here at Solitude I never cared how I looked. But to get on a train—to be in a crowded city with a handsome girl—to see every Tom, Dick, and Harry rubbering at the backwoods guy with her—gosh!"

But there was no help for it. At Illahe or Agness perhaps he could remedy in some degree the lamentable deficiency.

As he went out Beryl hailed him gaily from the porch of the other cabin.

"Laggard! Late on your wedding day!"

She was radiant. Keven was not prepared for the wonder of her this morning.

"I'd been here sooner if I'd known you were going to look like this," he replied.

"Like what?"

"So lovely."

"Kev, things have gone to my head badly enough. . . . I'm 'most packed. Oh, Kev—it's won—der—ful."

"Beryl, did you tell your father?" asked Keven, in eager anxiety.

"Not me. That's your job. But I'll back you up," she said, with an excited little laugh.

"Where is he now?"

"I hear him now—in the living room."

Beryl kissed Keven and then fled precipitously.

"Hold on! Is that backing me up?"

Just then Aard appeared on the porch, catching sight of Keven and the fleeing Beryl.

"Hey, son, what's all this rarin' around so early?" he queried.

Keven abruptly took the buck by the horns.

"Beryl and I are going away to be married," he blurted out. Then when the fearful truth had been imparted he grew suddenly weak and frightened. This stalwart, piercing-eyed trapper might take exception to the idea.

"Thank the Lord!" ejaculated Aard heartily. "It's about time. You pale-faced sighin' an' quarrelin' doves have bothered me a heap lately."

"Aw—I—we—it's sure sudden, Aard," stammered Keven, in the throes of changing emotion. "Last night it all came out. I'd spoken to you first, sir, if—if I'd had any idea. But it was just—just like a dam bursting."

"You found out you care a heap for my lass?" queried Aard, with straight dark glance intent on Keven.

"I've known for long. I fought against it," replied Keven frankly. "I—I felt I wasn't much of a match for Beryl. But it was too strong. . . . Aard, I love that girl so—so terribly it was killing me."

"Wal, son, I reckon you won't die if it's Beryl you want," said Aard, with a smile. "She's like her mother—a one-man woman. An' she's loved you for years, since you came to Solitude as a boy fishin'. As I see it she's all the better for that, since now you've declared yourself. . . . I'm downright glad, Kev."

"You're awful—good," rejoined Keven huskily, with a knot in his throat. "I hope I can repay you and Beryl—for your faith in me. I——"

"Chuck all that, son," said Aard. "It's no one-sided deal. . . . Let's go in to breakfast. I see Beryl ran off to let you brace the old man alone."

As they entered the living room, Beryl appeared from the kitchen. She was a very agitated young woman.

"Oh—Daddy—Kev . . . is everything all right?" she panted, her color coming and going. And then suddenly when the roses did not come back to her cheeks, Keven turned to look at Aard. He seemed a very stern and forbidding parent.

"Daughter, I've had a shock," he said gravely, and he indicated Keven.

"Shock! Why, Daddy—it—it oughtn't have been."

"Do you love this young man?"

"Love him? . . . Of course I do. I—I should think anyone could have seen that."

"You have acted sort of queer lately. . . . Wal, I reckon I ought to withhold my consent."

"Father!" The deep full-ringing word went through Keven like a blade. Beryl Aard was something to gaze at then.

"Keven is a mighty fine boy," went on Aard calmly. "How do I know you won't mistreat him? Lord knows he's had sorrow enough."

Enlightenment did not dawn swiftly upon Beryl. She was too deeply moved, and her father's totally unexpected statement required time to clarify.

"Lass, I might give you to Keven on one condition," went on Aard. "That you quit fishin' an' leave the river to him an' me."

Beryl stared bewildered. Then the blood came rushing back to darken her cheeks. "Villains! You put up a job on me. Oh, I went stiff and cold. . . . Never! *Never!* I can beat you both—and I always will."

She ran into his widespread arms. That was rather a beautiful moment for Keven Bell. He swore in his heart that he would die before he would fail this girl and her father.

"Wal, let's have breakfast," said Aard, and with an arm around the happy girl he led her to the table. "An', son, tell me your plans."

Keven soon told them.

"Wal, I reckon they can be improved on," replied Aard presently. "You might have the trip to Agness all for nothin'. The preacher comes there only twice a month. Likely you'd miss him. An' the natives down river are a gossipy lot. Of course, if you're not in any *hurry* to be married——"

"We are. At least I am," replied Keven quickly.

"So am I," said Beryl quickly. "You see, Dad, I'd better nail Kev before he changes his mind."

"Haw! Haw! . . . Wal, I've an idea. Suppose you go out by way of West Fork. There's a good trail that crosses the mountains up here. I'll go with you. So it won't look like you're elopin'. Haw! Haw! . . . You can catch a train goin' south to the Pass or goin' north to Portland."

"We must go to Portland first," spoke up Keven.

"I've gone to Roseburg several times this way, Keven. I think it's really the best way for us to go out. Long ride, but easy trail. How far is it, Dad?"

"Reckon about thirty-five mile. If we pack an' saddle up quick we can make it to West Fork by sundown."

"Fine. Let's go that way," acquiesced Keven.

"But there's one drawback," interposed Beryl, blushing rosy red. "We can't be married at West Fork. . . . It's only a station. No preacher."

To Keven that appeared vastly more than a drawback; it was an insurmountable obstacle.

"Beryl! We can't be married today?" he ejaculated.

"I'm afraid not, Kev," she replied mournfully.

"Wal, don't take on so," interposed Aard. "It's no great matter whether you get married today or tomorrow, is it? Now see here. Let me engineer this business. We'll rustle right on the trail. I'll see you off at West Fork. You'll get to Portland sometime tomorrow. Five o'clock if you catch the train I go on. Then you can get married—an' everything will be lovely."

"I—I g-guess that'll be all right," said Beryl dubiously, though her great eyes were wide and bright.

"But, Aard—it isn't just—the proper thing for me to take Beryl that way," objected Keven, quite flustered. "Suppose we meet someone on the train. People from Grant's Pass who know me. Gus Atwell, for instance or—or Rosamond Brandeth. I couldn't introduce Beryl as my wife."

"Sure, you could, if you got in a pinch," declared Aard.

Beryl gazed mutely at Keven and he stared back at her. They were in a quandary.

"Your old friends aren't goin' to ask to see your marriage certificate, are they?" inquired Aard.

"It wouldn't be beyond Rosamond Brandeth," returned Keven darkly.

"What do we—*you*—care about her?" asked Beryl, with wonderful eyes on him.

"Nothing. Absolutely nothing," replied Keven confusedly.

"If Dad says it's all right I'll go," added Beryl.

"Sure, it's all right," put in Aard coolly. "You needn't take a Pullman. There wouldn't be any berths anyway, that late. I always go in a day coach. Set up an' sleep some. You can do it."

"Well, that's better," agreed Keven, greatly relieved.

"I'll go out an' saddle up," said Aard, rising. "Lucky I have some horses in. Don't waste any more time, children."

Keven had almost finished his breakfast when Beryl transfixed him with eyes beautiful and penetrating.

"Kev, you looked and spoke sort of funny," she said.

"How so?"

"Was that Brandeth girl in love with you?" asked Beryl tragically.

"Oh, Lord, no!" exclaimed Keven.

"Are you ashamed to have *her* see you with me?"

"No, darling. On the contrary I would burst with pride."

She was reassured and the shadow faded. Keven was worried lest she might ask next if he had ever been in love with Rosamond Brandeth. What a fool not to have told her long ago!

"Honey, I had a queer burn deep inside me," exclaimed Beryl, with her hand over her heart. "I believe it was jealousy."

"Nonsense. It's indigestion. You've bolted your breakfast—what little you ate. . . . Come now."

"Wait, Kev. Let me give you the money before I forget. We'd be in a pickle without that. . . . And I must fix some sandwiches. But I'll be ready before you are."

"Say, Beryl, wouldn't it be funny if we didn't have time to change our riding togs for something respectable?"

"I wouldn't mind," she replied, and ran to her room.

In less than an hour they were riding north on the river trial. When the sun broke through the mist they had reached the lower end of Mule Creek Canyon. Keven felt himself in a state of transport. By nine o'clock they were climbing the slope above Winkle Bar. The higher they mounted the more glorious seemed the golden forest and the blue river. When Keven turned a last time from the summit the sweet singing voice of running water called to him to come back soon. Then he plunged after the others into the many-hued maze of the wooded ridgetop. From that time the hours and miles were exceedingly and marvelously too short. At Nine Mile they halted for lunch, with Aard making sly jokes, Beryl gay, and Keven trying to realize why he should have been so crowned by the gods. From Nine Mile the trail led downhill. For long they rode in the fragrant shade of giant firs, zigzagging the slope of an ever-widening canyon where the blaze of autumn leaves dazzled Keven's dreamy sight. When the early mountain sunset fell they rode down into West Fork.

A store, a station, and railroad track, set down between high dense slopes, where two streams met, constituted this place, West Fork, that had seemed such a goal.

How quiet and lonely! Even the iron rails and the telegraph wires made little difference. Beryl babbled like a running brook. Aard returned to where he had left them waiting with the information that they had ample time to change their clothes and have supper before their train time. Their difficulties seemed to dissolve into thin air.

Then, before Keven realized it, they were at the station. Aard was saying: "I reckon I better leave the horses here. No need of my comin' in for you. I'll expect you along in about two weeks."

A deep low, hollow whistle came from round the narrow turn.

"Thar she comes."

Keven felt Beryl squeeze his arm. Then she was kissing her father. The train rolled in with tremendous roar and clatter and halted with engine far beyond the station.

"Wal, son, it comes to every man once in his life," Aard said, gripping Keven. "Be good to her. . . . Lass, I 'most forgot somethin'. Here. A weddin' present for you an' Kev. . . . Good-by. Come back soon. Solitude will be waitin'."

Then they were on the platform waving. The train jerked. Faces passed out of sight. Keven thought it no less than miraculous when, a moment later, he saw Beryl sitting by the train window, gazing out with wet and softened eyes. He sat down beside her. The train gathered headway along the glancing yellow-bordered stream.

Dusk fell all too soon. The brakeman lit the car lights, which rudely tore Keven and Beryl from their dreaming oblivion. They let go of each other's hands and sat up to try to appear natural. Presently to Keven's amaze he discovered that none of the other passengers were paying any attention to them. It was a relief, but Keven could not understand it. He said as much to Beryl. She gave him a bewildering smile. They talked then of everything except the tremendous adventure upon which they were embarked.

The train thundered on. At length it passed out of the mountainous country. The flickering lamps of hamlets flashed by. At Roseburg a stop of several minutes was made. Beryl peeped out of the window at the throng on the platform, and it was plain to Keven she was thrilled. After Roseburg the brakeman turned off the lights, except one at each end. Passengers settled back in their seats in anticipation of the long night.

But it was not going to be long for Keven. He felt too excited for sleep, though he was tired from the unaccustomed ride on horseback. Beryl's presence was a continual delight. In the shadow she gradually nestled close to him, and then—wonder of wonders!—she went to sleep with her hand clasped in his and her head on his shoulder. After that, time seemed annihilated. Somewhere late in the night the train slowed abruptly with roar and jerk. It awakened Beryl, who, like a child, asked where she was. Keven kissed her, to her consternation and embarrassment.

On through the night rushed the train. Keven drowsily thought that at this rate he and Beryl would be married very soon indeed. Then all faded away. He awoke in the gray of dawn, to find that he had gone to sleep on Beryl's shoulder. Daylight came. Beryl presently told Keven that the train was running along a very pretty trout stream.

They had breakfast in the diner—a new experience for Beryl. She was all eyes, and so were a number of men who caught sight of her. No one appeared to notice Keven. In his Illahe suit, his plain flannel shirt, and with the black shield over his eye, he was not too prepossessing, he thought. But Beryl was too handsome, too flushed and radiant to escape close observation. On the way back to their car a hawk-eyed young man got between Keven and Beryl. He was very polite about opening doors. At the third platform Keven heard him accost Beryl. She replied promptly enough, but Keven could not distinguish what she said. At last they reached their seats in the day coach.

"Did you see that man?" she asked, with flashing eyes. "The fool!"

"What'd he say, Beryl?"

"He said, 'Dearie, haven't I seen you before?'"

"Ahuh. And what'd you answer to that?" replied Keven, with a grin.

"I said, 'You might have. I visited an insane asylum recently.'"

"I knew it—soon as we got out of the woods—men would run after you."

"Nonsense. Why should they?" rejoined Beryl, with heat in her cheeks.

"Beryl, you're so all-fired good-looking. Lord, but I'm proud of you! And jealous—whew! I'll bet I'll have ten fights on this trip."

And so they talked and gazed out of the window at the inspiring Oregon landscape, while the train flew on and the hours flew by. Then Portland, before they realized they were halfway there!

At precisely five-ten the taxi driver Keven had engaged

197

halted before a pretentious hotel. Keven hesitated. "Driver, I said a quiet, modest hotel."

"Boss, dis is modestest hotel in Portland. Shore, it's quiet, an' respectable, too."

Keven bade Beryl wait a moment. He went in with the baggage, checked it, and got a couple of addresses from the clerk. Then he ran back to Beryl. They drove off. At five-twenty they walked down the steps of a municipal building with a marriage license in their possession. And before six o'clock Beryl had a tiny circlet of gold round the third finger of her left hand.

The beautiful big city, the hurrying crowds, the canyon-like walls of the streets dazed Beryl. As for Keven, the climax of that journey had dazed him. They walked on. Glittering entrance to a restaurant caught Keven's eye. Strains of music floated out.

"Beryl, are you hungry?" he asked eagerly.

"Come to think of it, I believe I am."

"Can you dance?"

"I never tried with boys, but I've danced with girls."

Keven halted almost in the act of entering the place. "Gosh, I can't take you in there, I look like a hick."

That would not have mattered to Beryl. They wandered on and eventually found a modest little place to dine, where they sat in a stall, hidden on three sides. Beryl was opposite him, turning the ring on her finger. Her eyes were dark stars.

"How easy it was!" she murmured.

"What?" he queried.

"Getting married. I hope everything was all right. . . . Did I look queer?"

"You looked like an angel bestowing heaven upon a poor beggar. And that's just what happened. . . . Help me pick out something to eat."

"Is there any smoked steelhead?" asked Beryl merrily.

"See here, backwoods lady. You've got to eat lobster salad, caviar, mushrooms, and——"

"But they won't have that—that stuff here," interrupted Beryl, taking the menu. Sure enough, no sign of such fashionable dishes was there. They compromised on beefsteak and potatoes, bread and butter, ice cream and cake.

Night had fallen when they went out, but the streets were brilliant with colored lights. It seemed like fairyland.

"I've never been to a motion picture," announced Beryl, breathlessly. "Would you take me to see one, Keven?"

"Would I? Ha! Watch me."

The many street lights centered in a white-and-red sign which read *Their Wedding Night* in gorgeous letters.

"Oh," gasped Beryl, "I—I couldn't go in—here." She said that even before she saw any of the glaring posters of a sinuous siren wrapping herself round a lovesick swain.

Keven laughingly dragged her in, where amazement was added to shock. "I didn't know it'd be all dark. I—I like it. . . . Oh, Kev, look!"

Holding onto her, Keven found two empty seats, and when they were settled in them, he still possessed her hand. The picture was one of those fantastic and atrocious counterfeits of life which the producers foist upon twenty million lovers every night. But Beryl was mystified, affronted, enchanted. She laughed and she cried. Once after a climax, she whispered in Keven's ear; "It's perfectly terrible!" Keven whispered back in her ear. "But you're a married woman now!"

After the performance, and when they had walked at least a block, Keven asked:

"Did you like it, Beryl?"

"Oh, it was wonderful. . . . Crazy, and—and—Kev, if it hadn't been pitch dark in that place I'd have died. . . . Yes, I'm afraid I liked it."

"My word, it's going to be great to take you places!" ejaculated Keven, squeezing her arm. "Say, what was the name of that hotel?"

"What hotel?"

"Where we went first, and I left the baggage."

"I don't know—I didn't see any name."

"Gosh, I never looked!"

"What'll we do now?" asked Beryl, aghast.

"We sure are from Solitude. . . . Here's a cop. I'll describe the place. He can tell us."

Eventually they reached their hotel, tired and happy, with Beryl lagging a little, dragging at his arm, mute now where for long she had babbled like one of her mountain brooks.

Next morning they went out together, into a roseate world.

Beryl went to the oculist with Keven and waited in the outer room. Keven found himself well remembered. He sat in a darkened room, facing strange instruments, through which the oculist cast a pinpoint of white light upon his injured eye. He had to try to read letters of difficult sizes. He sat with his head in a brace and looked through bits of glass slid in a frame before him. And magically the moment arrived when he could see as well with his defective eye as with the other. That was a happy moment.

"Your general physical tone has greatly improved," said the doctor. "Likewise your eyesight. I will give you glasses for reading and close work. The right glass will be bifocal and quite strong. The left glass will have no power. I'll have them ready for you in a few days."

The oculist charged Keven sixteen dollars for the glasses, but refused anything for his services. Keven thanked him and rejoined Beryl. "Come. Ho, for that dentist! While my luck lasts!"

They found Dr. Ames in the same building. "Hello, Bell, how're the steelhead running?" was the genial doctor's greeting. And he certainly had two admiring and curious eyes for Beryl.

"Fine, Doctor. Twelve-pounders thick lately. . . . This—this is my—my wife, Beryl."

"I'm delighted to meet you, Mrs. Bell," said the doctor. "I didn't know my Rogue River informant had a wife. I fancy it's not been for long."

"About one day," replied Beryl shyly, and the ever-ready, telltale red spotted her velvety cheeks.

"You don't say! Well! My hearty congratulations! . . . Bell, there's a reason for you looking so greatly improved.

I'm glad. . . . Take a seat and wait a little. I'll get after you quick."

Keven had nerved himself for an ordeal, and when once in the operating chair he prepared for it.

After an examination, the dentist said: "Your mouth is in pretty fair condition. Ulcers gone. Very little stomatitis. We can go to work at once. And that's fine. I'll take a plaster impression first, before the tissue and bone become irritated. Then I'll have to burn and scrape. It'll hurt like hell."

"Go to it, Doctor. I can stand anything."

The doctor mixed plaster of Paris with water in a bowl. When it resembled whipped cream he poured it out into a metal cup, which he inverted and inserted in Keven's mouth, pressing it down hard. This did not hurt so much, but presently, as the plaster began to harden, Keven felt he would strangle. The doctor warned him not to swallow or cough or breathe through his mouth. When the plaster set it took considerable force to remove the cup, which came forth just in the nick of time for Keven.

"Gosh!" he exploded.

"That was nothing," replied the other cheerfully. "Wait till I tackle that bone." He repaired to his laboratory and presently returned with a plaster cast of the missing section of Keven's jaw. Over this he fitted soft wax and built it up. "I want to be careful to get the former fullness of your lip and the line of your cheek. You won't know yourself when it's done." He set the wax impression in place and bade Keven bite down naturally upon it. Then, with Keven's teeth set, the dentist rounded and trimmed the wax so that it filled out the flat and waving line of jaw which had been so hideous to Keven.

"This is like taking candy from the baby," said the dentist. "It's going to be easy to fix you up. . . . But now for the hell."

Cocaine helped some, but in spite of it Keven searched again the very depths of agony. The dentist feared necrosis. He bared the raw bone and scraped it. Blood flowed like water. He scraped and he dug and he chipped. Then he burned bone and tissue with something like fire. Lastly he packed and dressed the wounds. "Only

201

one more treatment like that. Then we're okay. Come tomorrow."

It was a wobbling, clammy-faced Keven that returned to Beryl.

"Oh, Kev, you've been hurt," she exclaimed anxiously.

"Hurt! Ump-umm! I'm only killed. . . . Beryl, that kick from the old cannon was nothing to what this kind gentle dentist did to me."

"Mrs. Bell, it was something of an operation, I admit," said the dentist. "But it was necessary. When it's over he'll be amply repaid."

Keven and Beryl went back to their hotel and stayed in for several hours, until his pain had ceased; then they went shopping. Beryl insisted on a complete new outfit for Keven. Protest was useless. He gave in despite misgivings as to Beryl's leaning toward extravagance. The well-tailored gray suit and accessories would be delivered to their hotel the following day. They still had an hour to look for something for Beryl. At the very outset this bade fair to be a stupendous task. The saleswoman, after the keen observance of her kind, brought forth gowns that dazzled Keven. But Beryl, though admitting their elegance, showed no disposition to try one of them on.

"But, darling, *this* must be an evening gown, or at least, something terribly nifty. It's to knock 'em dead in Grant's Pass," entreated Keven.

"Honey, I—I couldn't wear a dress with no top or sleeves in it," protested Beryl.

"Sure, you could. Why not?"

"It's indecent."

"Gosh! Well, maybe it is, but what do we care? If *I* can stand it, you ought to. You've got the loveliest neck and arms of any girl in the whole world. I'll be divided between pride and jealousy. . . . Beryl, please try on that shiny gold dress. Just to let me see how you look!"

"*That* one! Kev, there's not enough of it to cover half of me."

"Please try it on."

The saleswoman returned with more glittering fabrics. Beryl took up the shimmering gold thing and asked to try it on. She went away with the pleased saleswoman. Keven sat down, once more aware of the deep-seated throb in his jaw. He waited for what appeared a good while, and almost grew impatient. Then a vision glided into sight.

The vision turned out to be his own wife. Keven stared incredulously. Yes, this was Beryl. But so vastly transformed.

"Isn't she lovely, sir?" asked the saleswoman excitedly. "This gold suits her coloring."

"Kev, I tried it on—just to please you. But of course I—I couldn't take it," murmured Beryl.

"You're a queen!" he exploded.

"Do you—like me—in it?" she asked, and it was evident that his compliment accounted for her heightened color.

"Like you? Heavens!" And Keven found mere words inadequate.

"Kev, would you—buy it for me, if I would take it?" asked Beryl, quite composedly, with bright thoughtful eyes on his. "It's eighty-seven dollars. And slippers, stockings, etc., would fetch the cost to a hundred and over."

Keven never flinched. This was his wonderful bride, for whom nothing was too good. Her mere gesture repudiated the idea of cost.

"Well, I'll think it over and call tomorrow," said Beryl to the saleswoman. "It's too late to try on another today."

chapter twenty-one

EXCEPT FOR THE few trying hours in the dentist's chair the next few days were nothing less than enchantment for Keven Bell. The truth was that Beryl's unalloyed happiness seemed to substantiate facts which otherwise Keven could not have accepted. He took her everywhere, even to see a famed trout stream near the city. He quite forgot to be careful with money, and certainly Beryl did not help him to remember. Still she had not yet bought the dress that was to dazzle Keven's former friends and acquaintances of Grant's Pass.

He stopped at the oculist's office to pick up the new glasses. The happy moment when he first put them on came. Keven, hardly taking time to thank the oculist, rushed out to confront Beryl, unmindful of other people present in the waiting room.

"Beryl, that blank black place is gone!" he cried gleefully.

"Oh, splendid! How nice you look!"

The dental work, too, was completed at last. The artificial jaw and teeth of gold, platinum, and porcelain were inserted and felt comfortable. Keven ran his hand round his chin. Then he looked in the mirror an assistant held before him. He could not believe his eyes. Following the first flash of astonishment and delight, he thought of Beryl.

"Fine and dandy, Doc!" he ejaculated. "You've made a new man out of me. Gosh, I couldn't thank you if I tried. Hand over your bill now, quick. I've got to rustle back to the hotel. This job will sure please a little lady I know."

When Keven paid the bill he had only a few dollars left, but such was his state of elation that for the moment he did not even think of money. He rushed back to Beryl.

"It's done. . . . I'm all through. . . . What do you— think?" he panted, posing for her.

Beryl dropped whatever it was on her lap, and leaped up, her eyes glad.

"Kev! . . . Oh, you handsome man! I—I hardly know you. To think it would make such a difference! . . . I'm just too happy for words."

"Gosh, so'm I. But wait till I tell——"

She gave a little squeal and almost climbed on him, and kissed his chin, and the new line of his jaw, and lastly his lips in an abandon wholly unusual with her.

"There! I have been saving that," she whispered.

"Lord, but I love you, Beryl!" he cried, giving her an enormous hug. Then he added ruefully: "But listen, hon-

204

ey. It's great for us—to mend me up this way so I'm not ashamed for anyone to see you with me. But it took all the money we had left. Except this. . . . Three dollars."

"Oh," returned Beryl, not particularly impressed.

"Darling, you're a woman, all right. Money cuts no ice with you. But I'm darned sick. How'll I pay the hotel bill? Fortunately I had sense enough to buy round-trip railroad tickets. . . . We can't go to Grant's Pass. That is a disappointment. And the peach of an outfit for you! I did so want that. . . . Damn the luck!"

"Kev, are you swearing at me?" she asked demurely.

"No. I—I suppose I ought to thank God you're so good, so reasonable, so unselfish. It's all been so lucky for me. But I wanted something grand for you—I *wanted* it!"

He turned away so that she would not see the tears in his eyes.

"Honey, do you feel very badly?" she asked sweetly.

"Rotten! I'd rather you had the dress. Why didn't I make you buy it? The doctor would have trusted me."

"Look on the bed," said Beryl softly.

In surprise Keven turned as bidden. The bed appeared to be loaded down with a bewildering array of finery, in the midst of which shone the lacy golden gown he had so admired. He espied slippers and stockings to match. Then there was a blue traveling dress, a small blue hat, and gloves and shoes. And underneath all these shone silk lingerie.

"Isn't it lovely?" she asked innocently.

"Good heavens! Beryl, you didn't go in debt for all this stuff?"

"No. I—just bought it."

"Bought it! What with?"

"Well, naturally, it had to be done with money."

Keven sat down stunned. She looked so sweet and so pleased with the effect of her surprise.

"How much did all this cost?"

"I haven't figured up yet."

"Where'd you get the money? . . . Did your father give you more besides the wedding present, which, by the way, I spent on myself?"

"No. Dad gave me only the hundred dollars, which you had."

"Well, sweetheart, I hope you didn't rob a bank."

"I've had the money for a long time, Keven. . . . And I reckon I'd better give you what's left." Whereupon she extracted a roll of bills from her bag and handed it to Keven. "Don't look so scared, darling. It was honestly mine, and what's mine is yours."

"Thank you, Beryl," replied Keven huskily. "Was this a—a legacy?"

"Hardly," she said mysteriously.

"Did you work for this, too?"

"I suppose you'd say I worked Dad for it. Anyway I've saved it, a little at a time, during the four years you stayed away from me. I thought it might come in handy sometime. And it surely did. Behold my trousseau! And we're going to Grant's Pass."

"Oh, we are. . . . Is this *all* the money you had?"

"No, I've still enough left to buy you a rifle and the best fishing tackle to be had. . . . I wish you'd let me surprise you with them."

Keven counted the money she had placed in his hands. Nearly five hundred dollars!

"You see, Kev dear, we don't get married often. And we need a lot of things for our cabin. I plan to buy these at Grant's Pass and have them shipped to West Fork, where we can have them packed over to Solitude."

"By gosh! . . . I'm glad—I guess—but I'm sure flabbergasted," rejoined Keven, sitting down as if his legs had become weak.

"You *guess?* . . . Kev, I never knew any man would guess about feeling glad his wife had saved a little money."

"It is kind of churlish in me. Doggone it! . . . But I'm stumped."

What more he was besides being stumped he did not say. All he was sure of was that he was an extraordinarily fortunate young man. Once again he glanced at the finery on the bed.

"Beryl, you have excellent taste."

"I'd rather have a few really good things than a lot of

shoddy stuff. . . . As for the gold gown—that's for you. If only I can screw up courage to wear it! Perhaps I can."

"You bet you will. . . . Say, Beryl, what are you going to pack all this gorgeous stuff in?"

"I haven't had time yet to look for anything. A couple of strong grips might do."

"I think two of those heavy telescope cases with straps. They're nothing much for looks. But they'll stand packing across the mountains. Suppose I run out and buy a couple?"

"Do. While I begin to pack."

"I'll see about trains, too. We'll leave for Grant's Pass tonight."

"Oh, goody!" cried Beryl, clapping her hands like a child.

"It may not be so goody as I'd fondly hoped," returned Keven ponderingly. "I'd forgot about my arrest at Gold Beach."

"Arrest! You weren't explicit about that."

"I'm afraid there are a lot of things I never told you."

"What were you arrested for?" she queried, anxious dark eyes on him.

"Assault on Gus Atwell. I *did* tell you I punched him, for I distinctly remember you were very pleased. . . . Well, the sheriff at Gold Beach turned out a friend of mine. He wouldn't let them take me to Grant's Pass for trial. And the case was dropped."

"You think it might come up again if we go to Grant's Pass?"

"It probably would. But I believe we'll go anyhow. Beryl, I'm a different man now. I don't feel that I can let Atwell's enmity keep me away from my home town. I *am* innocent of what Atwell laid at my door. All I did was to knock him down. I don't believe I'd care if the case did come up again."

"I wouldn't, either. . . . But it never will, Kev, darling," she said, with one of her dazzling enigmatic smiles.

"Never? How do you know?"

"Well, it never will if you take *me* to Grant's Pass."

"Of course I'll take you. That's the main reason why I

want to go. But what will that have to do with the possibility of my arrest?"

"Kev, when Major Atwell sees me with you—that will be the end of his persecution of you."

"Indeed!" ejaculated Keven, almost stiffly. Just then Beryl reminded him of her father. Perhaps it was the Indian in her. She looked strong, resourceful, aloof. What a friend—what an enemy she would make!

"I'm pretty sure of it," she returned.

"May I ask why?"

"I know too much about Major Atwell."

"You mean the—the personal attentions he tried to force upon you, while you were at school in Roseburg?"

"No. That was nothing. To be sure he tried, but after that one time he saw me with Emily Carstone. And you bet he sneaked."

"Emily Carstone! Who's she?" exclaimed Keven, in a queer tone.

"She was my best friend in Roseburg."

"Any relation to that—that Carstone family in Washington?"

"A first cousin. Emily visited their ranch while the army training camp was there. That was early. But Emily said it was too swift for her. . . . A year later came the horrible disgrace. Five sisters ruined! Emily's father went out there, got the family away, and sold the ranch. . . . I know all about the affair. Emily told me. What's more her father told Major Atwell to stay away from Roseburg or he'd shoot him. That happened last May, just before I went back to Solitude. Now Major Atwell knows I know all this. And it strikes me the facts might be known in Grant's Pass by this time."

"Good heavens! Beryl, why in the world didn't you tell me this long ago? We talked about Atwell. I don't remember what else. But you had some hint of——"

"Yes, I did," interposed Beryl, her face flushing. "But I hated the whole thing. I didn't want to talk about it."

"You knew—all the time you knew Gus Atwell had laid his vile doings upon me!"

"All the time I knew, Kev. Also I knew what rot it was. Truth always comes out. No man can hide his crimes forever. Atwell is a—a—oh, I've no name dirty enough

208

for him. . . . And he'd just better look out or he'll have Emily Carstone's father and Daddy Aard to reckon with!"

Keven gazed mutely at Beryl. White-faced, with dark flashing passionate eyes bent upon him, she held him transfixed with her beauty and menace. Then she turned to the articles on the bed.

"I'm sorry it came up, Kev. But maybe that's just as well. . . . Now you run out and buy those bags for me. Don't stay long."

Pondering and bewildered, Keven left the hotel and went uptown to make the purchases. It seemed there was infinitely more reason for him to worship Beryl Aard than he had ever dreamed of. Moreover something strange was beating into his perplexity. Life or love or God was recompensing him for the misery and pain he had endured. He had been turned back from the precipice of failure— from the abyss of crime.

The following night late Keven and Beryl arrived in Grant's Pass. The long ride through beautiful Oregon and the gradual approach to his home and father, and to some thrilling adventure he anticipated, had heightened Keven's spirits to the utmost. He put aside dismaying and inexplicable questions. They drove to the best hotel, which was new to Keven, and there he laboriously registered as unintelligibly as possible. And he had the satisfaction of seeing that neither his face nor name had been recognized. He did not fail to note that Beryl, as usual, wherever they went, was the recipient of most admiring glances.

"Beryl, nobody knew me," said Keven with satisfaction, when they were alone in the spacious pleasant room. "Gosh, that clerk rubbered at you. And the other men, too."

"I didn't notice. But if I'm ever to be noticed I want it to be in your home town."

"Noticed? Good Lord, listen to you," declared Keven. "A blind man could see you're a bride. A beauty! A peach! A queen!"

"Thank you, Kev. That is fine on my honeymoon. But I fear you're a little hipped over my good looks."

"All right. I'm glad you're not conceited. And I'm glad you make such a hit with the men. . . . Doggone them, I'll show them you belong to me. I'm going to act differently here in my home town. I intend to hang onto you, fall all over you, gaze at you like a dying duck, hug and kiss you in public——"

"You can't scare me, Kev Bell. Go ahead. I dare you."

"You do? Very well, Mrs. Bell," he returned threateningly.

"I'd like nothing better than for your old girls to see you act that way. . . . And *I'll* show them."

"It's a bargain," cried Keven.

At sunrise he was up, gazing out of the window, from which he could see across the roofs of the town to the meadows, the pines, and the shining river, a ribbon of rose. What a magnificent thrill he sustained! He could look at the playgrounds of his boyhood with a new joy, with a surety that the regret and grief and bitterness of his first home-coming after the war had gone forever.

After a while he awoke Beryl.

"Wake up, angel. And put on that blue outfit. We're going to start knocking 'em dead."

"What time is it?" yawned Beryl, stretching her round arms.

"It's late. Eight o'clock."

"So late! Well, chase yourself, you wild-eyed bridegroom! I can't get up with you staring there."

"Gosh, but I adore you!" cried Keven, kissing the red lips. "I just know I'll come to presently and find this all a dream. . . . I'll wait for you downstairs in the lobby."

Keven took a last glance at himself in the mirror, to make sure that the immeasurable improvement in his features was real. It also reflected the well-cut gray suit, and the fact that never before in his life had he looked like this.

"Vain thing!" giggled Beryl, and as he rushed away toward the door: "But you are handsome."

Downstairs Keven found a number of men in the lobby, none of whom he recognized. He lounged about, apparently with casual interest, when inside he was bursting with excitement and glee. He walked out to the street corner and stood there marveling. There seemed to be a glamour over the whole world this day. Then he returned to the lobby. Beryl would be prompt and he did not want to miss her. Presently she entered and he was hard put to it to contain himself. Fine feathers did make fine birds. But he was unprepared for her blushing, adoring reception of his approach. At Portland she had been reserved, almost shy. Here she was a bride, wholly oblivious of anyone save him. It gave Keven a shock, but he liked it.

On the way into the dining room he whispered: "You look like a million dollars."

"If I do you're the millionaire."

All through a delightful breakfast they talked after that fashion. Then Keven said: "Gosh, let's get down to brass tacks. What'll we do now?"

"You'll go to your father at once."

"Yes, but oughtn't you come, too?"

"No. You see him first. Don't forget you said you were supposed to be dead. . . . Kev, I've an idea. Show me where to find your friend Minton. I'll go in and ask to see fishing tackle. He'll not know me from Adam."

"That'd be great. Gosh, I'd like to see you."

"It'll be all the better after I work him up, so to speak. I'll say, very loftily, 'I wish to purchase some fine tackle for my husband. He is a poor fisherman, but it's my wish that he possess a splendid outfit. Have you any really *good* tackle? Leonard rods, you know, and English reels, lines, leaders. He doesn't care for common things.'"

"Oh, that's rich!" gurgled Keven. "It'll be immense. Minton is crazy about pretty women anyway. Then, just when he's fallen, I'll bob in and chirp: 'Howdy, Mint, old geezer?' And he'll shout, 'My Gawd—is it a ghost? By thunder, it's Kev Bell! We thought you dead!' . . . And I'll say, 'Terribly exaggerated, Minton. I'm fine. . . . Meet my wife.'"

"I don't know," replied Beryl dubiously. "That about his being crazy about women! Is he very bold?"

"Bold? He's the mildest and kindest man you ever met."

"Very well, then, let's go," said Beryl, once more reassured. "You see your Dad. . . . Oh, I hope he's well. Then I'll meet you at Minton's. After that we'll buy our furniture."

"Okay. But see here, honey, you'll need some money to buy the tackle from Minton," rejoined Keven, his hand going to his pocket. "But I'll not give you much."

Beryl waved this offer aside. "Thanks. I've got some money left. Anyway you'd never give me enough."

"You've got some left!" he ejaculated.

"Sure."

"Beryl!"

"Kev!" she imitated impertinently. "Come, we're wasting time."

"See here, this—this is too much," declared Keven doggedly.

"What is—my little dab of money?"

"No, not the money itself. But your having it. . . . Beryl, I'm going to get angry presently. I'll be thinking I married you for your money."

"All because for nearly five years you had a loving, faithful, saving sweetheart—who's now your wife. . . . I declare men are funny."

They were now out on the street. Keven surrendered in despair. Then he pointed out Minton's store across the street. "I'll meet you there in a half hour," he said and fled.

He was so thoughtful that he did not look to see if he met anyone who knew him, and before he realized how far he had gone he was down the side street almost to his father's home. The drab little house had not changed; nothing had except the leaves of the vine that trailed over the porch, and they were dyed the russet hue of autumn. No one answered his knock, and the door was locked. Keven went around to the back. Then he heard hammering in the shop. Approaching he was able to reach the open door without being seen. His father, apparently not a day older, was at work on a boat.

"Hello, Dad," he shouted, stepping in. "How's tricks?"

Bell had his back to the door. He stiffened. The hammer fell. Slowly he wheeled, calling *"Kev!"* even before he espied his visitor. Then his gray old head jerked up, his eyes lightened. "My son! My son! . . . I never believed you dead."

The moment ensuing was more poignant than Keven had expected, and it was he who showed the most emotion.

"You're changed—well—a new man! . . . Why, Keven, what does this mean? An' the prosperous look of you! Son, I'd have thanked God to see you back home anyhow or any way, but——"

"Dad, take a peek at my new jaw," interrupted Keven, drawing down his lip. "Gold and platinum——porcelain teeth! Some class, eh? And look at my bad eye. I'll bet you can't tell which was the bad one."

"My boy, I can't, indeed."

"I've gained forty-eight pounds. Can you see it on me?"

"That didn't strike me, Kev. But now I do. . . . An' dressed in the height of fashion! For heaven's sake, explain."

"It's a long story, Dad. I'll save it for some other time. Enough to say, when I was down and out—a lost wretch ready to—well, never mind what—I met someone who changed me, body and soul."

"A woman!" gasped Bell.

"A girl. She's the loveliest—the noblest—Oh, wait till you see her. . . . I'm well! I'm happy! I'm married! I've a job!"

The older man sat down quite suddenly upon the boat he was building, overcome by Keven's wild utterances, and the manifest proof of some of them, at least.

"Dad, I'll get back my good name, too," added Keven triumphantly.

That stirred the old man.

"*Son*, you've *got* it back," he replied ringingly. "Garry Lord saw to that, God bless him!"

"*Garry Lord!* . . . Dad, what're you saying? . . . I saw Garry drown. With my own eyes I saw him."

"You thought so. But you didn't. Garry's alive."

"Alive!" cried Keven huskily. "Are you sure? It would be hideous—if—if——"

"Son, he was here last night," announced the father, his tone carrying absolute conviction.

Keven threw up his hands to send his hat flying. His face was beaded with clammy drops.

"More to thank God for! More! Where will it end? I'm—just—knocked—flat."

"Listen," said Bell, with the hurry of a man keen to give joy. "Garry didn't drown. The skiff floated out to sea. Next day it was sighted by a woman—daughter of a fisherman named Coombs, on his way to Crescent City. They picked Garry up, took your net an' let the skiff go. Garry had a bad knock on his head, but he recovered. He married the young woman, Mary Coombs. But that was afterward. As Garry told it he knew you were dead, murdered by a fisherman named Mulligan. Meanwhile, Mulligan's body was found, with your knife sticking in his throat. Then Garry knew you had stabbed Mulligan in that fight. He swore he would clear your name. But he laid low at first, working it out. Atwell went to Gold Beach—openly accused you of murder, an' sought to lay the stealin' of fish upon you. After a time Garry got proof of where that net came from an' who sold it to Mulligan. He even got proof about the eight-inch mesh at the top of the net, which Mulligan had added to it. Garry went back to Gold Beach an' stole another such net. He laid a trap for those crooked market fishermen. He had that Gold Beach sheriff hide on shore an' watch an' listen. Garry led the fishermen ashore, where, in the midst of the fight, the sheriff pounced down on them. One of them was Mulligan's pardner. The sheriff arrested him, made him confess to crooked nettin'. . . . Well, Garry an' the sheriff came here to Grant's Pass an' laid the facts before Judge Parsons an' the new chief of police. Garry told his story. It was believed. It went all over town. It cleared your name an' it cast a dark shadow on that of the man who has hounded you—who implicated you in that infamous Carstone scandal. . . . Kev, it is significant that Atwell is no longer associated with Brandeth—nor engaged to Rosamond."

"The world is coming to an end!" raved Keven, pacing the shop, tearing at his hair. "Oh, Garry! . . . What a man! . . . I see the hand of God in all this. . . . Where is Garry—where can I find him?"

"He runs a little fish market here, three days a week

214

an' another three days in Crescent City. Coombs supplies the fish, Garry sells them. They're doin' well. He'll be at his place on Thursday, this week. I told you he married Coombs' daughter, didn't I? She's a rosy-cheeked buxom girl, an' she manages Garry, believe me. She told me she allowed him only one spree a month."

Keven shouted his mingled mirth and joy. Then suddenly he remembered Beryl.

"Dad, I gotta beat it. I'll see you again today. I'll fetch her around." Then he rushed out and down the path to the street. And only when he saw that pedestrians were remarking his singular actions did he correct them. By the time he arrived at Minton's store he had gained some semblance of outward composure, nevertheless his mind was full of wild, whirling thoughts.

Keven peeped in before entering. Beryl stood in the center of the store, whipping a trout rod with no uncertain hand. Minton wore a most extraordinary expression upon his genial face. He was certainly fascinated by this new and lovely customer.

"This rod is no good," Beryl was saying. "It's too pudgy. My husband——"

"Pardon, lady," replied Minton, "that rod is good. It's a Leonard. There's no better made."

"I like the Grangers better," replied Beryl, laying the rod on the counter, where a pile of disordered tackle gave evidence of the condition of Minton's mind. "I'm sorry you have only two. They'll last my husband about two days."

"What kind of a—er—fisherman is he?" asked the dealer. "Is he an expert?"

"He thinks he is. But I can beat him. Of course I know the river."

"What river, Madam, may I ask? Rivers are different, and your river——"

"The Rogue."

"You know the Rogue?" queried Minton, beaming in spite of his astonishment. Manifestly he was learning that he did not know all about the famous river.

"I was born on it. I know every stone from Winkle Bar to Illahe."

Keven thought it was about time to enter, even if he

215

could have waited longer. So he rushed in like the wind.

"Hey, Mint, old boy, how are you?" he yelped happily.

Minton turned pale. His eyes popped out. His jaw dropped.

"My God! . . . Who're you?"

"Well, I like that! Don't know me! My feelings are hurt."

"It can't be—Kev Bell."

"Why can't it, I'd like to know?"

"But—he's dead."

"Dead nothing. Do I look dead?" retorted Keven.

Minton whooped and knocked everything off the counter getting at Keven.

"You ole fishin' son of a gun! Come back to life! . . . Oh, boy! . . . Kev, I never was so glad in my born days. And just look at you!"

"Well, I reckon I'll have to forgive you, since you are so glad," replied Keven, touched at the warmth of Minton's welcome.

Then the tackle dealer remembered his waiting customer, who stood there, far from calm, if he had not been too excited to notice.

"Excuse me, Madam," he apologized. "This gentleman is an old friend. He was reported dead. Naturally I was somewhat upset to have him drop out of the clouds, as it were. . . . Now, if you please, we'll get back to——"

"Hey, stop flirting with my wife," bellowed Keven fiercely.

Minton halted as if he had been lassoed. He was thunderstruck. Keven's ferocious aspect and Beryl's blushes caused him to sag in his tracks.

"Oh, Kev," murmured Beryl.

Keven laughed till his face was convulsed. When he recovered he espied the paralyzed Minton leaning against the counter for support.

"Beryl, this is my good friend, Minton, whom you have heard me speak of often. . . . Mint, old top, meet my wife."

"I'm very happy to meet you, Mr. Minton," replied Beryl, overcoming her confusion.

216

"Wife—husband! . . . Say, you put up a job on me," burst out Minton. "Of all the surprises! . . . Mrs. Bell, I am delighted to make your acquaintance. . . . Kev, you old wizard, you're about the luckiest man on earth. How'd you do it? You get chased out of Grant's Pass under a cloud. You get pinched at Gold Beach. Then you're drowned. Then your home town clears your reputation. Now you bob up well, handsome, prosperous-looking, with a queen for a wife!"

"Gosh, it is a fairy story, Mint," declared Keven. "But no wonder. Look at my fairy!"

"I've been looking."

Between Minton and Keven they gave Beryl a very flattering if embarrassing few moments. Then Keven remembered his great news.

"Oh, I almost forgot. Beryl, I've got the most wonderful news. Dad is well and fine. I sure surprised him, but he said he'd never believed I was dead. And listen to this. Garry Lord is alive! Some girl saved his life. He married her. If that doesn't beat me. . . . Beryl, Dad says Garry cleared my name here in Grant's Pass."

"Bless him!" exclaimed Beryl.

"Mint, has Dad got that straight?" went on Keven anxiously.

"You just bet he has," declared Minton emphatically. "It's late in the day, Kev, but the old town has made amends. You'll be a lion. And when they see your wife—good night!"

chapter twenty-two

KEVEN AND BERYL spent most of the rest of that day in the stores of Grant's Pass. Beryl did the buying, while Keven accompanied her, a silent partner. If she had wanted to purchase the moon he would have made no objection and would have believed in her ability to get it. She bought furniture, utensils, and other household articles, a host of little things to make a cabin comfortable, and groceries, canned fruit, and vegetables. Then she spent as much time in a bookstore as she had at Minton's, and considerably more money. But at last she turned to Keven with a relieved and happy smile.

"Kev, now I *am* broke. But oh, wasn't it fun? I've had this in mind for years. Won't we have a dandy cabin? Won't we have a happy time this winter?"

"Well, Beryl, if we don't it'll not be for lack of work on my part, and prayers, and devotion to you," he said fervently.

"I'll have it all shipped to West Fork at once, so it'll be ready to pack when we get there. I'd say about ten pack horses, Kev. Won't Dad whoop when he sees them bobbing down the trail?"

"Dad won't be the only one who'll whoop."

"I'm sure we've forgotten something. . . . Oh, yes, your rifle."

"So we have. I'll need that. And some shells. A pair of heavy boots—a raincoat. Rubber boots, too, and gloves . . . . Beryl, you've made me careless with money. Gosh, when I think——"

"Don't think," she interrupted sweetly. "Just be gay. You're so—so nice then. You run along. I'll leave instructions here about packing and shipping our goods. Then I'll go back to the hotel."

Keven hurried back down Main Street towards Minton's. It was late in the afternoon, with the weather perfect. The sidewalks were thronged. A string of automobiles flashed down the street. Keven expected to meet someone he knew, but he did not. He noted, however, that he was observed by many people, quite curiously, it seemed. He was glad to escape into the comparative safety of Minton's store.

"Say, Mint, I forgot a rifle, ammunition, gloves, boots, and what not," he announced gaily.

"Suppose I just sell you the store," replied his friend beamingly.

"Doggone if you oughtn't. Isn't Beryl a wonder?"

218

"Kev, she surely is, and she is shrewd, too. She's a good sport, but don't you get an idea anybody can trim her."

While they were selecting Keven's concluding purchases the telephone rang. Minton answered the call: "Hello. . . . Who? . . . Yes, he's here."

He returned to Keven with a bright face. "Call for you, Kev. That's the tenth person who's rung me up to ask if you were really alive and in town. Men have run in here, too, asking the same. The news of your return has spread like wildfire. But nobody seems to ask about your wife. Gee, this is immense."

"Call for me? Wonder who," returned Keven, and walking across the store he took up the receiver and said, "Hello."

"Is this Mr. Keven Bell?" asked a woman's voice, rather low.

"Yes, I'm Mr. Bell. Who is this calling?"

"Kev—don't you—know my voice?" came the query, in unmistakable agitation.

A queer shock ran through Keven.

"No, I'm sorry, I don't," he replied hesitatingly. "Still your voice seems familiar."

"Oh, it should be—you fickle soldier. . . . Guess."

"I—I'm not good at guessing."

"Rosamond!"

Keven nearly dropped the receiver. He looked up wildly, to see Minton waving his hands in the most ridiculous manner.

"Rosamond! . . . Not Rosamond Brandeth?" he ejaculated weakly.

"Yes, indeed it is. . . . Oh, Kev, I'm half crazy. I was in a car just a few minutes ago—when I saw you. I nearly fainted. You know—don't you? We thought you dead. You don't know, of course, that that nearly broke my heart. . . . Kev, I—I made a mistake. I found it out—only too late, I thought. But surely it isn't, now you've come to life. . . . I broke with your old Major here long ago. He's a flat tire, Kev. . . . But heavens, I can't go on like this over the phone. I must see you—to tell you everything. May I run down there in my car and pick you up?"

"Aw—I—we—thanks awfully, Rosamond," floundered

219

Keven. "But I was just leaving. I'm in a rush. Tomorrow maybe——"

"Oh, so! I get you, Keven. . . . In a rush, eh? Didn't I see you with a girl?"

"I surely walked down the street with one. You might have seen me."

"Same old devil with the girls, eh?"

"Not exactly."

"Bah! Don't try to kid me. Who was she?"

"Which one do you mean?" countered Keven, absolutely powerless to tell her what he should have told her. "Was it the—the blonde?"

"No. She was dark. And jealous as I am, I've got to hand the laurel to her."

"Thank you."

"Well, you matched her for looks, if you ask me. . . . Kev, where can I see you, quick? I'll run down to the hotel. . . . Don't try to stop *me,* Kev Bell. So long."

Keven fell away from the telephone, to gaze in consternation at the grinning Minton.

"Rosamond Brandeth! What do you know about that?"

"It's great. It tickles me pink."

"But it doesn't tickle me. It scares me limp. . . . Mint, she wants to make up with me."

"Let her want. It'll do her good. But to be square with Rosamond, I'm bound to tell you she gave Atwell the gate last spring, and she's running pretty decent—for her."

Suddenly Keven felt the very roots of his hair stiffen and freeze.

"My Lord! If she happened to meet Beryl! She'd cook my goose."

"Not with that little lady, I'll gamble. Buck up, Kev. Hang round here with me till after six. That'll dodge her. Of course you'll run into her while you're in town. You ought to be glad to. And make a point of having Beryl with you. . . . Now let's get back to guns and things. I advise a 30 Gov't 1906 Winchester for that mountain country. You want a high-power rifle, with flat trajectory and long range. The 30 takes several grades of shells."

In the interest of his requirements, Keven recovered his equilibrium and his gay spirits. He spent an hour with

Minton and, finally making his choice, he paid the bill and asked that the articles be sent to the hotel. Whereupon he left, promising to see Minton on the morrow. Among the cars parked in front of the hotel was a beautiful little roadster of a make unknown to Keven. As he came abreast of it a smartly dressed young woman came out of the lobby. In one flash Keven recognized Rosamond, the same attractive dashing creature she had always been.

He halted to meet her, hat in hand, sure of himself before the watching idlers.

"How do you do, Rosamond?" he said, bowing, and he met the hand she extended.

"Well, Kev Bell! Hello, you lost soldier," she replied, with apparent cordiality, and drew him to the edge of the pavement where the bright car was parked. There she looked reproachfully at him. "I went into the lobby here and asked for Keven Bell. They sent down your wife. . . . Why didn't you *tell* me you were married and not let me make a damn fool of myself?"

"You didn't give me a chance," protested Keven, deeply embarrassed.

"Bunk! You didn't have the nerve," she returned scornfully. "But I can take my medicine. Serves me right. I didn't appreciate you when I had you. She's a peach, Kev. I wish you joy."

She shut the door and drove away, leaving Keven standing there, bareheaded and stricken. Remembering Beryl, he ran into the hotel and up the stairs. He found Beryl lying across the bed face down. A moment he stood aghast, conscience-stricken. Then all the sense and wit and nerve he ever possessed rushed to his aid. This was the crisis of his life. He turned the key in the lock.

"Beryl," he called, bending over the bed. She was not weeping. Her body appeared stiff. He shook her, then lifted her to a sitting position. Light from the window fell upon her face. It was white. And her eyes, at sight of him, became blue-black blazing orbs, so fierce with the primitive passion of her blood inheritance that he almost quailed.

"Flirt! Liar! Leave me, before I kill you," she cried, with indescribable bitterness.

221

Keven reproached himself. Why had he not told her? But staggered as he was, he did not weaken. This was the hour when he must win or lose, and he swore he would never lose. That would be too horrible. It would be no less than death. Still he never knew what guided him. Falling on his knees, he gripped her hands.

"Beryl, what did she tell you?" he asked.

"She asked when I had met you," replied Beryl, in a low voice. "I told her. . . . Then she informed me you made love to her—engaged yourself to marry her—*after* you left me at Solitude. . . . I told her she lied. She laughed in my face. . . . Oh, God, she could afford to laugh. . . . Keven, you are free to go back to her. She wants you. I *felt* it. . . . And I—I don't."

"Darling, don't——"

"How dare you call me that?" she cried furiously, as if stung.

"Well, you are—my darling wife," he said, in earnest simplicity.

"Is it *true?*"

"Is what true?"

"That you—you made up to her after the week you spent with me—four years and more ago—at Solitude?"

"Beryl, to my shame it is true," he replied hurriedly. "I——"

"Then go. I hate you!"

"But listen. Surely you will hear my excuse—if it be one. . . . I fished with you at Solitude that week long ago—played with you—made love to you—oh, I took liberties with you. And then like the wild, careless, crazy boy I was I rode away and forgot you. I became infatuated with Rosamond Brandeth. In the excitement of leaving to go to training camp, I—I proposed to her. And she accepted me. Then I went away. As I might have expected—with her, out of sight out of mind. She never wrote. Then I was injured. I lay between life and death for months. Two years I spent in hospitals. Then I was mustered out—sent home—you know the rest. I became an outcast here in my home town. I assaulted Atwell and fled. You remember when I passed through Solitude on my way to Gold Beach. There——"

"Oh, I do remember!" she moaned. "But I didn't know *why* you would not stop."

She rocked to and fro on the bed, her hands clinging to his, her eyes dilating.

"There I went from—bad to worse," continued Keven shudderingly, yet he gathered hope with the sense of his power over her. "You know how Garry and I were nagged and cheated, our labor made useless. Atwell was back of that. Then came the night when I killed Mulligan and thought Garry was lost. I fled up the river, my one resolve to shoot Atwell before they caught me. . . . *You* met me at Solitude. *You* stopped me there. *You* saved me. . . . But you know it all. Memory slowly came back—and hope and faith and health. Love, too, Beryl. I had never loved Rosamond Brandeth. I was only a boy. It was nothing—at least nothing—a candle flame before the sun, compared to my love for you. Once or twice, late in the summer I felt that I should have told you. But I didn't. I just didn't. It was cowardly of me. But I hated to hurt you. That's all, Beryl. You and Solitude saved me— changed me. I couldn't go on without you. If you can't— forgive me—I'll walk straight out—into the river."

He ended brokenly, beseechingly. Beryl loosened his hold of her hands. Suddenly she drew his head to her breast.

"I believe you, Kev, I forgive," she sobbed. "But, oh, how could you do it!"

Next morning they sought out Garry Lord. They had located his shop, a stall-like little compartment between two stores just off the main street. They were waiting for Garry to open up, watching from a doorway. Promptly at eight o'clock an ice wagon stopped before the place and unloaded ice on the sidewalk. Soon after that, the sturdy market fisherman appeared, ice tongs in his hand, and dragged in the cakes of ice.

"Now, Beryl," said Keven eagerly, "you go first. Walk right in on Garry. Tell him you want to buy some steelhead. Say your husband loves steelhead and won't eat anything else in the fish line. Look at Garry's big sign, 'Terms Cash.' That's like Garry. Well, after he wraps up the steelhead you tell him you haven't any money and ask him to trust you. You'll get some kick out of this. Then I'll amble in."

Keven went down the opposite side of the narrow street and watched Beryl enter the store to accost Garry. She was a capable actress, and evidently her appearance struck Garry as Keven had calculated it would. Then Keven crossed the street. When he entered the open door of the spick-and-span little shop Gary was behind the counter, his weather-beaten face shining, and he was wrapping up fish.

"I had a pard once who loved steelhead like this husband of yours," Garry was saying. "I'm sorry he's hard up. But you shore don't look it. All the same, lady, I'd trust *you* for anythin'."

"Oh, thank you, so much," murmured Beryl, and very likely she was making eyes at the hypotized Garry. "I knew you were a gentleman and a good sport."

"You did? How'd you know that?"

"I had only to see you once."

Garry fell. He looked it. Blushing like a girl, he replied: "Lady, I—I'm a married man—but——"

Just then Keven picked up a small trout from the window shelf and threw it at Garry with a whoop. Garry looked up to see the missile at the same instant he saw Keven.

Bam! The fish took him squarely in the middle. Garry doubled up and froze in that position.

"Say, you upriver salmon ketcher," yelled Keven, "are you trying to make a date with my girl?"

Beryl trilled out her merry laugh. But for Garry the situation held no humor.

"*My—Gawd!* . . . Who're you?" he gasped, shaking like a leaf. His dark rugged countenance turned a greenish white.

The fun of it for Keven suddenly ceased. The agony of appeal in Garry's faithful blue eyes was too much to bear.

"Pard. Don't—you know me?" he asked huskily.

Garry began to jump and yell like a maniac. "Mary! Mary! I got 'em again. I knowed I laid off the bottle too quick. . . . *Mary!*"

A door at the back of the shop quickly opened to

disclose a buxom young woman, whose ruddy pleasant face wore a look of concern.

"What ails you, man?" she demanded severely.

"I swear I ain't had nothin', sweetie," replied Garry, who reacted significantly to her presence. "But I either got 'em again or the dead has come to life. Look at that feller. Is he there, Mary, or am I seein' things?"

Keven stepped forward. "Gary, old pard, it *is* Kev. Come back to life in more ways than one. And this is Beryl, my wife."

Then for Keven, and surely for the two watching women, there dawned the realization that for some of the grief and longing in life there was recompense.

On the long ride over the mountain ridges, above the flaming canyons, Keven and Beryl lived over their three wonderful days in Grant's Pass. Dreams had come true. Hopes that had seemed vain were fulfilled. They hardly exchanged a word until they came abruptly out of the forest, upon the open mountainside above Winkle Bar.

In the sunset flush of gold and red the shining, singing river was revealed, as a promise fulfilled, as a goal reached. They sat long on their horses watching, listening, while the sun sank. Then when they started down the trail Keven raved and Beryl babbled.

Darkness overtook them when they were about abreast of Missouri Bar. By the time they reached Mule Creek Canyon they were talked out. Thereafter they rode on in blissful sillence, always aware of their river.

It was eleven o'clock when they arrived at Solitude. Old Moze gave tongue, and his deep rolling bay awoke the echoes of the steep slopes. The other hounds chimed in, making the welkin ring.

"Hyar, you prodigals," called Aard from his window. "All well with you?"

"All well, Daddy," sang Beryl, in tired happy tones. "Ten pack mules on the trail, due tomorrow."

"All well, indeed," rang out Keven, hoarsely, and that ended the strength of his voice for this never-to-be-forgotten day.

They slept in Keven's cabin. When Keven awoke the sun was up, and a golden-purple glory poured in door and windows. Beryl lay asleep, her dark pure profile and black hair outlined against the pillow. Keven hovered over her, possessed of a longing to kiss her awake. But he tiptoed out, to encounter Aard in the yard.

"Wal, bless my stars, son! You look made over new. Honeymoons must agree with you."

"My Lord, but it's been great," exclaimed Keven. "But I'll let Beryl have the joy of telling you. . . . Now Aard, it's enough for me to say I've thanked God a thousand times for guiding me to Beryl and you. . . . Give me work. I owe Beryl a lot of money. It doesn't matter how long it takes to pay her back. But I must get on the job. Only she won't let me help you trap fur. I'm sorry, but I can't go against her wishes."

"I reckoned she wouldn't. Wal, it ain't so important. Any hurry about this hyar job?"

"Hurry? I guess yes. Right now I want it settled. What with your accumulating stock and the growing orchards there's plenty of work. Then I'll branch out for myself, some way or other."

"Wal, son, I'm glad you're so keen about it," replied Aard, his piercing eyes on Keven. "I've a job you haven't reckoned on. Come along."

Wonderingly Keven followed the trapper out of the yard, past the first orchard, and up the creek trail to the heavily wooded bench. Aard crossed the gully on the boulders, and taking to a fallen fir tree he walked its long length, presently to step down into another trail, well defined and deep. It led to a shallow gully, out of which a tiny brook ran to leap down the mountainside. The timber was heavy here, forming thick shade. They proceeded up the brook, soon to come to banks of reddish-yellow earth, where there were unmistakable evidences of placer mining. Keven's curious groping mind began to be illumined.

"Son, this claim pays about five dollars a day, workin' six hours," said Aard quietly. "I never work it in summer, because packers or prospectors ridin' the trail would see muddy water an' get curious. But it's safe from November till April."

Keven had no voice to answer. But he was thinking this must solve the mystery of the Aards. Presently Aard drew some brush carefully from in front of a hole in the slope of the ridge above the brook. It was a tunnel—a shaft like hundreds he had seen up and down the river.

"This is another claim of mine," went on Aard. "I've only dug in about sixty feet. Average cleanup a day from ten to fifteen dollars. I'm bound to admit it gets a little richer the farther I go in. There's a chance of runnin' into a pocket of gold. In which case—wall, enough said. But there's moderate work hyar for years. Good wages, an' shore the chance of a strike. Though I never gamble on that."

Keven found it convenient to sit down on a stone. His legs wobbled and there was a riot in his breast.

"Aard—your trapping is only a blind?" he queried.

"Sure is. But I like the woods. When I was a boy, huntin' an' trappin' got into me. . . . I find it advisable to keep them up. Years ago, as you know, there was a big company placer minin' across the river. They gave this place the name Solitude. But that company was crooked. Prospectors have dug around hyar some since, mostly pannin' down by the river. They never struck anythin' good. So I've had this all to myself. An' I've worked to keep it so. Shore these claims are on my land. I proved up on this land years ago an' someday will get my patent from the government. So we're safe. But, son, we don't want the peace of Solitude broken."

"No—indeed," said Keven thickly.

"So, son, this is your job, an' I reckon you needn't worry none about your debt to Beryl."

"Oh, that girl! She drove me near crazy. Every little while, when I was distracted about our expenses, our extravagances, she'd laugh and dig up more money. If only she had told me!"

"Well, she had her way. An' that was to surprise you. Now, Kev, you're in the family. Hyar's your job. But don't get gold-mad an' spoil it. Don't work too much. Wintertime is enough, when the rain an' snow fall to keep the ground wet. Our wants are reasonable. Shore you'll need to take Beryl out a month or so every year. I'm right glad you've come back to us, for my sake same as the lass'."

227

Keven was deeply moved. "Aard, what can I say—what can I *do?*" he queried.

"Wal, you needn't say nothin'," returned the trapper. "An' shore you see what there is to do. Make my lass happy. I know you can. I've seen that ever since you got well. Before, I had my doubts. Beryl is like her mother. Just love her, Kev. That's all. An' Solitude will be—wal, Solitude for many years to come."

They worked their way back to the creek trail and began the descent. Keven halted at the open spots to look. Indian summer had fallen on the valley. He felt that he might be seeing it through magnified and glory-hued glasses. But the colors were really there. Black sheered up the dense slopes of firs, without a break, clear to the blue sky. But that was straight across the valley to the vast mountain wall. On Keven's side it was a broken slope, not at all forbidding. And here Indian summer reigned. No eye could take in all that color without being blinded to actualities. But by limiting his sight to this slope or that bench, to canyon and ridge and ravine, to open oak knolls and stretches of madroña, to any of a thousand vistas, Keven made some approach to appreciation of the glory of Solitude. He seemed surrounded by bright areas. Gold now encroached upon the green, and both were slashed by red, by cerise, by flame, by magenta, by scarlet. Winding bands of yellow bordered the river, their continuity broken by gray amber-mossed, brown-ferned, red-vined rocks. A drowsy warm sultry air mantled the valley, and far up, near the bend, the smoky haze began, deepening to purple.

Once more in the enclosure Keven espied Beryl sitting on the porch of his cabin, her dark head bent. He saw the glint of a fishing rod.

Aard drew Keven into his living room and directed his attention to a rude bookcase built along one of the logs.

"See anythin' queer?" he asked.

"No," replied Keven wonderingly.

Aard shoved the books to one end of the shelf. This disclosed a section of log, apparently identical with the other timbers of the cabin. But Aard inserted his finger in a knothole and shoved aside a cunningly concealed slide.

The log was partly hollow. Inside reposed a number of gray buckskin bags, neatly tied and tagged, and significantly bulging. Aard removed one.

"Heft it," he directed Keven.

Keven's unprepared hand sagged markedly.

"Gold!" he whispered.

"Wal, it ain't anythin' else. Son, I reckon we can keep the wolf away from the door. . . . Now go out an' fetch Beryl in to breakfast."

Keven slowly crossed the yard like a man in a trance. He approached Beryl, gazed down upon her. Old brown blouse, overalls, heavy shoes, all the worse for water and wear, signified her intentions this first morning at home after her honeymoon. Her lap was full of fishing tackle, comprising envelopes full of flies, packets of leaders, reels and lines—a showy assortment. She was examining a shiny fly rod, which she had not yet jointed. These articles were part of the precious pack she would not trust to the mule drivers they had engaged at West Fork.

"Morning, old dear. Gosh, you look funny," she said brightly, and this was one of the occasions when she imitated his peculiarities of speech.

"So I've married an heiress?" he asked, in awed accents, putting his hands in his pockets to keep them off her.

"So Dad's told you? . . . Kev, I'm afraid you *have* married an heiress—in a small way. Aren't you glad?" She seemed somewhat concerned about this amazing circumstance, though there shone a twinkle in her eyes.

"No gold could make you more precious, Beryl. I'm so happy that—that——"

"Oh, so am I. Isn't it lovely to be home again? Indian summer at Solitude! And I've come back your wife! Dear God, I don't know why I deserve to be so happy."

Keven knew, but he could not find words to express his knowledge.

"Hey, you turtledoves," called Aard. "Come to breakfast."

Keven listened with many a thrill to Beryl's recital of their trip to Portland and Grant's Pass. And Aard, with eyes both glad and sad, lived in her story over his own poignant past.

"Come down to the river and watch me try out my new rod," invited Beryl afterward.

On the way down the trail she turned to Keven with soft dark eyes.

"I'm sorry for Rosamond Brandeth. She found out too late that she loved you best."

"Don't waste your pity, Beryl."

"Well, if you made love to her like you did to me—and villain that you were, you must have!—I don't see how she could ever, *ever* get over it."

"Don't block the trail," retorted Keven, and as Beryl continued to walk backwards, suddenly he seized her in his arms and carried her.

He expected a protest, not to say more. But she liked it. She nestled her head against his shoulder.

"Kev, darling, do you know—when you first came back to Solitude and for a long time after—you couldn't have packed me like this?"

"No, indeed. But it's easy now."

"I'm a husky piece. One hundred and twenty-eight!"

"You're a feather. . . . Beryl, you haven't kissed me yet this morning."

She rectified that neglect. And her kiss brought on the impending deluge of Keven's bursting love and pride. As always with Beryl, his surrender to emotion induced a corresponding lapse in her.

"Oh—honey—am I riding or flying?" she murmured, at last breaking away and slipping down. "Listen, Kev, once for all," she went on, very sweet and grave. "It's heavenly for me to hear you rave like that, but I'm no goddess, no noble creature, no angel. I'm just ordinary Beryl Aard, lovesick for you. Please don't spoil me."

"Gosh, there comes the pack train," ejaculated Keven, gazing up the trail. "I'll bet those half-breed drivers saw us. They have eyes like hawks."

"What do we care? . . . Say, they sure rustled along. We'll have to go back and unpack all that stuff. Such fun! But I've time to make a few casts. You stay here, you critical, masterful fisherman. *My* fisherman, whom I've

230

promised to love, honor, and *obey* all my life. Oh, dear!"

Soon Beryl stood back from the edge of the bar, casting down alongshore with her inimitable grace. She forgot the arrival of the pack train. She no longer heard the bells on the mules. She grew oblivious of Keven. He, too, fell under the spell. And the river glided on in an endless solitude, its eternal song, low and musical, near at hand, droning sweet melody from the rapid at the bend, and filling the distant drowsy air with its soft thunder.